THEIR B
BEAUTIFL

ML-I00775316

Henry Dana was a young artist on the cusp of success. I lis agent knew Dana was a sure thing and planned a big art show to show off his client's talents. But the day before the show, terrible things began to happen. It started when Henry narrowly escaped being run over by a train. And there was no mistake about it—he had been pushed! Then, returning to the studio, he found the walls and floors indiscriminately blanketed with oil paints. However, the biggest blow was the discovery that Henry's best works—paintings he had slaved endless hours in the creation of—had been shredded to ribbons! Henry Dana was crushed. What kind of heartless wretch would do this, and most of all…why? No, things were not adding up, and soon even Henry's closest friends became suspect. And when the dripping red paints of death flowed onto the scene, Henry found himself the prime suspect in a macabre murder. And when his own brush strokes promised to reveal the killer, by then it was too late!

FOR A COMPLETE SECOND NOVEL, TURN TO PAGE 147

POLICE LINEUP:

HENRY DANA
Painting was his livelihood; but when his life was threatened and his work destroyed, he followed his first instinct…and ran!

CHARLIE POWELL
After a crippling accident he had lost much of his will to be an artist, but his hidden agenda was quite another work of art.

PETER NORCROSS
Being the husband of Kay Norcross wasn't easy. It took great patience, undaunted will power—and quite a lot of money!

KAY NORCROSS
This shameless, sex-crazed vamp seemed to derive a sadistic pleasure out of flaunting other men in front of her husband.

WILLIE TEMPLE
Stealing enormous amounts of money from his clients didn't bother him in the least…until he was caught.

SHEA MASON
She'd been dumped by Henry Dana years before—but now she was back in his chaotic life again, as a soothing force of calm.

PRESTON MARQUISS
A bitter ex-husband who constantly fought off feelings of jealousy and hatred—feelings that threatened to drive him to murder.

LOTTIE HIGGINS
She was trying to make a big splash in the modeling biz, but this kind of splash was definitely not what she'd bargained for!

THE ART STUDIO MURDERS

By
EDWARD RONNS

ARMCHAIR FICTION
PO Box 4369, Medford, Oregon 97504

CHAPTER ONE

THERE WAS AN instant of freezing fear and rage before he fell. One moment he was simply standing there, aware only of the dim, unsavory heat below ground and the dull-eyed people on the platform; he wasn't thinking about anything at all. The next moment the tunnel vibrated and filled with sound, a trembling roar and mechanical clatter that rushed down on him like a wave. His hands went out, fingers splayed, clutching the empty air. Afterward, he remembered the fleeting moment of dismay and pure white anger as the world pin-wheeled in giddy lights around his head.

His shoulder hit first, jarring on the greasy ties between the rails. His legs sprawled, his knee slammed on something sharp and angular that ripped the cloth from his gabardine trousers.

From somewhere on the platform a woman screamed and screamed again. The track-bed shook under him. The rails sang, and the air thundered. He felt the vibration in every bone, shaking him to little bits as he lay dazed between the track.

He lifted his head and stared down the tunnel with stunned eyes, watching the subway train as it slammed toward him, watching the green lights on the lead car, the shower of sparks from the wheels and the brush on the third rail.

Something had happened to his knee; there was no strength left in it. He sprawled there and saw the train thundering down on him, smelled the grease and dirt of the track floor, felt the angular tie jammed into his ribs. He had to move. But he couldn't move. The train was screaming like a frustrated animal, roaring to a stop; but it couldn't stop any more than he could get out of its way, and the sparking, enormous wheels slashed down on him like giant knives.

Somehow, from somewhere, he gathered the strength to pull his elbows under him and heave sideways, over the rail and under the dark overhang of the platform. There was a crash of sound, exploding inside his head, screaming all around him, filling the air with its uproar.

Nothing touched him.

The train halted with a last and final groan. He heard the hiss of pneumatic door controls, the scraping of feet on concrete directly overhead. He couldn't move in the niche he was crouched in. Voices babbled and filled the air with hysteria. A flashlight sent a feeble beam of yellow down the dark crevice between the subway car and the platform. He stared in dull horror at the huge steel wheel that glittered before his eyes and drew a strangled breath of air into his lungs after an eternity.

Someone called down and asked if he was all right. He didn't answer. He swallowed dust and dirt in his throat and at last be began to crawl forward, hugging the cold, rough, dirty concrete. The coarse surface hurt his hands and knees. He could see nothing but a dim crack of light ahead, flanked by the endless row of wheels and the platform base. The voices followed him, the feet scraping overhead. His left leg regained some movement, and he stopped to feel his knee, cramping his arm around so he could touch it. His fingers came away warm and wet from the torn cloth and skin. He went on crawling.

At the end of the train he scrambled out and stood erect, swaying, his hands torn and his face scraped and blackened. A sea of awed, frightened faces peered down at him from the subway platform. Someone leaned over and extended a rough, gnarled hand, and he reached up and felt himself hauled over the cold, grimy edge of the concrete. He could see the legs of the curious excited people, watching him with avid, morbid eyes as he clambered to his feet. Their mouths were open, talking and exclaiming, but for a moment he couldn't hear anything. The world was without sound. He shook his head and boxed one ear. Someone grabbed his arm, and a red, angry face was thrust into his. A subway guard. Gold-capped teeth glinted in the yellow light. The man's mouth worked, and suddenly his words were audible.

"What's the matter, mister? What's the matter with you, anyway? You trying to kill yourself?"

"Kill myself?" he echoed.

"What did you jump for?" the man shouted.

"I didn't jump."

"He didn't jump," the guard announced, to the crowd. His attitude was one of patient exasperation. "He says he didn't take a flying jump in front of that train."

"I didn't."

"Well, what was it, a gag?"

"No, no gag."

"Then you're a—nut," the guard decided. "What's your name, mister? You got a name?"

"Dana. Henry Dana."

He could still feel the vibrations, all through his body. He couldn't stop shivering. He boxed his ear again and clamped his jaws hard shut to keep his teeth from chattering.

The guard was saying something else, asking more questions, and Dana looked at him with blank eyes. The gold teeth glittered in the guard's angry face. He looked around at the spectators, the men and women, their sweaty features and staring eyes devouring him. He looked at them keenly and anxiously, but he didn't see anyone he knew. He felt a sudden nausea.

"What did you say?" he asked the guard.

The man with the gold teeth gripped his arm. "Look, Mac, you feel all right? We got to make a report. You got to go to a hospital, see a doctor. You look all right, but we can't take chances. Maybe you're figuring on a lawsuit, I don't know; or maybe you're hurt bad. You act a little dopey."

"I'm all right," Dana said. "I wasn't hurt."

"You still got to see a doctor," the guard insisted.

"All right," Dana said.

He was at a hospital fifteen minutes later. He lay on a table, naked under a bright light, smelling the pungency of antiseptics, the crisp starch of the doctor's white jacket. He was still shivering, although it was warm in the examination room, stuffy with the mid-summer city heat. Someone gave him a jigger of brandy, but it didn't help much. Two clean, masculine hands with little dark pads of hair between the knuckles of each finger gave him a cigarette, gave him a light, touched his shoulder. Sharp, stinging pain went through his knee. He heard remote voices, as if from a great distance.

"Nothing serious, just contusions. Scraped the knee, but I don't think any damage was done to speak of. Primarily, we have to watch out for shock in these cases. These people are always in a difficult emotional state."

"Yes, Dr. Taylor."

The voices ended. The hands stopped touching him. He lay still and waited, but when nothing more happened, Dana sat up. It was quiet in the room. The room was small, a white painted cubicle with the examination table, a desk lighted by a gooseneck lamp, a clock on the wall with the hands at nine. Dana looked at the doctor. He was a young man with sandy hair and a quiet, impassive face, evenly tanned. He was selecting forms from a cubbyhole in the desk, unscrewing the top of his pen, smiling quietly at Dana.

"Hello," he said. "Like another cigarette?"

"Yes, thanks."

The doctor lifted his short, white jacket and produced a pack of cigarettes from his trouser pocket. A fraternity key glittered on the end of a linked chain. The doctor got up and stuck the cigarette between Dana's lips and struck a match. Then he took a cigarette for himself and looked at the clock and smiled at Dana again. He had a deep, quiet voice. He looked very young. "This is just to fill out the forms. Pertinent data for your record. You don't mind a few questions?"

"I don't mind."

"We'll get the formalities over with. Your name?"

"Henry Dana."

"Address?"

He gave the sandy-haired doctor the address of the studio he shared with Charley Powell. The doctor's pen scratched noisily, and the doctor tilted his head back to blow smoke at the ceiling. Dana held on tight to the edge of the table.

"Age?"

"Twenty-nine."

"Occupation?"

"Artist."

A sandy eyebrow arched up. "Oh, you're that Henry Dana. I've seen some of your work. Very good. Interesting color." An apologetic laugh. "I'm just a layman, though. You're having a one-man show next Saturday, at the Willi Temple Gallery, aren't you?"

"Yes," Dana said.

"I saw the announcement in the *Times*." Dr. Taylor pinched his chin and poised his pen and frowned. He put his cigarette away, very deliberately, in a copper ashtray on the desk. "Well, let's see. You jumped or fell from that subway platform, didn't you?"

"I didn't jump," Dana said.

"Oh?"

"I didn't jump."

"Then you fell? You slipped?"

"No, I was pushed." Dana drew a deep breath and met the doctor's eyes. "Somebody pushed me."

"Pushed." The doctor put his pen aside now. Dana looked around for a place to crush out his cigarette. He didn't feel as though he should get off the table. The doctor got up and took the cigarette from him and put it with his own in the copper bowl and smiled. "You sound quite sure of yourself. Someone pushed you from the platform into the path of that train. Was it an accident, then? Was the station that crowded?"

"No, I wouldn't say it was particularly crowded."

"Then how—?"

"Someone pushed me deliberately," Dana said. The doctor's gaze was blank and clinical. "I felt hands on my back, shoving me—hard and suddenly. It couldn't have been an accident. I don't see how it could have been—I mean, I'm not mistaken about it. But I didn't have a chance to see who it was."

The doctor glanced at the electric clock on the wall as if it annoyed him. Dana became conscious of the whirring sound it made. From beyond the window came the cacophony of street traffic, then the solitary blare of a taxi horn, startlingly loud. When the doctor spoke again, his voice was casual.

"Are you implying that someone attempted to kill you?"

"I'm not implying anything," Dana said. "I'm just stating the facts as I know them."

"But you just said someone deliberately pushed you."

"Yes."

"That would be an attempt to kill you, wouldn't it?"

"All right," said Dana. "Put it that way."

"Do you have any enemies, Mr. Dana?"

"No. None at all."

"Then who do you think wants you to die?"

"I don't know," Dana said. His voice was stubborn. "I have no ideas about it at all. But it happened. I felt the hands. It was deliberate. I'm sure of that."

The doctor sighed and ruffled his sandy hair.

"Were you drinking earlier this evening?"

"No."

"Do you drink at all?"

"Occasionally. Do you?"

The doctor grinned. "Just questions, Mr. Dana. I'm only trying to help you get things straight in your own mind if you don't have any enemies and you don't know why anyone should want to kill you, then you must be mistaken. Don't you see?"

Dana's blocky face looked dark and angry. Dr. Taylor stood up, pushing away from the desk. He pocketed his cigarettes.

"Very well, then. You'll have to stay here overnight, of course. You're suffering slightly from shock, which is only natural. And you need a tetanus shot, just to be on the safe side. I hope you didn't have any important engagements for this evening."

"I planned to have dinner with Peter Norcross and his wife."

"That's Peter Norcross, the art critic?"

"That's right."

Dr. Taylor shrugged. "I'll telephone them if you'd like me to. But just now, I think I'd better get you settled with a bed for the night. Excuse me a moment while I get a nurse."

The doctor went out. Dana looked at the four walls of the room. There was a small mirror behind him, and his dark face and blue eyes stared back at him. His naked, muscular body still reflected the athletic training he had undergone in years past, and, at twenty-nine, he was just a little more solid, that was all. He looked away from the mirror. The blank, antiseptic whiteness of the room was disagreeable. He looked down at his hands, and they were shaking a little but not so much as before. He felt somewhat better. He ran his fingers through his thick, dark hair and scowled at the clock on the wall. He thought Of Peter Norcross, with whom he'd intended to dine tonight. He thought of Kay Norcross, Petey's wife.

The hell with it, he decided.

The sight and sound and scent of her. The little smile on her lips, and the bold, direct stare of her green eyes. The scarlet of her fingernails, the soft touch of her hands...

There was another door near the doctor's desk, and Dana slid off the table and crossed toward it. His legs felt weak, as if he had just climbed a dozen flights of stairs; his knees were almost liquid. The door opened into a closet, and he found his clothing there, his gray gabardine suit and white shirt and dark blue necktie. He piled them on the examination table and then dressed. It didn't take long. There were grease stains from the subway tracks and a triangular rip over the left knee. Not too bad. Not too good either, for visiting Kay. He left his tie off and opened the door the doctor had gone through. A white corridor with green wainscoting stretched ahead of him. No one was in sight. He walked down to the corner where the corridor turned and heard voices from behind a nearby door. He walked faster and found himself in the street lobby of the hospital.

A moment later he was out on the avenue, the hot muggy night enveloping him in a moist steam. A taxi swerved and pulled in to the curb as he waited. Dana climbed stiffly inside.

"Central Park South," he told the driver.

KAY and Peter Norcross lived in one of the few remaining old houses on the street that faced north toward the park. There was a self-service elevator, and Dana punched the button marked 5 and then stared at his hand as if seeing it for the first time.

A thought crossed his mind, sickening in all its implications. *I should be dead. Right now, this minute. I should be dead and gone.*

He shuddered. He had faced death before, during the war, and it had come perilously close to him on other occasions. But this was different somehow. This didn't make sense.

He got out of the elevator and rang the bell to the Norcross apartment without exactly knowing what he was doing. The apartment, occupying the top floor of the house, was luxuriously furnished, designed as an exotic background for Kay Norcross' exotic beauty. Most of the money that had gone into it came from Kay, too. Petey's salary as an art critic could hardly afford that zebra-striped settee, the lush mirrors the Sarouk carpet in the octagonal foyer.

"Well, Hank! Are you tight?"

Kay Norcross smiled, extending both hands for his. Her dark hair shimmered down around her shoulders. She was tall and dark, in a green dinner gown that was like transparent silt matching the seas that laughed in her green eyes.

"Sorry I'm late," Dana said. "I was just thinking—"

"Why, you are drunk," she said happily. "You've been in a brawl!"

"No I—"

"Come in, darling. Let's see if the other fellow managed to put a hand on you."

He let her pull him into the long, narrow living room with the tall French windows that opened on a balcony overlooking the park. It was cool in here. And he was immediately aware that Kay was alone. Petey wasn't here.

"You'll have to forgive my appearance, Kay," he said. "I had a slight accident."

"Not so slight, judging from those torn trousers. But I'm glad you came up anyway, no matter how you look. You aren't hurt, are you?"

"No."

"Too bad. I'd love to play nurse to you."

He felt uncomfortable under the bold stare of her green eyes. "Where is Petey?"

The eyes smiled coolly, mocking him.

"Hank, darling... Peter won't be here. He knows you're coming. I told him to stay away."

"Look, Kay..."

"Don't be a cross-patch, Hank. He knows I love you. Why do you insist on being so naive?"

"I simply insist on being honest," he said.

"Oh, pooh. Wait a moment. I'll fetch drinks."

He swallowed his anger. His eyes followed the smooth rhythm of her hips as she crossed the room to the bar. He knew what was coming. It had happened before. Dinner for two, when there should have been three, in a little dining room beyond the arched doorway, served by a maid whose feet whispered back and forth as if she weren't there at all. Just the two of them, dining across the glittering table and watching the candlelight. The room would be cool, an oasis in that hot summer night.

Dana shook his head savagely, aware of a slow ache in his left knee, of a momentary light-headedness. Then Kay was back, green eyes smiling, a frosted daiquiri in her slim fingers.

"Drink up, darling. What kind of an accident was it?"

"I may tell you about it some time," he said.

"Why not now?"

"When Petey is here," Dana said. "I'll tell you both at the same time. Where is he, by the way? Where does he hide out—when you send him away like this?"

Kay shrugged pale, smooth shoulders.

"Does it matter? I'm not curious. That's one of the difficulties with Peter, darling. He is so plain and simple—oh, cultured, of course—but transparent and guileless in personality. Not like you. You are full of secrets, Henry Dana. Perhaps that is one of the reasons why I love you."

"Don't talk that way," he said sharply. He should put down the drink and leave, he thought. He might have known Kay would have arranged something like this. The thing to do was to get out of here, fast. Which was crazy, because Kay wasn't the sort of woman any man could run away from. If any man would. He drank the daiquiri, grateful for it, and sat down, listening to Kay's liquid laughter as she leaned on the mantel before him.

"You always look so shocked, Henry, when I tell you I'm in love with you. And how many times must I repeat to you that Peter knows all about it?"

"You've told me too many times," he said. "Last winter it was Charley Powell; now it's me. Give it up, Kay."

"Poor Charley," she said. "Does he still think of me?"

"Not in a very complimentary fashion," Dana said.

She laughed. "But you do like me, Hank?"

"Of course."

"But I'm not desirable to you, is that it?"

"You're very lovely," he said, and he meant it then. "But you're not for me. I shouldn't stay here."

"But you will," she said gently.

"It won't mean anything. You know how I feel."

She said, "Henry, I generally get what I want. You know that, too. And I mean to have you, because I want you. I'm going to divorce Peter."

"No," he said.

"But I've already told him, darling. You're not in love with anyone else, are you?"

Frowning, Dana shook his head.

"Then the only difficulty," Kay said. "is that you are not in love with me either."

"No," he said.

"You will be," she said confidently.

"Kay, you know—"

"Hush," she said.

He left ten minutes later. He knew Kay was angry and puzzled, but he was no longer concerned with what she thought. He punched the street-floor button with deliberate care and let the cage slowly descend with him. Kay's eyes, when she closed the door after him in the foyer, were a cool, remote emerald. He limped a little as he crossed the small lobby to the street door. There were six brownstone steps down to the broad pavement, and in the light of the passing traffic he saw a man seated on the second step up from the bottom. He went on down, and the man got to his feet.

"Hello, Henry," he said. "Welcome back from the dead."

Dana stood very still. A taxi hooted behind him. He looked across the street into the warm, dark reaches of Central Park, and then he swung slowly on his heels and faced the little man on the brownstone steps.

It was Peter Norcross. He looked soft and mild and amused. Or perhaps tolerant. He was small, about forty, with a thin body and a weak face. He wore horn-rimmed glasses with wide straight bars poked back into his gray hair. His hands were in his pockets. His round, intellectual head seemed far too big for his shoulders.

"What are you doing here, Peter?" Dana asked.

"I live here, Henry."

"On the steps?"

"I was waiting for you to come out."

Dana said, "Peter, how did you know what happened to me tonight?"

Norcross smiled. His eyes swam behind his lenses. "If I don't choose to tell you, you will probably think I'm the one who pushed you into that train. Do you think I would do that, Henry?"

"I'm not thinking anything about it, yet."

"Well, I might have done it."

"Did you?"

The small man shrugged. "As a matter of fact, I heard about it in the city room. The flash came in about it just ten minutes after you slipped away from the hospital. The way our legman got it, though, you simply fell. But the doctor told me you insist you were pushed."

"I was," Dana said.

"That's quite interesting, don't you think?"

"I'm wondering how you happened to be in your newspaper office at such an opportune time."

"Where else would I be? Surely Kay told you she had sent me away. Didn't she?"

Dana made no reply. He sensed something unhealthy in the little man's smile, an expression that was bland and friendly and totally wrong, though what exactly was wrong was difficult to locate. Involuntarily, he glanced up at the fifth floor windows. From across the street, in the park, he supposed that one could see a small segment of the living room through the thin summer curtains. He wondered about little Peter Norcross, watching those lighted windows up there.

"I think you'd better go upstairs," Dana said. "Kay is probably waiting for you."

"I'm sure she is," Norcross nodded. He sat down on the steps again and laughed, a sound that was almost a giggle. "I'll go home when I get damned good and ready."

Dana stared at him.

"All right," he said. "Have it your own way."

"Good night!" Petey called after him. "Sweet dreams!"

Dana seemed to hear the man's giggling laughter halfway down the block. At Columbus Circle he hesitated, and then he knew what Petey had laughed about. Petey was expecting him to avoid the subway. Dana's jaw tightened. Then he turned left and found the subway entrance and went underground.

Nothing happened. He had an uneventful ride home.

CHAPTER TWO

In the morning Dana dreamed, and awoke from the dream smoothly, without effort, not moving or opening his eyes. The day was young. He knew as much from the light in the big north window that disturbed him through his shut eyelids. All his senses were alert. He heard the whirring of the fan, suspended from the ceiling overhead, and the muted discord of traffic sounds from the street four floors below. It was going to be a hot day, but for the moment he felt chilled, his naked shoulder blades damp with sweat, the pillow wet under the back of his neck.

He lay without moving, savoring the memory of his dream. He had dreamed of blue water and a seagull gliding along on the feathery edge of a breeze. There was a girl in his dream, her face one that he had long forgotten. Not a beautiful face, not exotic or glamorous, but clean and fresh and framed in chestnut hair that stirred a little by the same breeze that lifted the seagull high above the blue water.

And then a man's shadow crossed the girl's face, and it was not Dana's shadow. The girl turned toward the newcomer and her eyes became the eyes of a stranger.

A funny kind of a dream, a vignette out of the long ago. Thinking of it now, aware of the hot morning that smothered the city, he wondered about it and remembered the girl, and smiled. Still smiling, he rolled over and opened his eyes and looked up at the man who stood over his cot.

"By God," Charley said. "You're an animal."

"Am I?"

"How long have you been awake?" Charley asked.

"A few minutes."

"That's what I mean. The way you wake up, like an animal, all in one piece, so to speak."

Dana grinned. "Anything wrong with that?"

"I envy it," Charley said. "Me—I usually wake up with a hangover and spend half an hour picking up the pieces—an arm here, a leg there. And I don't have a built-in alarm clock, either. Do you know what time it is?"

"Eight-thirty," Dana said, without looking at his watch.

"On the nose. How do you feel?"

"All right. Stiff. But all right."

"I read about your accident in the papers this morning, on my way down. You're lucky to be alive."

"I know that," Dana said.

He slid his long legs off the cot and searched for his clothes. There was a quiet, relaxed virility about all his movements that fascinated Charley Powell.

"Did you see Kay Norcross last night?" Charley asked.

"Can anybody avoid it?"

"I thought you were going to work."

"No. I went to see Kay."

Charley sighed. It was hot in the studio even with the fan going. He sat forward in the chair, chin cupped in his hands. Charley was a big man with blond hair and a herculean physique. He had a square, friendly face, all straight lines and angles, and the ridge of his sandy eyebrows was thick and precise. His jaw was massive, pugnacious.

His presence irritated Dana, for some reason.

"I thought you had a date yourself," Dana said.

"I'm just a hard-working, commercial artist," Charley said. "The K.V.B. Company suddenly squawked about that last immortal oil I did for them. Monday is the deadline for a new shot at it, according to the agency. So it's slave labor for Charley. I worked last night. I envy you, Hank."

"What for? You make three hundred a week. What are you squawking about? On the other hand, if you didn't let me chip in for this loft, I wouldn't have a place to work or hang my hat. You should kick."

Charley grinned. "As for sharing this loft, the only condition I maintain is that you listen to my gripes. Anyway, after next week you'll be famous. You'll be a real artist. You'll hang in the museums. And I? More immortal lingerie for K.V.B."

"You're optimistic." Dana smiled.

"No, I'm not." Charley took his cupped hands from his chin and looked earnest. "You've really done some good work, Hank, really good. I'm glad Willi Tempel took you on. Me, I'm only good for projecting commercial nonsense."

Dana had no reply. It wasn't that he felt ungrateful, but he wished Charley Powell would go away. Still, when you occupied one half of your host's quarters and dined too often at his expense—it had been going on for six months now—there was nothing you could say. He felt impatient for the exhibition of his paintings to be over, to know the verdict. Whatever it would be— fame and fortune, or more obscurity—he wouldn't stay here. He would have to get out of New York, not only because of Charley, but because of Kay. Kay was a far worse problem than Charley could ever be.

In the bathroom, Dana splashed water on his face and con- templated the dark bristle of new beard on his jaw. While he shaved he heard Charley wander about among the canvases stacked against the walls. The loft occupied the entire fourth floor of the warehouse east of Washington Square, and Dana grinned faintly as he thought of the jibes endured for living over a feather merchant. The second and third floors of the old building were crammed with the manufacturer's stock of pillow feathers. A fire hazard, Kay had said. But it was only a hop, skip and a jump through the big windows to the roof of the next building.

He had seen the possibilities of the place the moment Charley invited him to work and sleep there. Charley's apartment was uptown, on the east side of Central Park, but he always worked down here. A wallboard partition divided the barren floor space into two studios. A cot, a mahogany dresser from the Salvation Army, and Dana had all he needed.

Finishing shaving, he soaked his head under the cold-water tap, gaining momentary relief from the hot, sticky morning. Charley was gone when he crossed the studio and finished dressing. Color sang to him from the four walls, from all his canvases stacked in disorder about the huge room. The slanting window on the north wall shimmered blue with the morning light and reflected his tall figure as he knotted his tie.

Charley was waiting in the other studio, beyond the partition that separated their working quarters. Charley had a girl with him, a redhead. Dana hadn't heard her come in. She looked as if she had moved in permanently. She was dressed only in black lace panties and a half brassiere, and she lolled on the little platform that served as Charley's modeling dais, eating chocolates that apparently had no effect on her ripe figure.

"Hello, Lucky." She moved her long body in the chair and reached behind her for a soft-drink bottle. "Have a snort?"

Charley said, "You're drunk on root beer, baby."

"There's nothing else to do until you make up your mind to work." She kept her eyes on Dana, eyes that reflected a cool resentment. Her name was Lotti Higgins, Dana recalled, and she had been hanging around Charley quite a bit lately, ostensibly serving as a model for his K.V.B. lingerie ads.

"You going to see Kay again?" Charley asked.

Dana paused. The blond man was sprawled in a wire chair, glumly surveying an easel on which he had thumb tacked a sheet of rough white sketch paper. The paper was blank.

"I'm going to breakfast," Dana said.

"Stay away from her, Hank. She's no good for you."

"You think so?"

"Don't get sore. But she's Petey's wife…"

"Just what do you think has been going on between us, anyway?" Dana asked quietly.

"I don't have to think. I know Kay, boy. I know—"

"Shut up, Charley," Dana said. "You don't know what you're talking about."

Charley Powell lifted the straight lines of his brows in mild surprise. "Touchy aren't you?"

"I suppose I am."

"All right, then. Sorry I said anything."

Lotti Higgins made a small sound of disgust and twisted her firm-fleshed figure in her chair upon the dais. "You two are so damned polite to each other, it's revolting."

Charley said, "It's that mixture of root beer and chocolates you've been swilling, baby. Keep out of this."

"Charley, dear, you're such a bastard." Lotti stood up, her figure slim where it should be slim, round and supple in the right places. Her long red hair was a cascade of light. Dana wondered how Charley got any work done with Lotti Higgins around. Lotti went on, "What gets me is how two eligible males like you fall for the same dame, and ignore a gal like me. What's this Kay Norcross got that I haven't got?"

"Not a thing," Dana grinned. "You've got it, Lotti."

"And ten percent dividends, too," Charley added. He seemed concerned over Lotti's temper. "Have another drink, baby."

The girl's mouth was sullen. "I will. A real one, too."

Dana's irritation over Charley's questions vanished as swiftly as it had come.

"Look," he said. "I know how you feel about Kay, yourself. And I know all about Petey's problem, keeping her in line. Would you believe it if I said I am not interested in her?"

"No," Charley grinned.

"Well, I'm not. For your information, I went to their place at Petey's invitation, not Kay's."

"Better look out, then. Petey is little, but he's mean."

"He can't complain about me," Dana said. He opened the door. "Go to work, Charley. Forget it."

"Sure thing."

Lotti Higgins said, "Ta-ta, handsome."

There were four flights of stairs going down to the street, and he felt better with each landing he reached. The heat of the day didn't bother him. He felt fine. He wasn't troubled by any memories of what had happened last night. He was getting too damned sensitive about Charley, he thought. A temperamental artist. He grinned to himself and walked toward Washington Square, then swung into a corner cafe and had breakfast. He didn't bother to read the newspapers. After breakfast, he walked for perhaps half an hour before returning to the studio.

A detective waited for him there.

Charley Powell and Lotti were gone. Dana found the detective when he paused at the bottom of the stairs to pick up his mail from the box. There was a letter from Willi Tempel, his agent, and he felt a paper clip through the heavy, extravagant stationery and felt quick gratification. The paper clip meant there was a check inside from a sale Willi must have consummated—a sale of one of his paintings.

The detective didn't look like a cop. He wore a blue pinstripe suit and a white shirt and a black tie. His hands were small and clean. He took off his hat and mopped his forehead.

"You're Henry Dana, aren't you?"

Dana nodded. "That's right."

"My name is Evans." The man flipped open a leather card case and exhibited a badge. "We have to check up on what happened to you last night."

Dana hesitated, turning Willi Tempel's envelope over in his hands. "Come on up. It's four flights."

"Can do," Evans said.

He had smooth, silvery hair and pale, slightly bored blue eyes. He looked like a shoe clerk, and he wasn't too obviously interested in Dana's makeshift quarters. His glance flickered over the virile colors on Dana's canvases, and he poked his head into Charley's room. Charley's sketch paper was still blank. Recalling Lotti Higgins, Dana was not surprised.

Evans said, "You share this studio with Charles Powell, don't you? A commercial illustrator?"

"It's his place, really. We split the rent, though."

Evans asked many of the same questions the doctor had asked the previous evening. He didn't take any notes. He filled a pipe and tamped the tobacco down carefully with a clean fingertip, but he didn't light it.

"You were in the army, weren't you, Mr. Dana?"

"Yes." Dana nodded.

"Saw lots of action?"

THE ART STUDIO MURDERS

"Some. I was in the Third."

"As what?"

"Engineers."

"That's right. I remember seeing your sketchbook. They published it right after the war. Good stuff."

Dana said, "Sketching wasn't my regular duty. I was a corporal in the engineers. That's what I chose."

"You've been a civilian for how long now?"

"Five years."

"Honorable discharge?"

Dana felt a growing irritation. "Yes. I wasn't Section Eight, if that's what you're driving at. No nervous disorders."

"You're nervous now, Mr. Dana."

Dana looked down at his hands. His fingers were trembling, slightly. He tightened them over his knees.

"So I'm nervous. Wouldn't you be?"

"Well, I just asked, checking up. Artists are supposed to be high-strung and sensitive."

"I'm not," Dana said. "No more than the next fellow."

"No offense." Evans looked thoughtful. "What made you skip out of the hospital last night? The doctor was pretty worried. He kept talking about what a man in shock might do to himself, wandering around loose."

"I was all right," Dana said.

"I suppose you were. Anyway, a Mr. Norcross phoned in that you'd been up there to see his wife and that you seemed to be fine, so we didn't bother." The detective put his unlit pipe down carefully on a small table, moving aside some tubes of pigment to find a place for it. Strong sunlight beat in through the slanting window and made his, hair shine like a silver casque. Dana watched him take a dog-eared notebook from his neat blue suit. "Let's see. You think somebody tried to kill you, but you don't know who, and you don't know why. Is that it?"

"I'm not so sure, now. I guess so," Dana said.

"We have to look at all the angles here. Maybe you were mistaken for someone else."

"That's possible," Dana said.

"You sure you didn't see who pushed you?"

"Quite sure."

"It could have been a woman?"

"Maybe."

"You wouldn't care to name anybody you think might want to push you, would you?"

"No."

Evans frowned and pulled at his lower lip

"Well, what would you like us to do about it?"

Dana grinned. "Is there anything you can do?"

"Not much, under the circumstances. There's nothing to go on, except your story of what happened."

"And you don't believe me," Dana said flatly.

"I didn't say that."

"It's understandable," Dana said. "I find it a little difficult to believe myself, now."

Evans smiled. It was a thin smile. He looked bored again, and after another moment, he departed. Dana got up and rearranged the pigments Evans had disturbed. His knee felt stiff, but that was all right. He wasn't shaking at all. He thought of the envelope he'd received in the mail from Willi Tempel, and he slit it open with his thumbnail. He had been right about the check inside, attached to a brief note with a paper clip.

The check was for two hundred dollars.

The note read: "My dear Henry, This is all I could get for your *Death Mask*. Still, it is a sale, and every bit helps. Willi Tempel."

Dana was conscious of disappointment and then a sharp, stinging anger.

KAY NORCROSS moved to the ivory telephone with swift, decisive steps. She wore a long housecoat of scarlet, embroidered with Russian designs in gold thread. Her dark hair swung as she turned her head sharply to stare back at the bedroom. Her mouth was red and sulky as she picked up the telephone.

"Put it down, my dear."

Peter Norcross appeared from the kitchen doorway, surprising her. He looked disheveled, a thin, gray mouse of a man. Without his glasses, his eyes were disconcertingly large and protruding. His smile was only slightly amused.

"Don't call Henry now," he said.

Kay's voice shook with fury. "How dare you, Peter? How dare you do such a thing!"

"Do what?" he asked innocently.

"I've just seen the newspapers. Henry didn't tell me what really happened last night."

"So?"

She looked at him, suddenly confused. It wasn't possible. Not Peter. Not this erudite little mouse. She became aware of the dial tone in the telephone and she put it down, avoiding a decision now. Turning, she clasped her hands and faced her husband squarely. He still smiled. A clock chimed somewhere softly and sedately, and the light that came in through the windows facing the park was gray and sultry, warning of rain during the day.

"Peter, he says he was *pushed* into that train!"

"Perhaps he was," Peter said mildly.

"But..."

He said, "Haven't you the courage to ask me, darling? You think I pushed him, don't you?"

She felt frightened. "Did you, Peter?"

His answer was unexpected. "I love you, Kay."

"Don't—"

"You don't think the two things are related?"

Her lower lip trembled and she caught it between her teeth. She was very frightened now.

"You wouldn't, Peter. Not you."

"Perhaps not."

Her voice screamed, "Tell me the truth, damn you!"

Peter still spoke mildly. "I'll let you think about it, sweetheart. Let's have breakfast now."

"I have to call him first."

"He isn't at home."

"I don't believe you!"

She lifted the telephone again, and this time Petey just stood there, small and thin, watching her. He looked pathetic. Kay dialed Henry Dana's number with a stiff forefinger, not looking up. She heard a series of clicks, and then the depressing ring of the other telephone far across the city. There was no answer.

Kay hung up and stared in wonder at her husband.

It was going to rain. Charley Powell swung his London-made trench coat over one arm and hung a hip on a corner of Willi Tempel's elaborate antique kidney desk. Through the open windows over Fifty-Seventh Street came the sound of noontime traffic and a dull rumble of thunder. Powell looked big and casual. He leaned across the desk to crush out his cigarette in Willi Tempel's immaculate cloisonné ashtray.

"Willi, my fat little pal, you are a conniving, unadulterated rascal, and a crook of the first water."

"Of course," Willi Tempel agreed blandly. "Everyone in business is a crook. That is the very essence of business. Cheat your fellow man. Get a bigger profit. And kindly keep your filthy cigarette butts out of my antiques."

"There are ethics even in business," Charley Powell went on. "Even in an art agent's business."

"I never heard of them," Willi smiled.

When he smiled, it was with his entire face and all four chins. Willi Tempel came from a long line of New York's public exhibitionists. Outdoors, he flaunted a broad-brimmed black hat and an impressario's cape of midnight blue, lined with red silk, and he was never seen without his ebony staff—it was not a cane— tipped with its solid knob of gold. He liked to have people stare. It was good advertising, he said.

His salon and his office were patterned after himself. The furniture was dramatic, on a colossal scale to fit his huge bulk, with crashing, jarring colors that made his artists wince. This private sanctum into which Charley had intruded was even more flowery and Oriental than the outer salon, and in the big cushioned swivel chair behind his desk. Willi Tempel sat like an Eastern deity, calm, cunning, and patient.

"Perhaps you didn't understand me, Willi," Charley Powell went on. "Let me repeat it. I called you a crook."

"Harsh words," Willi murmured. "Elaborate, please."

"I've just seen Mrs. Barnabus Neal, one of your Park Avenue clients, Willi. She is a very happy woman."

"She has ten million dollars. Why not be happy?"

25

"She has more than ten million dollars," Charley said. "She has a painting called 'Death-Mask,' by Henry Dana. She bought it from you two days ago."

"Quite correct," Willi nodded. "I was happy to convince her that she should own that canvas. Very encouraging for young Dana. A promising painter should be stimulated by occasional sales."

"How much did Mrs. Barnabus Neal pay you for that canvas?" Charley asked quietly.

"That is none of your business."

Charley said, "I've made it my business, Willi."

The fat man shifted in his swivel chair. He put his pudgy, dimpled hands flat on the green blotter of his desk and studied his pink fingernails. Charley regarded him curiously, reflecting that Willi Tempel, the sybarite, was also an ordinary coward. His analysis was correct. When Willi Tempel looked up, his eyes were resigned, although that did not lessen the bitter downward swoop of his little mouth.

"All right, Charley. She paid me seven-fifty."

"Hank got a check from you for only two hundred."

Willi's smile was apologetic. "Perhaps I feel that Dana owes it to me, as my protégé. On the other hand, it may merely have been a clerical error."

"But you will correct that error, Willi."

"Of course."

Powell stood up. Thunder crashed over the street outside. "The three of us can have dinner tonight. You explain it to Hank then—about your error; I mean. But leave me out of it, please."

"At Kolevici's?" Willi Tempel asked.

"Good enough. At seven."

Willi Tempel smiled. "I'll be there. Now please remove yourself from these premises. You have an aura of ugly hatred, Charley, and it revolts me."

The breeze lifted a seagull high in the air and it poised, trembling, before it slid down the slope of the wind and skimmed over the dory grounded on the beach. The girl in the dory had chestnut hair and a face that seemed scrubbed clean by the sea and the wind.

She leaped nimbly from the dory and drew it up beyond reach of the tide, then paused to brush her hair from around her face. She carried her mail, picked up at the Stone Cove post office across the harbor; and wrapped around two circulars was a New York newspaper. She had already scanned the news, and Dana's name had leaped at her from an obscure story on the fourth page.

Shea Mason turned and walked purposefully to the cottage that stood just beyond the yellow sand dunes. The island was small, and from this point she could see most of the curve of the northern beach, from the abandoned lighthouse on the rocky seaward point to the thick growth of pine and oak that faced the red roofs of Stone Cove and the fishing piers across the blue harbor.

The cottage was a man's place, and from a casual glance one might think it was still occupied by its original owner. Nothing had been changed since the day Hank Dana left it, so many years ago. His first easel still leaned against the wall, with the experimental painting still on the rack. His pipes stood on the old cobbler's bench that served as a table, and the bunk in one corner was neatly made up. There weren't many days that Shea Mason missed in visiting the cottage.

She sat down near the stone fireplace and stared again at the newspaper story she had read. Her blue eyes were troubled. She sat still and listened, wondering if Abel and Sarah, in the house just beyond the knoll, had seen her return. But there was no sound except the roar of the surf. Abel would be out tending to his lobster traps, anyway. And Sarah was busy getting dinner.

She counted again the years that had gone by since Hank Dana was last here on Kettle Island. And then she rummaged in the desk for stationery and pen. It wasn't merely a matter of pride, Shea Mason thought. There were times when pride had to be swallowed. Dana was in trouble. But she realized with a rueful sigh that her own motives were hardly unselfish. She wanted to see Hank again. He belonged here. And if there was anything she could do to bring him back, she would do it. Pride be damned.

She started to write her letter to him.

A shadow fell across the open doorway. A tall man with dark red hair and a deeply tanned face stood there for a moment, watching her. He was near forty, but his craggy face and burly body still held a youthful mastery of his years. He wore a light, checked sport coat and gabardine slacks and water-stained sneakers. The heavy-knuckled fingers of his hands snapped restlessly as he waited for Shea to notice his presence.

"Pres! You startled me!"

"I always seem to do that, don't I?" the man said.

"What are you doing on Kettle Island?"

"Waiting for you, Shea. Sarah said you would head for this place first, as soon as you got back from town. She was right, although I didn't believe her."

Shea Mason flushed. The burly man came into the cottage, his eyes curious as he glanced about at the easel and paintings in the room. His voice was heavy with hatred.

"You've never forgotten him, have you, Shea?"

"No," she said bluntly. "I never shall."

"You're still in love with him?"

"I've always been, although I didn't always know it." The girl turned over the sheet of notepaper she had started to write upon, her whole body defensive as Preston Marquiss drew nearer. She looked at him and tried to control an inner shiver of apprehension. She made her voice light. "I certainly didn't expect you back today. I thought you were in New York."

"I was."

"Did you read about—that accident? He fell in the subway…"

"I heard about it. A close call. He was always lucky. I'm going back to New York immediately, by the way."

"Today?"

"In an hour. Want to come along?"

"No."

The man's eyebrows quirked. "You might see him there."

"I don't want to see him." Shea said. "It's too late—for everything. And I don't want to see you here, either, Pres. You don't belong on this island any more. You have no more claim on me, you know. That's all over with."

"Not with me, Shea," the man said. "Not ever."

"Our decree became final almost a year ago. I'm no longer your wife."

"That's what the law says," Preston Marquiss agreed. "I choose to ignore the law. You're my wife, Shea. No scrap of paper can change that. I'll never give you up."

"We've been over this so many times—"

"And will again, until you see my point of view."

"No, Pres."

"There will come a time," the man said. His voice was confident, suddenly cheerful. "I'll be back in Stone Cove by the weekend, no later. I'll see you then."

"No," she said. "Don't come here again."

"Who will stop me?" he asked. "Sarah? Abel?"

Shea's voice was suddenly harsh. "I'll stop you, Pres."

The burly man laughed. Shrugging, he turned away, quitting the cottage without another word. Shea Mason sat very still for a long time. She considered tearing up the letter. She felt physically ill, weighted down by an intolerable burden carried over from errors in the past.

After awhile, however, she resumed writing to Hank Dana.

CHAPTER THREE

DANA MET Charley in Kolevici's at the appointed time. They chose a table near the window, where they could watch the broad sidewalk of Fifth Avenue under the summer awnings and the drumming beat of rain. Umbrellas bobbed and taxis splashed leisurely up the glistening street. Inside, it was cool and dry, the air annoyed by the struggles of Hungarian fiddlers to provide entertainment.

Charley Powell looked bigger and more powerful than usual as he stripped off his thin tan raincoat. They didn't shake hands. Charley grinned and ordered a Manhattan and sat down, his athletic body straining within his light suit. He wore no necktie, and his throat was thick and bronze.

"Well, you're perfectly all right now, Hank. You seem to be lucky with your accidents."

For the first time in a long while, Dana deliberately looked at Charley's hands as the big man placed them on the table. He felt an inner explosion of pain. He never wanted to look at Charley's hands, the way they were twisted and distorted. It was the one flaw in the big man's physical perfection. He nodded toward them, his face a little pale.

"How are they, Charley?"

"Getting better—so the doc said, anyway. Forget 'em, Henry. I know how you feel about them."

Charley's square, planed face was friendly. He took a breadstick from a wicker basket and watched with approval as an attractive girl walked head-down into the rain on the sidewalk beyond the window. Dana kept looking at Charley's hands. The accident had happened over a year before, when he had been driving Charley's car. Charley was the only one injured when the car skidded in the Connecticut snow and went over an embankment. Charley's hands would never be the same.

"Forget 'em, will you?" Charley grunted. "It wasn't your fault. Look, Henry, how was Kay last night? I saw Petey Norcross at the museum this morning—he was looking at some of Jabonski's work—non-objective stuff, pretty interesting; I might try it myself if I ever—" Charley interrupted himself with another grunt. "Listen Henry, did you know that Petey Norcross once killed a man?"

Dana felt his jaws begin to ache. He deliberately sipped at his drink. His voice seemed only casually interested.

"No," he said. "Little Petey Norcross?"

"He was telling me about it again today. He isn't at all reticent; almost brags, actually. He's such a little rooster. I suppose it inflates his ego."

Dana said carefully, "What was it all about?"

"Oh, technically he was innocent. He was never bothered about it. The poor victim, as he phrased it, met with an accident—even as you, Henry. He was one of Kay's flames at the time—again, even as you."

"If it was an accident..."

"Technically. But Petey as much as told me that he engineered it. That part of it was veiled, of course, but—"

"What sort of an accident, Charley?"

"In the subway," Charley said quietly.

Dana listened to the rain on the window and the squeaking of the Hungarian fiddles. He thought: *It didn't take much strength to push me off that platform.*

Charley Powell said earnestly, "It's something to think about. I know how Kay has been pestering you, the same way she used to pester me, and Petey knows all about it—she rather publicizes her efforts to win you."

"Yes, I know," Dana said. "So you think Petey is the one who pushed me?"

Charley leaned back. "That's for you to decide, Henry. Just be careful, that's all."

Willi Tempel came in then, with his usual flourish, wearing his wide-brimmed hat and swinging cape and carrying his ebony staff. He was loud and boisterous enough for heads to turn and stare at him. He wheezed as he took off the wet cape, hung up his hat, and squeezed into a chair at the table.

"My dear clients," he sighed. "Rest easily. This dinner is on me."

"Fair enough," Charley said drily.

The waiter took their orders and went away. Willi Tempel cursed the weather in several languages, because it had interrupted his daily stroll down Fifth Avenue. Dana stared with fascination as Willi regaled his monstrous appetite with double portions of everything.

"You have your paintings ready, Henry? Tomorrow is the big day. We shall make a fortune, you and I."

"Everything is set," Dana said. "I'll bring them over myself, first thing in the morning."

Charley nursed his cocktail and looked at the fat man from under his straight brows. "Willi, don't forget about that clerical error."

"Dear boy," Willi said between mouthfuls. "I had no intention of forgetting it." The fat man took out his wallet and withdrew a check, which he shoved, with just the faintest trace of reluctance, toward Dana. "Henry, far be it from me to let myself open to a charge of knavery. A stenographer's error, my boy—that was all. You may tear up the check you received from me in this morning's mail. And let us hear no more about it."

Dana would have liked to say more about it, he thought later, but the conversation between Charley and Willi Tempel overwhelmed his tentative questions. Yet he had a pretty good idea of what had gone on. It had been bothering him for some time, this laxness of Willi's in keeping finances straight. And he had heard disgruntled comments from other artists whose work Willi handled, about the way Willi kept half his books in his head—and half the income in his own pocket.

The dinner, however, turned out to be Charley's idea of a minor celebration over Dana's brush with death the night before. Lotti Higgins, the red headed model, showed up and joined them at their table, evidently by prearrangement with Charley. The tall girl looked smart and attractive in a cocoa-tan raincoat and hood, and a series of thin silver bracelets jingled on her wrist when she sat down between Charley and Dana.

"Still hard to get?" she asked Dana.

"Stop annoying the man," Charley said. "Don't you know when you haven't got a chance?"

"A gal can try, can't she?" Lotti pouted. She leaned close to Dana, and he knew she'd been drinking again. "What do you say, Hank? Is Charley right? Don't I have a chance?"

"Drink up," Dana said. "You'll feel better."

"You're hateful," the girl snapped.

Charley laughed. "Henry was in love once, a long time ago. Some other bloke won her, and he's sulked ever since."

Lotti looked interested. "Is that a fact?" She glanced at Charley suspiciously, and then returned to Dana. "Were you actually in love once?"

"My heart was broken," Dana said. "And Charley talks too much."

"A man with a secret sorrow," Lotti gloated. "How charming! That makes you even more intriguing."

Charley said grimly, "He wants no consolation, baby. Leave him alone."

Over the brandies, Willi Tempel recalled an engagement and departed. The rain had stopped, and darkness had fallen. Dana and Charley and Lotti remained, talking about other artists they knew, remembering college days and past rivalries. Eventually,

Charley got impatient with Lotti and decided to leave. Lotti went with him. Dana watched them enter the bar and then he found his hat and coat and went out alone.

The night was warm after the rain. The wet sidewalks dried rapidly, and Dana chose to walk, with no particular destination in mind. For some reason he felt no desire to return to his studio, nor did he want the company of friends. He dropped in to a newsreel theater for an hour, became impatient with the innocuous shots of fashion models that passed for news in a world trembling on the brink of disaster, and walked out to spend another hour in a bar, drinking rum-cokes. He drank alone, on a stool at one end of the bar, watching the video screen. He didn't drink too much.

He wasn't drunk when he finally reached Washington Square and turned east to his studio.

The offices of the factory on the first floor were locked and dark. The little entry to the stairs that led up to his quarters had a dim bulb burning over the staircase. He paused on the sidewalk and looked up at his windows, but they were dark, too. It was almost midnight. The street and the building were quiet, although from a block away he heard the sounds of a man and a woman quarreling on the street corner. Dana reached for his keys.

Since the building was not designed for residential purposes, no lights were maintained on the stairs beyond the single lamp at street level. For his own use, Dana kept a three-cell flashlight hooked to a nail on the second landing. He reached automatically for it, where it should have been, in its usual place.

The flashlight wasn't there.

He paused in sharp surprise. Below him, the stairs angled sharply down in a distorted geometrical pattern to the street door, where the entry was buttered with dull light. The way up was swallowed by deep darkness.

He listened, but there was no sound. He looked on the floor of the landing for his flashlight, but he knew he wouldn't find it. Someone had taken it. The street door had been locked below, and it had to be someone who had a key.

Lots of people had a key to that street door. Charley Powell had distributed over a dozen to his friends—mostly women. Dana himself had handed out three that he knew of. It could be Charley up there, with Lotti Higgins. The absence of light on the fourth floor would mean nothing then; Charley would have taken the flashlight with him.

On the other hand, there might be a completely different explanation. The darkness brooded above him, waiting.

His indecision lasted only a moment. Then he started up the second flight of stairs to the third floor. He tried to make no sound at all, but the ancient treads creaked no matter how he tried to place his weight. He knew the way well enough to do without the light. On the third landing he paused and listened again. He heard the sound of his own breathing. From far across the city he heard the wail of a siren, belonging to a world other than this one of enveloping darkness.

He went up the last flight of stairs a little faster. He had to feel for the door, and then he let himself into the darkness of his studio, not breathing, ready...

The air was heavy with a perfume that was familiar—Lotti Higgins. But no one spoke to him from the darkness, and nothing happened.

He reached for the light cord near the door. The lamp over Charley Powell's easel sprang into existence and he looked at the big room. Nothing was wrong. Nobody was here.

He went on into his own studio at the rear, shrugging out of his coat. His arms were still in his coat sleeves, his shoulders hunched forward and upward in the act of seeking release, when he paused.

Things were changed.

Dim light crept ahead from Charley's room, but he needed no more light to know what had happened. He could feel it, sense it, and see it. He could almost smell it, the fear and the danger. The insanity in the room. It seemed to giggle and gibber at him from out of the shadows.

Yesterday, before the subway incident, he had stacked the paintings he planned to exhibit at Willi Tempel's against the opposite wall, in preparation for crating them. He had placed a dozen of the canvases against the wall, where he might look at them alone, perhaps for the last time. He had left them that way this morning, after Evans, the detective, left.

The frames were still there. But each painting had been slashed and tattered and ripped and clawed as if by a wild animal, chewed to bits in a fit of berserk rage.

Nothing else had been touched. There was just the silent studio, the makeshift furniture, the big plate of window in the opposite wall reaching from floor to ceiling, with nothing but the starlit night beyond. One of the casements stood open, swinging over the gravel flat of the adjacent roof. There was that, and the torn fragments of his paintings.

He didn't believe it. Four years' work couldn't be destroyed like this. It couldn't have happened.

But it had happened.

He wanted to run. A voice screamed in the back of his mind, telling him to get out of there, to run as fast as he could from the danger of those motionless, tattered colors. Deliberately he shrugged his coat back on again and stood still. He let the air out of his lungs in a long, exhausted sigh. Then he stepped into the big room and turned on the lamp over his easel. He looked at the torn paintings. He couldn't take his eyes off them. It seemed worse in the bright glare of light, the insanity of it standing stark and naked, laughing at him.

Nausea made his stomach squirm.

Slowly he crossed the room, feeling anger mount with his helplessness. All that work, a complete loss. He paused and touched his palette knife with his toe. It lay on the edge of a gray carpet on the inner floor of the big room. The rest of the floor was bare, where his easel stood, except for another knife, a bread knife, and he touched that with his toe, too. But he didn't pick up either one.

The breeze suddenly slammed the casement window shut, and he went toward it, worked the catch, and pushed it open again. The studio stifled him. He felt again the impulse to turn and run. It was almost as if the vandalism itself had a tangible entity, sharing the place with him.

Or as if someone, or something was in the apartment.

There was a dim glittering on the tar and gravel roof beyond the open window. Dana stepped out into the starlit night. The gravel crunched underfoot as he walked toward the glittering object and picked it up. He stared carefully all around before he looked at what was in his hand. It was his flashlight.

He stood with his back to the window for a moment, feeling a faint, cool breeze, and he knew someone was in the studio behind him. He could feel it. It was in the air, a silent, screaming danger.

He started to turn. There was a cold knot in the pit of his stomach. His body twisted a little at a time, head turning first, shoulders twisting, shoes scraping the gravel. His skin tingled. And abruptly someone turned out the lamp over his easel. The darkness came like a soundless explosion. For a moment he didn't move. Then he slid quickly back through the window. He turned to face the darkness.

"Who is it?" he called softly.

He could see nothing, hear nothing. He strained all his senses. From far away across the city he heard a siren again. He felt a cool breath of air sweep around him from the open window at his back. He heard the ticking of his wristwatch; he heard the thud of blood in his arteries.

"What do you want?" he called again.

Senseless.

He expected no answer.

Light seeped in from the window behind him. He was staring into darkness, with the glow of the night sky making him a clear silhouette. Even as the thought came to him, he knew that was what the intruder had been waiting for. Even as he lunged to the protective wall, the attack came, a sudden burst of movement, something white and round hurtling at his head. He ducked. It went past his head, crashing into the window frame. It shattered explosively, tinkling to the floor. It was one of Charley Powell's decorative vases, taken from his studio.

He reached the wall and stood flat against it, his hands open, palms hard against the cold, painted plaster. There was no further sound or movement. The darkness brooded all through the building. Dana wondered if the other person was armed. He felt a sudden fierce exultation in what was happening. It was something he could understand, at least partially, an open attack on his life, a definite fact.

He looked into the dark studio. Someone was there. He thought of the kitchen knife on the floor, the knife that had been used to slash his paintings. He kept his shoulders flat against the wall and slowly flexed his knees; he put out one hand and groped along the floor for the edge of the rug.

He was too far from it. He couldn't reach the knife. Straightening, he took a sideways step into the room. A faint rustling came at last from the darkness. A scraping footfall. Dana paused. Nothing more happened. He reached down again, and his groping fingers found the edge of the carpet. He could see the big dim rectangle of the window, a shadowy gray island against the darkness surrounding it. His fingers searched along the edge of the rug, fighting time and frustration, and then they touched metal and closed triumphantly around the heavy knife.

Dana stood erect. His voice rang out.

"Now!" he called. "Come out, damn you!"

Something had changed in the texture of the atmosphere in the studio. It was no longer charged with threatening danger. He moved into the center of the room—

Footsteps scurried from him through the doorway to Charley's quarters. Dana sprang forward, forgetting the knife in his hand. A shoulder hurtled into him, slamming the breath from his lungs. He staggered and threw away the knife, after all. He wanted his hands free. He charged after a shadow in the doorway. A fist came out of the darkness and caught him high on the cheek. Dana swung, felt his knuckles slam into something soft and yielding, heard a grunt of pain. Something scraped off the mahogany chest of drawers, where a lamp stood. The lamp crashed down on his scalp...

He was on hands and knees, shaking pain and noise and whirling color from his head. He could hear himself curse in a futile monotone, cursing in the dark as if his voice was a disembodied thing that didn't belong to him. Footsteps rapped sharply on the floor, and a door slammed.

Silence flowed back into the room. It was empty again.

Dana got to his feet, weaving. His shoes scraped in the broken shards of porcelain from the lamp. He bent painfully and found the shattered base, the switch. His fingers seemed to be all thumbs when he turned it on.

It worked. The light glared, shooting nakedly up from his feet. The intruder was gone. He just stood there, not giving chase. Following the attacker down those stairs was useless. It was too late.

His tattered paintings jeered at him from the walls.

Insane, he thought.

Then he thought: *But who? Why?*

He had no answers. None at all.

Afterward, he had to think back to remember what he did. He had a drink. He went into the tiny, makeshift bathroom and plunged his head into ice-cold water from the tap, bathing his lacerated scalp. He had another drink, salvaged from a bottle in Charley's quarters. The rye burned a hole in the pit of his stomach. It didn't stop his shivering. He went to the little electric hot-plate that Charley kept and heated a stale pot of coffee and laced it with some more of the rye and poured it into a cup and drank that. He had trouble holding the cup in his shaking hands.

After awhile he locked the staircase door and closed the studio window and searched the entire loft thoroughly. He didn't find anything. When he looked at his ruined work, be felt a dead, tremendous weight of complete despair.

He expected nothing when he went to the telephone. He dialed Kay Norcross' number and listened to the other instrument ring. It kept on ringing. No one answered it.

He called Willi Tempel's apartment. A woman's voice answered, high and shrill. He could hear the sounds of other voices and music and the clatter of dishes in the background.

"Let me talk to Willi Tempel," he said dully.

"Veelee?"

"Yes, please."

"He iss not here. Wait a moment, yes?"

Dana stood with the telephone in his hand, waiting. In the receiver he heard someone's shrill, high laughter. Something tinkled and crashed. It was quite a party. He waited a long time. Then a man's voice suddenly spoke up.

"Mr. Tempel has gone out somewhere. Come on up and join the crowd, whoever you are."

"Thanks," Dana said, and hung up.

He tried Charley Powell's number. No answer.

Eventually, he got around to calling the police.

EVANS, the detective, showed up. He wore the same neat blue suit and polished brown oxfords. His white shirt gleamed immaculately. A dark red, knitted tie was carefully held in place by a leather and steel clip, the steel ornament shaped like a pair of handcuffs. Dana hadn't touched anything in his room. Evans' silvery hair shone like polished metal as he looked at the violence in it. His eyes touched the open window briefly, swinging over the tattered paintings, the knife on the floor, the wrecked furniture. His eyes came back invariably to the paintings. His expression was neutral as he looked at Dana's tall impatient figure. Beyond the detective, a uniformed cop lounged in the doorway, doing nothing at all.

"I asked for this call, especially," Evans said quietly. "I told them I knew you. Strictly speaking, it's none of my business. It doesn't come under my division. I'm Homicide. Nobody's been killed, right?"

"No," Dana said.

"I didn't think so. On the other hand, we ought to work on preventing crime just like the medics are trying to institute preventive medicine. It's a good idea, but there are a lot of kinks in it," Evans sighed. "Cigarette?"

"Thanks," Dana said. "You get around, anyway. But why pick on me?"

"I was interested," Evans said. "On that subway deal, your story had a lot of cute angles. This is a funny one, too."

"Not funny," Dana said. "This is the second time someone has tried to kill me. And there's a lot of work ruined on those walls. My life's work, you might say, although I'm not shedding any tears of self-pity. All those paintings were to be shown tomorrow at the Tempel Gallery."

"That's tough," Evans said.

"It's hell."

"Were you drinking tonight, Mr. Dana?"

Dana felt the shock of the question like a sudden blow. "I've had a few, mostly during dinner. I don't drink much. What are you trying to make out of it?"

"Nothing."

"You harped on it before. That…and the army."

"I just like to look at it from all sides, that's all. You're pretty touchy, Mr. Dana." Evans walked slowly around the studio, his small feet making no sound. He looked at one picture after the other, lifting the flaps of torn canvas and holding them together to study the paintings. He saw the knife on the floor and looked down at it and pinched his chin. "What do you suppose he used? This knife?"

"I imagine so."

"When he slugged you, were his hands bare? Or was he wearing gloves?"

"I think they were bare. I don't know."

"Well, then, it's easy, Mr. Dana. There would be fingerprints on the knife. That ought to settle it."

Dana swallowed an ache in his throat. "No, that's no good," he said. "I picked up the knife, too. In the dark, when he came at me. I didn't use it, but I picked it up. It will have my fingerprints all over it, if it has anybody's."

Evans said, "I see." Then he said, "You don't have any idea what the guy looked like?"

"It was too dark in here."

"But it was a man, you're sure of that?"

"Pretty sure."

"I thought I smelled perfume."

"It's possible. Charley always has girls up."

"No girl was here when you got home?"

"No."

"Can't you guess who the man was who attacked you?"

"I don't want to guess about a thing like that," Dana said. He crushed out his cigarette. He was beginning to regret his call to the cops. There was a subtle antagonism in Evans, as if he was trying to prove something inimical toward Dana himself. "All I know is that someone deliberately ruined my paintings, and then jumped me."

Evans said, "It's too bad about that knife. You shouldn't have handled it. The way it shapes up, this thing could be just a coincidence. You might be working it up inside yourself, building it into something that doesn't exist. Take that subway business, for instance. You say you only had a sensation of those hands pushing you. You didn't see anybody. Maybe you were pushed, sure, but it could have been an accident, say, by a complete stranger, who was afraid to come out with it afterward. It could have happened that way, you see. You might be mistaken about this personal angle, the idea that someone is out to get you."

Dana said, "Maybe I was mistaken about the subway thing. But I'm not mistaken about tonight."

Evans said, "Well, look. Tonight it could have been a prowler, some nut. A coincidence, like I said."

"No," Dana said.

"Well, it's worth checking into. Of course. I'll do what I can, try to locate anybody seen prowling the premises. But I'd suggest you see a doctor, Mr. Dana."

Dana felt sick anger in the pit of his stomach.

"Why should I see a doctor?"

"Well, you've been working hard on these paintings. You might be overwrought, too imaginative. This show of yours is like a climax to your life, isn't it? It means too much to you. Besides, you haven't given me any real reason why anybody would want to kill you. You haven't given me one concrete item of evidence to back up that idea."

"What about this studio?" Dana demanded.

"You could have done all this yourself."

Dana trembled. "You're a hell of a cop."

"Don't get sore. I just look at all the angles."

Evans looked worried. He glanced back at the cop posted in the doorway. The cop was beginning to appear interested.

"I'll work on it straight, Mr. Dana. But if you're right, the best thing you could do would be to take a vacation, maybe. Get out of town. Let me handle it here."

Dana said, "It will follow me, wherever I go."

"If anybody follows you, then you'd have some proof."

Dana said harshly, "If I saw him first."

He remembered the silence that had come between them after that. There didn't seem to be much to say. He almost lost interest in the routine questions that followed. He sat there in the wreckage of his studio, listening with only half an ear, answering questions about the dinner with Charley and Willi Tempel, about Peter Norcross and Kay. Most of the time he was just listening to a vast, deep silence…

It couldn't be a coincidence, he thought. It was easy enough to kill a man in the city. Almost impossible to prevent a thing like that, if the killer was determined. It could happen anywhere—on the street, in the subway, when he stopped to buy a newspaper. How could he cope with a thing like that? And he would have to handle it himself, because Evans wasn't going to be much help, he could see that. Evans needed tangible clues to work on. Give him a corpse, give him fingerprints, give him a storybook set of motives. Motives…

Who wants to kill me? Dana wondered.

Evans suggested that he might have buried within his own consciousness a convincing knowledge of the killer's identity. Evans acted as if he was sure Dana knew the real facts behind the two incidents. Dana wondered. It came back to him now, an odd sensation he'd felt when he went down and out, in those brief seconds after he'd been slugged here in the studio. He had felt almost happy, relieved, as if he were atoning for something.

Atoning for what?

He didn't know.

It was as if he were trying to remember a dream already faded. Why should he have felt relieved when that lamp came crashing down on his head? It didn't make sense. The memory of his emotion was fragmentary and confused, as if a veil were drawn across his mind when he tried to penetrate further.

Eventually, Evans left, saying something about keeping the doors and windows locked. He had gone all over the adjacent roof and found a fire escape by which anyone could have entered the studio or escaped to the street. But nothing else was found.

He tried to get Willi Tempel on the phone again, but the party in the fat man's apartment was still going strong and Tempel didn't answer. Neither was there an answer in Charley Powell's place. He was about to try Kay when the telephone rang of itself.

The shrill bell echoed through the emptiness of the loft. His shadow slid long and distorted on the wall, as he picked it up.

"Hello?"

The receiver hummed—a faraway sound as if a giant were breathing.

"Hello?" he said again, impatiently.

"Dana?"

It was a woman. There was intolerable amusement in the one word—and relief, too, as if he hadn't been completely expected. He looked at his watch and saw that it was well after midnight.

"Mr. Lucky Dana?" the girl insisted.

It was Lotti Higgins, Charley's redheaded model.

"Lotti," he said. "Charley isn't here."

"I don't care. I want to speak to *you.*"

"I don't think—"

"Don't hang up," the girl warned. "Don't be so damned hasty. I don't know why I like you, Hank Dana, honest I don't. But you're going to be nice and polite, my dear boy. Oh, you're going to be ever so nice to Lotti."

"What are you talking about?" he asked sharply.

"Your paintings," the girl said. "What a shame, all your beautiful paintings! I'm glad nothing happened to you, though."

Dana stiffened. He lowered the telephone for an instant, staring at its black, impersonal shape. He fought down excitement.

"How do you know about it?"

The girl laughed. The laughter sounded shallow, as if she were frightened by a memory.

"I was there. I went to your place to pick up my compact—I'd forgotten it this morning—and I saw what happened to your paintings. I was hiding on the roof. I saw the whole thing."

"Who was it?" Dana rasped. "Who did it?"

"Over a drink, darling. I'll tell you all about it."

"Tell me now," he insisted.

He could almost see her full red lips in a pout when she spoke again. "And then you'll ignore me. Oh, no. This time you're coming to see *me*. And you'll be nice about it, too, my sweet."

"Lotti, listen, what you know may be dangerous."

"It is, darling. I wish I'd never seen it. That's why I want you with me when I get home."

"All right. Where can we meet?"

"At the Kalico Kat. In twenty minutes?"

"I'll be there," he said.

CHAPTER FOUR

THE KALICO KAT was a cellar joint on the west side of Greenwich Village, and Dana walked there through empty streets. Once or twice he turned to look back, but no one followed him, no one he knew. His nerves were still jangled, and he paused at a juice stand near Greenwich Avenue for a cup of insipid coffee. A tall man in a worn blue suit came up and stood next to him and ordered a lemonade.

The man said, "My old lady thinks I'm out bummin' around when I can't sleep. She should only know. All I do is walk and walk." The man had a hard, flat face and expressionless eyes that raked Dana's features. "You got insomnia, too?"

"Yes," Dana said.

"Walkin' it off?"

"No. I've got a date," Dana said.

The man ran his tongue along the bottom of his front teeth. "Sullivan's my name. I'd have a date, too, but my old lady would know it, sure as shooting."

Dana didn't finish his coffee. He put the cup down and it clattered in the saucer, spilling a little. The man beside him looked at the puddle of muddy liquid on the counter.

"This hot weather makes everybody nervous."

"Sure," Dana said. "Good night."

"Have fun," said the man named Sullivan.

"Thanks."

Dana walked away and this time he didn't look back. He went up Greenwich Avenue and then west for half a block. The Kalico

Kat had a green neon sign that hung from the first floor of the brownstone it occupied. The light from the cellar entrance cut a slab of yellow out of the dark pavement. From inside came the murmur of voices, the smell of stale beer. Dana went down five steps beside an iron railing and pushed open the door. The place was crowded, and he had to squint a little to see through the haze of tobacco smoke. He walked slowly behind the men and women perched on the bar stools and looked in all the booths. He didn't see Lotti Higgins.

He ordered rye and squeezed onto a vacant stool and settled down to wait. Now and then he glanced toward the entrance, but no one came in that he knew. It was just one thirty...

At one-thirty-five the man named Sullivan came down the sidewalk outside the Kalico Kat and kept going. There was a drugstore open at the far corner, and he went in to use the telephone. He waited for his connection with a tired, vacant look in his eyes. Finally he said,

"Evans? Sullivan here. I'm keeping an eye on him, like you said. He's jumpy as a mouse. He's in a beer joint now—said he had a date. Do I go in, or do I sit and wait?"

Evans sounded interested. "A date? You talked to him?"

"Sure, why not?"

"All right. Stay where you are, unless he comes out. I'll join you there. Give me the phone number you're using, in case you have to move. Then you call me there, if you're gone by the time I arrive." Evans paused. "And be careful. There's a nut in this fruitcake, somewhere."

"You ain't kidding," Sullivan observed.

He went out to the hot, dark, vacant street. Somebody had put a nickel in the jukebox in the Kalico Kat. Sullivan sat down on a doorstep nearby and watched the entrance...

At the bar, Dana looked at his watch and saw that he had been here more than ten minutes. There was no sign of Lotti. He felt impatient. The smoke and smells and noise had given him a headache, and when he rubbed the back of his head he winced at contact with the bruise there. One of the waiters touched his shoulder and he swiveled around fast.

"Mr. Dana?"

The waiter was a little man with a sallow face and tired, bloodshot eyes. His apron was dirty. At Dana's nod, he went on: "Telephone. Back room, please. A dame."

It was Lotti Higgins. It was her voice, and yet it was different. She wasn't flip or playful or beguiling, this time. She was frightened. He sensed it with her first words.

"Dana, I can't make it. I was there, but I had to leave."

"Why."

"I couldn't stay there. I was scared, that's all."

"What scared you?"

"I saw someone."

"The man who ruined my paintings?"

"I—I had to get out of there. I started to go home, but—I'm afraid to go up to my apartment alone. I don't know what to do."

"Tell me who it is," he urged. "If you saw something in my studio. It's dangerous, and you ought to tell me—tell anyone, as fast as you can. Why don't you call the police?"

She said, "Because I want to tell it to you."

"All right, tell me now."

"If I do, you won't help me."

"Yes, I will," Dana promised. He felt himself sweating. When you came right down to it, he decided, he was afraid, too. Not just for himself. He was afraid for Lotti Higgins He said, "Lotti! I'll come at once. Just tell me where you are."

"I'm calling from a coffee-and-sinkers place near my house. Number 21-A, Myrtle Street. Will you really come?"

"As fast as I can."

She sounded relieved. "I'll want you to stay with me tonight, darling. Will you mind?"

"I'll talk about it when I see you."

Dana hung up after a moment and pushed out of the back room into the smoky confusion of the bar. The waiter was helping someone out of, the men's room. The man was drunk. He clung to the waiter's thin shoulders and his legs dragged on the floor as he was eased into a nearby booth. Not many of the patrons bothered to spare the drunken man a second glance.

The man in the booth was Petey Norcross. His weak face was slack with liquor. His head rolled too big and round for his spindly shoulders. One bow of his horn-rimmed glasses had slipped from his ear, but he didn't seem to notice.

"Petey," Dana said.

"You know this little toad?" the waiter asked

"Yes, I know him. How long has he been here?"

"He came in about half an hour ago."

"Drunk?"

"Cold sober. But then he takes one drink at the bar and just look at him."

"All right," Dana said. "I'll take care of him."

The waiter went away. Dana slid into the bench on the opposite side of the booth from Petey Norcross. The little man didn't seem to be aware of him. His thin, sandy hair fell in loose strands down over his scholarly forehead.

"Petey, wake up," Dana said sharply.

"Whass at?"

"Look at me. It's Henry Dana. Snap out of it!" Dana reached across the table and lifted Petey Norcross' head so that the little man was staring directly at him. "You're not drunk. You're not fooling anyone."

"Huh?"

Dana said, "You came in sober and now you're carrying quite a load. I know your capacity, Petey."

A glimmer of understanding came into the little man's owlish eyes. He blinked and pulled his head away from Dana's supporting hand.

"Hi, Henry. What are you doing here?"

"Let me ask you that one," Dana said. "You're a long way from home."

Petey giggled. "Long, long way. So are you."

"Did you meet Lotti Higgins in here?"

"Lotti Higgins? Lotti? Who is she?"

"Don't give me that," Dana said roughly.

"Never heard of her," said the little man positively.

"You're sure you didn't meet her here?"

"Should I have?" Petey leered.

Dana gave it up. Petey Norcross might be the man who had frightened Lotti away from here, but Petey wasn't dropping his drunken mask. That it was a mask, Dana was sure, but short of hauling the little man to his feet and shaking the truth out of him, there was nothing he could do within the limits of avoiding a public scene. He stood up and watched Petey's head sag to the table.

"Give my regards to Kay," Dana said quietly.

"To hell with you, Henry."

Ten minutes later he stood before Lotti's address on Myrtle Street. The house had a colonial facade that hid its brownstone origin only up to the level of the second floor. A few of the windows fronting the street were lighted, but blind with shades. The street was quiet. A lamp almost directly opposite the house made a pool of yellow on the dark, hot sidewalk.

Dana went up the steps into the doorway. The door had an automatic lock and a buzzer arrangement, but the pneumatic stop on the door had failed to shut it completely. Lotti's was 1-C. That would place her on the first floor, rear. He thumbed the pearl button and waited.

Nothing happened.

He wondered if he had arrived ahead of the girl. The corner coffee shop had been closed and dark. She must have come here. He heard a muted sound inside, beyond the lobby door that wasn't quite closed, and he pushed against the brass plate and went inside. Steps angled up into the dimness of a night light, going to the second floor, and he thought he glimpsed movement out of the tail of his eye. But it was gone when he reached the foot of the stairs. High up, perhaps on the third or fourth floor, a woman was talking in a querulous, whining voice. He couldn't make out the words.

He waited, listening to that remote voice, and then he walked silently down the narrow lobby to the rear door. Like the lobby door, it stood ajar, and light streamed from the shattered room beyond.

He didn't have to check the nameplate to be sure he was in the right place. This was Lotti's apartment. It was too much like the shattered state of his own studio, in its insane disorder. One of the lamps flanking the couch lay broken on the floor; the rugs were disheveled, pushed aside by frightened feet; a chair was overturned near the bedroom doorway.

Dana left the hall door open behind him.

"Lotti?" he called.

His stomach was tied in a convulsive knot. There was a light in the kitchen; the window was open there, and he saw a fire escape beyond, the lowest platform of the four landings that went up to the roof. From the areaway beyond came the sound of the woman's querulous voice. Another voice had joined her—

Dana heard the scream as he put his hands on the windowsill and looked out.

He couldn't tell its direction at first—it seemed to echo from everywhere, bouncing back in ululating horror from the brick walls of the houses surrounding the back court.

And then he looked up toward the roof.

He was in time to see a dim, dark shape come spinning down out of the rectangle of night sky, far overhead. A shape that was contorted and struggling against the thin air as it hurtled to the hard concrete below.

And then the scream was cut off by an ugly, unforgettable sound...

DETECTIVE EVANS walked around the drum table in Lotti Higgins' living room and looked at the shattered lamp on the maroon carpet. The white shards of porcelain looked milky in the light from the kitchen doorway. Sullivan stood there, big and beefy, his face red and perplexed, his brows scowling.

"Too late," Sullivan said. "Way too late."

From beyond the open kitchen window came the sounds of activity in the courtyard. Men were busy out there, and other men worked the rooftops of adjacent houses. Evans sighed. He didn't think they would find anything that could be of help.

"Any marks on her?"

"She lost her shoe," Sullivan said. "They're looking for it now. Otherwise, she jumped or fell."

Evans looked wry. "Screaming bloody murder all the way."

"As far as the doc can determine," Sullivan said stubbornly, "she wasn't hurt before she jumped."

"Or fell," Evans mocked.

Sullivan said, "Go prove something, Ed."

"Somebody may have seen her go up that fire escape. Lots of them heard her, anyway. We may have some luck."

"Don't count on it," Sullivan muttered. He turned his heavy, red face toward Dana. "What have you got to say?"

"Nothing," Dana said. "I can't help you much."

He sat on the big couch in Lotti's living room. His face was tight and tired. Too much was happening for him to keep track of. Only one thing stood out with clarity. He had been too late. If he had arrived a minute or two earlier, Lotti Higgins might still be alive. She could have told him then whatever she knew about his studio. She had gambled on seeing him first instead of calling the police, and she had lost her gamble. The fact that Evans and Sullivan had materialized so hard on his heels left him beyond surprise. He looked at Sullivan carefully and recognized him as the man who had talked to him at the juice stand on Greenwich Avenue.

"You were tailing me all the time?" he asked.

Evans said, "I told Sully to keep an eye on you. That shindig up in your studio was too much to swallow. It didn't seem finished to me, coming on top of your subway accident."

"That was no accident," Dana said.

"I'm inclined to agree with you now," Evans nodded. "But that doesn't mean we know any more than we did before. You've got some explaining to do, Mr. Dana."

"I got here after she was dead," Dana said.

"You got here a minute ahead of me," Sullivan corrected. "That would have given you enough time to chase that poor dame up to the roof and push her over the edge."

"But I didn't," Dana said. "Why would I? She was going to tell me what she knew about the person who destroyed my paintings earlier tonight. She said she had seen him."

"Then why didn't she tell the cops about it?"

"I don't know," Dana said. "I gathered she wanted to talk to me first."

"That doesn't make much sense," Sullivan grunted.

Dana said, "I never paid much attention to her, because she was Charley Powell's girl—anyway, she worked for him, not for me, and I kept hands off. I think she saw a chance to get me interested in her. That's the only way I can figure it."

Evans smoothed his thick, silvery hair. He started to say something, then turned to the uniformed cop who came in from the kitchen. Behind the cop were others, crowding in from the courtyard. The cop whispered something to Evans and they both went to the front door and stood there in conversation. Dana stirred restlessly. The eyes of the other detectives were impersonal. They were just doing a job. Dana as a person meant little or nothing to them. But as a source of information, he meant much more. He wished he knew something definite to tell them. He watched Sullivan go out in answer to another cop's whisper. Somewhere on the street beyond the lobby an ambulance clanged. Through the open kitchen window he could hear a hubbub of voices, from spectators who crowded the windows of the surrounding apartments.

Evans came back, pinching his lower lip.

"It shapes up this way," he said. "This girl called you at your studio and said she'd seen something, or had information that you should know about; but she'd give it to you, personally, or not at all. And she asked you to meet her at this bar, the Kalico Kat."

"That's right."

"But she wasn't there?"

"No. That's where I got the second call from her."

"Who was the little drunk you were talking to in there? Sullivan says he saw you get chummy with a fellow in one of the booths who was just about passed out."

Dana moved restlessly. "That was Peter Norcross."

"Did he know Lotti Higgins?"

"He might have met her around town. Charley often took her out on dates. Peter might have known her."

"Did he say he'd seen Lotti in this bar?"

"He was too drunk to give me a straight answer."

Evans paused. "It's possible, though, that Norcross is the lad who scared Lotti Higgins away from this meeting place she'd arranged with you?"

"It's possible," Dana said.

"Well, we'll talk to Norcross later. Let's get down to this corner cafe, here on Myrtle. That was closed when you arrived. You waited a minute or two and didn't see anybody around, and then you came down to the apartment house."

"That's right."

"Sullivan says he found you in here. Correct?"

Dana nodded again.

Evans said, "How did you get in?"

"The door was open."

"You didn't have to use a key?"

"I don't have a key. I just walked in."

Evans said, "I'll tell you why I asked about the key. We know the girl let herself in with one. We found one in her purse. But we found another key still in the door lock, on the outside. It's being checked for fingerprints now. We figure the murderer—I guess we can call him that, if he scared the girl so that she jumped off the roof—we figure he had a key and slipped in here and in his hurry he didn't take the key from the lock. Well, you don't find keys to redheads' apartments just by picking 'em up off the street. We figure the guy always had one; maybe Lotti gave him one herself, a long time ago. So he was somebody she knew pretty well."

"She knew a number of men," Dana said.

"Intimately?"

Dana said angrily, "How would I know about that?"

"I'm only asking. You never had a key?"

"I told you once, no."

"And you didn't notice the one in the door when you came in?"

"I must have overlooked it. I didn't notice it, no."

Evans turned away abruptly. There were men in Lotti's bedroom, ransacking the closets. Evans sent out pickup orders for the cafe proprietor, for Petey Norcross, and for any neighbor who might have seen Lotti return home. In the midst of it, Sullivan came back again. Evans swung to him.

"Find her shoe?"

"We went over the courtyard with a fine-tooth comb, Ed. It's not in the apartment—I thought maybe she'd started to undress when the guy slipped in here, but the mate to the one she's wearing is gone. I checked the fire steps, too, figuring she might have caught the heel in one of them iron slats. No dice."

Evans looked grim. "If it's gone, it's gone. It couldn't have walked away by itself. You know what that means, Sully."

"Sure," Sullivan said. He looked at Dana. "Up to now, it could be suicide. Jumped or fell. Now it's murder."

Dana met Sullivan's hard gaze for a moment, until the big man looked back at Evans.

"We'll find that shoe," Evans said. "Check all the ash cans in the neighborhood."

"Sure thing."

Dana said, "What makes Lotti's shoe so important?"

"Because it's missing." Evans looked harassed. "Anything that doesn't make sense might be important. It makes this murder, as Sullivan says." He turned to his big assistant. "Any witnesses rounded up yet?"

"A few," Sullivan nodded. "That corner cafe proprietor is outside."

"Hell." Evans seemed to settle himself, as if bracing for a long siege. "Send him in."

CHAPTER FIVE

HIS NAME was Armand Spiros. He looked frightened and uneasy, yet somewhat self-important as he faced Evans in the battered room. He had dressed hastily, and his shirttail hung out over the back of his trousers.

Questioning the man, Evans was thorough and incisive. Yes. Spiros knew the girl they were talking about. Sure, she'd been in his place before he closed up. She'd made a phone call; he guessed it was to a man. Frightened? She sure was.

Slowly the scene was reconstructed until Dana almost saw Myrtle Street, twisting crookedly under a stifling blanket of midnight heat. Lotti Higgins stood in the doorway of Spiros' restaurant and hesitated. There were two street lamps, one about a third of the way down the block on the east side, and another at the far corner opposite her apartment house. Lotti looked at her watch; it would soon be two o'clock in the morning. Behind her, the restaurant proprietor made impatient, muttering noises.

"All right," she said. "I'm leaving. But I wish you'd stay open ten minutes more. My friend will be here by then."

"This ain't no hotel lobby," said Spiros. "You want to meet your boy friend, go hire a hall. I'm closing up."

He was a short man, very stout, with a dark face and drooping moustaches. Maybe he'd stay open if she ordered something to eat, Lotti thought. She turned back and placed her handbag carefully on the marble counter.

"I'd like some apple pie," she said.

"Look, lady—"

"And coffee, please."

"The fire's out, lady. No more coffee. The apple pie is stale; it's for the garbage pail. Once and for all, I'm closing up, see?" His voice whined up on a querulous note. "What's bothering you, anyway? If your friend is coming, he'll show up in ten minutes, you say. What's ten minutes?"

"Stay open until he comes," Lotti urged. "Please."

"You scared of the street?"

"Yes," Lotti said. "I'm scared."

He looked her over deliberately, and she had to endure his probing little eyes that seemed to take advantage of the fact that she didn't dare run, that they were alone together in an empty coffee shop that was like an island of light in the vast darkness of the city.

Lotti looked at herself in the yellow mirror beyond the marble counter. She was wearing a tiny hat and veil tipped over her long red hair; her light summer suit was smart and expensive; but under the veil her face was white and drawn.

I look scared, all right, she thought.

The lights in the cheap little restaurant suddenly grew dimmer and then almost completely blacked out as the proprietor snapped off the switches. Lotti swiveled on the stool, and it squealed under her.

"Please…" she said.

"I'll walk you home," the little fat man decided.

"But I told my friend I'd wait here!"

"That's up to you, lady. I'll walk you home, or you can stand outside by yourself. Take your choice."

Lotti wondered if she were jumping at shadows. Perhaps most of her fears were imaginary. The empty street was almost preferable to this leering little man with his dark drooping moustaches. She slid off the stool quickly.

"I'll wait outside, then."

"Suit yourself," he shrugged.

Evans stirred in his chair as Armand Spiros stopped talking. In the courtyard outside, the hubbub still went on. Evans leaned forward a little and spoke again to Spiros.

"That was the last you saw of her? You left her out there on the street?"

"Sure. I went home. She didn't mean nothing to me."

"Did you see the friend she was waiting for?"

"Nobody was around." Spiros' little eyes looked hot and black. Did he knock her off, lieutenant? Or maybe she did the Dutch, huh? I kind of think her boy friend did it, though—"

Evans looked at Dana. "That's what we're trying to find out. All right, Spiros. Thanks a lot. You've been a help."

Sullivan had someone else waiting for Evans' questions after the cafe proprietor was gone. Dana controlled his surprise when he saw the twelve-year-old girl ushered in. Evans' manner changed instantly with the girl. He had children of his own. Obviously, he knew how to handle them.

"You knew Miss Higgins, Polly?" he asked.

"Oh, yes, Sir. I knew her very well."

"And you recognized her on the street a while ago?"

Polly Cain was emphatic about it. She was tall and thin and awkward, wrapped in a mousy flannel robe, her pinched pale face more curious than fearful. Sullivan came in with a glass of milk for her, and she sat on the very edge of her chair sipping the milk. She hadn't been able to sleep, she told them. No, nothing special had aroused her. Her bed was by the window overlooking Myrtle Street, and she had been looking out and watching. No, not for any special reason—not until she recognized Miss Higgins.

The last light went out in the restaurant and Lotti stood on the warm, dark street, listening to Spiros' footsteps hurry away. The street seemed empty. From far away she heard the rumble of an elevated tram, and from closer at hand the shrill hoot of a tug on the North River. Lotti stood very still in the shadows of the doorway. There was nothing to be afraid of. She'd seen what she had seen; but no one knew she'd been on the roof outside Dana's studio. Remembering it, she shuddered in deep, primitive horror. Maybe she should have gone to the police right away. She looked at her watch again, but the light was too dim to see by. What was keeping Dana? He should have been here by now. Maybe he wasn't coming at all. He didn't like her, he never had, and he doubtless knew all about her affair with Charley Powell. Maybe that was why he'd been so indifferent. But things would change now. He'd have to help her, they were in this thing together. He'd have to pay attention to her now—if he ever came.

She began to feel a deep conviction that he wasn't going to show up and then she heard the footsteps. They were coming from around the corner, and she listened to the deliberate click of heels, a steady, implacable pace that ate up the distance toward her shadowed doorway. Whoever it was, he was bound to discover her there. If it was Dana, that would be wonderful. But she didn't think it was Dana.

She left the doorway and looked around the corner.

The man was midway up the block, walking in the center of the sidewalk. A street lamp behind him kept his face in shadow and threw a long, distorted outline of his figure almost to her feet.

It wasn't Dana.

Lotti stood paralyzed, staring at him. She wanted to scream, but she could not. In one sickening moment, she knew that all her plans had been childish and infantile, deliberately blind to danger. She gasped, as if someone had struck her a stunning blow. For an eternal instant, she and the man stared at each other. And then he started forward again, not hurrying, his pace deliberate, sure of himself and of her, sure of what he had to do.

Her legs refused to function. She wanted to run, but she couldn't run. And then she twisted around, not wasting the breath to scream, not throwing away a precious moment more in which she could save herself.

The man ran lightly behind her, his swift pace eating up the time and distance between them.

Lotti threw herself forward. Muscles she had forgotten about came into play as she ran down the sidewalk toward the door of her apartment house. Terror made her mind race on ahead of her gasping body, to the five steps, to the doorway in the fake Colonial facade of the brownstone. If the door was locked, she would never have time to get the key from her purse and open it. She would be trapped there, unable to escape or get inside. But sometimes the pneumatic stop on the door failed to shut completely. This had to be one of those times. If it wasn't, she was lost. She might as well stop running now and face her pursuer here on the deserted street.

Her high heels made a quick, frantic drumming as she cut across to the building entrance. Behind her, the man's footsteps pattered faster in a sudden burst of speed, a desperate sprint to catch her before she gained safety.

The steps, now. Don't trip, don't stumble! Lotti ran up them heavily, lunging into the lighted entryway, gulping air in a great gasping sob as she pushed against the shiny brass doorknob. *Please, let it be open!* And then she was through, the door hissing back as she threw her weight upon it, opening into the lobby beyond, with its lights, with its safety...

Little Polly Cain answered Evans' last questions without much interest and looked at her empty glass of milk.

"And that's all you saw of Miss Higgins? She ran inside the building and the man ran right in after her?"

"Yes, sir. I didn't see her again." The child's eyes were round and wide. "Did she—I mean, is she d-dead?"

Evans said, "She had an accident."

Sullivan took the girl out of the apartment. Dana lit a cigarette as Evans moved with angry, restless steps about the room.

"Well, we got her into the house, so far. And as far as we know, she still had both her shoes. And we know she had company—up to the lobby, anyway. It was no accident, her falling off the roof. It's easy enough to figure what happened to her in here."

Dana nodded. The reconstruction of Lotti's last movements was fairly obvious. It was too clear. He kneaded his fingers together as Evans went on describing what had taken place…

Her door was in the shadows, the brass lock shimmering against the dark green panel. Her heels made echoes vibrate up the stairway, her fingers fumbled in her purse for the door key. There was a scream in her throat, but no sound came from her. She didn't have the strength to scream. A wave of weakness made her stagger as if drunk, approaching her door.

The key! Compact, lipstick, a balled handkerchief, her change purse, the cloth of the bag's inner lining. Her mouth was open, sucking air deeply into her exhausted lungs. She could feel the wild, impossible beat of her overtaxed heart. And then her fingers closed over the cool metal of the key.

She had it in the lock and her door was open when she looked back at the street entrance. The street door, with its pneumatic stop, had almost closed. Almost. A hand had caught it, holding it open. All she could see was the hand and an arc of white shirtsleeve. She gasped and threw herself into the apartment, slammed the door shut and leaned back against it, exhausted, thoroughly beaten.

She stood in the darkness for what seemed forever. Fear twisted inside her. The foyer was silent. She swallowed dryness in her throat, swallowed again and again, her breath catching.

Slowly the pounding of her heart grew easier and steadier. No one approached her door. Her wild entry into the building had aroused no one; or if it had, nobody was going to mix into any peculiar business that didn't concern them.

But she was safe now.

Safe? she wondered.

She remembered, when she had called Dana, how the urgency of his warning had left her feeling remote from it all. The reality of danger hadn't really touched her. But now the reality had come, it was out there in the foyer, or on the street, watching and waiting for her.

Lotti moved into her living room and lit the lamp on her drum table. The everyday furnishings reassured her. Reaction set in, leaving her limp and helpless, annoyed at herself. Why hadn't she screamed or called for help? Surely someone would have replied; people would have come to her aid. And the danger was still near.

The telephone stood in a little niche at one end of the couch across the room. She started toward it, then paused. She wondered if she should call the police now. The thought of that figure prowling the building made her shudder. Phone in hand, she looked at her watch. It was incredible that so few minutes had actually gone by since she had called Dana at the Kalico Kat. Given every possible break in transportation, at best he could be just arriving at the corner of Myrtle Street. He would find the restaurant closed and deserted. It would take him a moment to realize that she had come here, to her own apartment.

She would wait five more minutes, she decided. She was safe here. She would let Dana decide what to do about the police and what she had seen.

Her fingernails scratched noisily on the cloisonné cigarette box. Her hands shook as she put the cigarette to her lips and looked about for a light. Her lighter was in the bedroom. It looked cozy, frilly, and feminine, when she snapped on the light in there. The silver cigarette lighter stood on the bed table. The cigarette didn't help much, though. What she needed, Lotti decided, was a drink. Dana would want one when he arrived, too.

The liquor was in the kitchenette. There was an overhead light in there, and she groped for the cord that dangled from the ceiling, with its little plastic bowknot tied to the end. She couldn't find it. She felt around over her head, annoyed. Sometimes when there was a draught through the apartment, the cord kept swinging to the right, toward the kitchen window. She reached in that direction and found the gently swinging cord.

But she didn't put on the light.

She stood very still.

A draft through the apartment. That only happened when she opened both the kitchen window and the front door. The front door! Had she locked it? Had she snapped the chain bolt when she stumbled inside? Or had she been too exhausted to think of it?

The front door was open. She could feel the sluggish stir of air about her legs, sweeping toward the open kitchen window. Beyond the window was a little courtyard and the lowest ladder of the fire escape that led up five flights to the roof.

Lotti dropped her hand from the light cord. Somehow the darkness in here was friendly, making a sanctuary for her. She stood still, straining to listen. The current of air swept silently around her legs, bringing with it a faint clicking sound, so faint that she thought she imagined it. It was the front door, closing again.

Someone was in the apartment.

She wondered for a desperate moment if it was Dana. His name was on the tip of her tongue, she was about to call out to him, when she heard the footsteps, methodical and direct, crossing the living room. They were the footsteps of her pursuer on the street. He came straight for the kitchen, as if he sensed her presence there immediately.

She screamed now. The sound ripped from her throat in a frenzy of terror, shattering the silence of the night. But even as she screamed, she knew it wouldn't frighten him off. Not after what she had seen him do.

Twisting, she lunged for the open kitchen window, pushed the flimsy screen out with a brief, ripping sound of wood and copper mesh. Behind her, she heard a crash as a piece of furniture was overthrown. The light in the other room went out. But she was through the window now, groping on the steel platform of the fire escape, hesitating in the dark. It was like being at the bottom, of a deep, deep well. The surrounding buildings rose sheer up, ugly and drab, on all sides. The fence of the little courtyard behind the house was far too high for her to climb, and the door in it was padlocked. There was only one way to go. Up.

Until now it had been fairly easy to follow Lotti's movements and motives. Dana sat still while Evans moved about the apartment, pointing out evidence to verify his reconstruction. But it was Sullivan who brought in the final witness.

"This here is Gustav Stein," Sullivan said. "He's an amateur astronomer. He sews it up for us, all right. He was on a roof across the way and saw the whole thing."

Gustav Stein was a small man with a mop of bushy gray hair and an excess of nervous energy. His answers literally crackled out before Evans finished putting the questions to him. His broken English didn't matter. He knew what he had seen, and described it with a scientific accuracy that left no room for doubt.

Stein had been up on the roof in the hope of witnessing a scheduled meteor shower. He had seen Lotti climb from her kitchen window and go up the fire escape. He had seen the man pursuing her—but no, he could not identify him. It was too dark. But he could hear them talking, up there on the roof.

Evans glanced at Dana. His nostrils looked pinched. "Look, was she limping at all?"

"Limping?"

"As if she'd lost a shoe."

"Ach, that I did not notice. But I saw her come up the fire escape, and that man was close behind her…"

Lotti could hear the footsteps rap harshly on the kitchen floor, only a few steps away. She flattened against the brick wall. She knew at once it was useless. He would know where she had gone. With the thought, she turned up the fire escape, careless now of any sound she might make. Behind her, the sash squealed as it was thrown up still higher by her pursuer.

The windows of the second landing were dark, tightly shut. Lotti looked into the well of darkness. The shadows plunged upward to meet her. She screamed, clinging to the iron rail, and her voice raised queer, garbled echoes in the narrow space between the buildings. Turning, she scrambled up to the third landing one of her shoes came off and fell, but she didn't hear it strike anything below. There was nothing in the world but the labor of her strained lungs, of forcing her legs to climb one more step, and then another. She heard the sound of her own continued screams as if from a great distance, overlaid by the roaring in her ears…

The fire escape trembled with the weight of her silent enemy. He was half a flight behind her when she reached the third landing. He was only two or three steps below when she reached the fourth. His hand came out and grabbed at her dress and the hem ripped with a queer, dry sound. Somewhere across the areaway a lighted window appeared and a woman stuck her head out and called out a question. Other windows went up, other heads appeared. But Lotti couldn't stop; nothing was going to halt the man behind her. She knew it with a dull, deadening agony, and there was nothing to do but keep on climbing in the hope that she would find a window open on the last landing.

None of the windows were open. She was at the top now, stepping out onto the roof, the tar and gravel crunching under her left shoe. She was aware of the pain of the pebbles in her bare right foot, but it seemed unreal, as if her foot, like the sounds she made, no longer belonged to her.

The man's head appeared over the edge of the roof. Lotti moved backward toward the rear of the building, unaware of the wide sweep of starlit sky overhead. From below came a clamor of voices, and someone called shrilly for the police. But they didn't know she was up here; they didn't know anything about *him*. Or what he had done earlier tonight, and what he was going to do now.

"No," she whispered. "Don't…"

The back of her foot struck something hard and she tottered for an awful moment. She had come to the small coping that bordered the edge of the roof. There was nothing but dark space below her…

Her lips moved. "Please…I won't tell…I wasn't going to tell…"

The man seemed content, now that she was finally trapped. Under the stars, he was only a shape, the head curiously indrawn on his shoulders, his arms limp and loose at his sides. "You saw me," he said.

"Yes but I—"

"You were on a roof once before, this evening. Another roof. You looked in through the window, didn't you?"

"I didn't see anything," she whispered desperately. "I wouldn't tell anybody, even if I had. You know I wouldn't. I don't care what you did, or why. Only, please…"

"I'm sorry," the man said.

He came toward her again, and Lotti tried to shrink back, but there was no place to go. He was going to touch her, and the thought snapped her last thread of reason. She couldn't let him put his hands upon her.

Turning, she flung herself away from him, from the hands that reached for her. There was nothing above or below but air. She felt herself falling, sucked into a vortex that wheeled about her head, and she screamed as she dropped...and dropped...

Evans said sharply, "Then she lost her shoe, you think, on the fire escape?"

"Yes, it seems so to me now," Gustav Stein said.

"Now, what happened to the man on the roof with her?"

"I do not know."

"Didn't you see where he went?"

Mr. Stein shrugged regretfully. "It was a horrible thing to watch, you understand. But one's eyes sometimes follow ugly sights to their conclusion. I watched her fall. When I looked up again to the other roof, he was gone. Just gone, you understand."

Evans looked discouraged. He thanked Mr. Stein and waved him out of Lotti's apartment. Sullivan came back inside and looked at Dana first, then Evans, and shrugged. "The newspaper boys are outside, Ed. They want to see you."

"Not now," Evans said. "We're moving back to my office." He jerked his head toward Dana. "You're coming with me."

"Why?" Dana asked. "Am I under arrest?"

Evans stared at him. "Damned if I know—yet."

DAWN touched the windows of Evans' office with a dirty gray brush. The room smelled of stale cigarette smoke and disinfectant. On the walls were framed photographs, groups of uniformed police, a college diploma. On Evans' desk, in addition to a white blotter, was a copper inkwell, a clipboard of typed reports, and a photograph of a slender woman with two small boys. Evans looked at the photograph and wondered if he should call his wife. She would be asleep, but it would be a light sleep as she waited for him to come home. She would have to wait a little longer, he decided. He thought of the dawn that must also be touching the bedroom window where she slept. The air was cool now, but the day was going to be another scorcher.

"This whole thing smelled of murder from the very first," he said heavily. "I should have kept a man on you from the start."

Dana leaned forward in his chair near the desk. There was dull shock behind his eyes.

"You didn't seem to believe me," he said.

"I thought you might be a nut," Evans sighed. "We get lots of them. Persecution complexes, psychopathic inferiors, people who pervert their own failings into some pretty horrible channels." He paused. "We might be up against somebody like that here. I always figured crime prevention can start before a crime is committed, given any decent breaks, and the more I thought about you, after you missed getting killed by that subway train, the more I thought you might be a case to test my theory. But I failed. I fouled it up, all right."

"You couldn't help that," Dana said.

"I didn't follow through," Evans said bitterly. "I didn't have the courage of my convictions. Now we got a dead girl on our hands and she's just an innocent bystander, so to speak, because you're the lad our murderer really wants to kill."

Dana didn't reply. Evans became brisk.

"Well, we've got something tangible now. Now we've got a girl who's been murdered, one way or another. It might be difficult to prove first-degree homicide in Lotti Higgins case, though. Who's to say she didn't just have a case of the screaming meemies?" He waved a hand downward in dismissal. "All right. I want to start this at the beginning, when you first returned to your studio."

"That was about midnight," Dana said.

"And you called all your friends right afterward?"

Dana nodded. "It was about twelve-thirty when you showed up. About one o'clock when Lotti Higgins telephoned me."

Evans said, "What time did you leave the Kalico Kat?"

"Make it one-thirty."

"And we find the girl dead twenty minutes later. Let's go on from there. Let's talk to your friend, Mr. Powell."

A uniformed cop brought Charley into Evans' office. He looked sleepy. He flipped a hand toward Dana in greeting and took a chair near the window, his heavy body relaxed, legs thrust out straight before him.

"On with the inquisition, commissioner," he said.

"Do you feel this is an occasion for flippancy, Mr. Powell?" Evans rapped.

"I'm just tired, lieutenant. You kept me waiting in your anteroom long enough."

"We'll try not to take up too much of your time. Perhaps Miss Higgins' death is only a trifling matter to you."

"Lots of people die," Charley said. "Every day, everywhere. Lotti worked for me. We were friends. So what? I've had other friends who died, too."

"Were they also murdered?" Evans asked softly.

Charley looked shocked. "Of course not!"

"Lotti was murdered. That makes this a little different, doesn't it? Particularly when I understand that she was more than just a model to you."

"What of it?"

"Did you have a key to her apartment?"

"No."

"Are you sure of that?"

Charley said, "I never saw her at her apartment. She always came either to the studio or to my uptown place."

"You knew where she lived, though?"

"I had her address, if that's what you mean."

"But you never went there?"

"Maybe, once or twice. Just to pick her up, or to take her home. I never lingered. I didn't like the place."

Evans leaned across the desk and snapped off the gooseneck lamp. It was broad daylight now. Dana felt as if someone had thrown a handful of sand in his eyes.

Evans said, "As far as we knew, you were the last person of consequence who spent any time with Lotti Higgins last night, Mr. Powell. What time did you leave her?"

"About eleven."

"Where was that?"

"Kolevici's."

"You didn't see her home, to her door?"

Charley scowled. "We had an argument. I guess there's no use trying to hide that. Half the people in the bar got mixed up in it;

65

but it wasn't anything serious. Lotti was hard to get along with. So I walked out on her."

"What was the argument about?" Evans asked.

Charley hesitated, looked at Dana, then down at his hands. His twisted fingers moved uneasily. "She wanted to come to the studio. I told her no, because I knew Dana would be there and I didn't want to disturb him."

"Yet she was at the studio shortly before Dana returned home," Evans pointed out. "How do you account for her going there after you refused her?"

"She was stubborn," Charley shrugged. "She made up her mind to go somewhere and do something, and there she was."

"Then she expected you at the studio, anyway?"

"No," Charley said sharply.

Dana interrupted. "Charley never slept there. She'd have no reason to come to the studio to find him."

"Not unless Mr. Powell made an appointment to meet her there."

"I didn't," Charley said. "I was sick of her. And if, by any chance, you're trying to pin all this on me, you've got a little paradox in your reasoning. I'd hardly invite Lotti to Dana's studio if I planned to cut up his paintings."

Evans said, "I'm not trying to pin anything on anybody, yet. What time did you get home to your own apartment?"

"About eleven-thirty."

"Then what?"

"Then nothing," Charley snapped, annoyed. "I turned in and went to sleep."

Evans said, "At a little after twelve, Dana tried to reach you by telephone. There was no answer."

Charley Powell looked startled.

"I couldn't have been asleep that soon. I'd had more than a snootful, but it made me wakeful instead of knocking me out. I didn't hear the telephone ring, though."

"Then how do you account for it?"

"I can't," Charley said. "Maybe Hank dialed the wrong number."

Dana felt Evans' eyes on him. "It's possible," he put in. "I was pretty upset at the time."

There were more questions, some of them reverting back to the evening before the murder, when Dana had been pushed from the subway platform. Evans didn't seem to be getting anywhere, Dana thought, and a slow, creeping discouragement entered his mind. He felt tired now, watching the new day brighten and grow warmer with each passing minute. Sullivan came in and Charley was sent into the anteroom to wait again. Sullivan turned his red face toward Dana and unwrapped an object he had carried in under his arm.

It was a high-heeled, red leather pump. It was Lotti Higgins' missing shoe.

"We found this in a trash can a block from her house," Sullivan said. "The way it figures, she lost it while running up the fire escape, and the killer was so close behind her that it fell and hit him, and he instinctively caught it. Maybe he didn't quite know what he was doing because, he was so anxious to get his paws on the girl. So he stuck it in his pocket. Afterward when he made his getaway, he discovered the shoe he still carried. So he dropped it off in the trash can in the next alley."

Evans nodded. He turned the shoe over and examined the heel. The little rubber lift on the bottom of the high spike was missing. "You notice this?"

Sullivan said, "We looked for the lift, too, but it hasn't shown up yet. We turned that trash can inside out, but it wasn't there."

Evans said, "Well, maybe it doesn't mean anything at all. Send it down to the laboratory. Let them use their imagination on it, if any."

Sullivan took the shoe with him on his way out. Evans told the uniformed cop at the door to let the rest of the people in.

Dana was surprised to see Kay Norcross, Petey, and Willi Tempel trail in after Charley Powell. It hadn't taken Lieutenant Evans long to round up everyone concerned. He wondered what persuasion he had used to rout Willi Tempel out of bed at this ungodly hour. Willi's air of pompous, outraged indignity suffered a sharp deflation in the harsh dawn light; he merely looked old and fat and frightened.

Evans laid the law down promptly. "I'm just as tired of sitting around here as you people are. This is only a preliminary inquiry, but it sometimes pays to get the basic facts as quickly as possible, even," he added, with a trace of sarcasm, "if it costs us a few hours' sleep. I don't want any bickering. All I want are straight answers to some simple questions. Is that understood?"

No one said anything. Dana looked at Kay Norcross. She was pale and drawn. Petey Norcross, standing beside her chair, was disheveled, his straw hair awry, his horn-rimmed glasses slightly askew. He held Kay's hand in a tight, child-like grip.

Evans said, "We'll take you first, Mr. Tempel, since you were at Kolevici's with Powell and Dana last night. You saw Lotti Higgins then, didn't you?"

"She was with Charley," Willi nodded. His chins doubled and redoubled as he leaned forward, wheezing over his great paunch. "I protest your questioning me, lieutenant, but I shall cooperate. I left them early, as you doubtless know. I had an affair of my own to manage."

"Then you were at home from eleven o'clock onward?"

"We ran out of champagne," Willi smiled. He spread his fat, dimpled hands apologetically. "Most of the neighbor liquor stores were closed. I had to search rather far afield."

"You went yourself?" Evans asked.

"Of course. I wanted the air. It was a stuffy night. And then, unfortunately, I was entertaining some rather stuffy people, too. It was a good excuse to escape from them, even for a few minutes."

"What time did you get back?"

"Quite late. I met some people I knew, on the street, and we talked for some time. The party was over in my place by the time I returned."

"We can check the time, you know," Evans warned.

"I shall give you a list of all my guests. You may question them, if you wish. But if, as you originally explained the matter, the young lady's death is due to the fact that she saw the person who destroyed Dana's paintings, then you should rule me out of your riddle at once. I stood to gain a considerable sum of money from young Dana's show, and I would be the last to destroy that source of income, inasmuch as I am without doubt the greediest man in the world."

"But you and Dana had a difference over money," Evans pointed out.

"Who told you that?"

"Mr. Powell mentioned it, and Dana confirmed it."

Willi turned venomous little eyes toward Charley. "Mr. Powell is a frustrated Casanova who had a perfectly good motive not only for destroying Dana's paintings—sheer professional jealousy—but also due to jealousy in love, as well. Charley was always chasing after women who, in turn, preferred Dana, although Dana does not encourage them."

Charley said, "Why, you fat ape—"

Evans voice was sharp. "Sit down! Both of you!"

"You seek motives, lieutenant," Willi added with satisfaction. "I have given you an excellent one."

"Yes, and tried to side-track the fact that you've cheated more than one of your clients financially, according to the record," Evans went on.

"You can prove nothing of that, and I warn you—"

"Sure," Evans held up a weary hand. "Sit down, will you? Powell, keep your mouth shut. I thought all you people were such fine friends!"

Petey Norcross spoke up unexpectedly. "We are, as a matter of fact. It is just that this matter has put us all under a heavy strain. I wish you would conclude this as quickly as possible, lieutenant. I'm tired, and my wife needs some rest. This has all been a shock to her."

Dana looked at Kay Norcross. The morning sunlight was not kind to her. Her lips were bloodless. She clung to Petey's hand with a desperate grip.

Evans said, "Mr. Norcross, all we want from you is an explanation of what you were doing at the Kalico Kat last night?"

Petey blinked. "I was there. I won't deny it. But I drank too much, unfortunately, to be reliable in memory."

"Did you see Lotti Higgins at the bar?"

"I think I would remember it, if I had."

"What were you doing there in the first place?"

"Drinking."

"Alone?"

"My wife was—otherwise engaged. She was at home."

Dana thought of the fact that the Norcross telephone had gone unanswered to his ring at midnight, along with all the others. But he said nothing. Kay Norcross avoided his eyes.

Evans said, "Then your presence in that bar at the time the girl was waiting there for Dana was purely coincidental. You want me to buy that?"

"I don't care what you do with it," Petey said mildly. He adjusted his glasses and looked calmly at the glowering detective. "What I've told you happens to be fact."

There were many more questions, but they were mainly repetitious, and it became obvious to Dana that Evans faced a blank wall. There was a curious uniformity to the answers Evans received, answers that should have said much but actually led to very little. Dana lost interest in the proceedings. No one had an alibi for the times involved. Everyone had a motive, of sorts.

Evans didn't stress the fact that Dana was the murderer's real target. Maybe, Dana thought, he still didn't believe it. Looking at the others in the grim little office, he found it a little difficult to believe, himself.

It was a little after nine in the morning when Evans gave it up. He made it plain that he was not through with any of them, but they were all sent home.

Dana was the last to leave, and Evans stopped him with a touch on his arm.

"You're going back to your studio?" he asked.

"For the time being," Dana nodded.

"Then what?"

"I haven't made any definite plans."

"You want a man to keep an eye on you? I can detail Sullivan—"

"Sullivan has more important things to do, I'm sure," Dana said. "I can take care of myself from now on."

"You've just been lucky up to this point; you realize that, don't you? You still don't have any helpful ideas on who wants to see you dead?"

"No," Dana said. "But I intend to find out."

CHAPTER SIX

ON TUESDAY, following that weekend, the letter arrived from Shea Mason.

Dana read it several times. It brought back the odd dream he'd had of a girl and an island and a seagull winging on the breeze. He felt a queer shock at the coincidence. Several phrases of Shea's letter remained fixed in his mind.

"I know what a tremendous disappointment...the loss of your paintings must be...and knowing you as I do, I am sure you will not remain in New York. Stone Cove is little more than two hours from where you are—but only you can travel that distance. Hank...Kettle Island is your home..."

"Perhaps it is forward of me appealing to you to come back, but I don't care...when Pres Marquiss and I were married, it was one of those mistakes people sometimes make; but I blame no one but myself."

Dana put the letter away and spent the rest of the morning packing his clothes. He cleaned out the studio closet and his old laundry and everything that belonged to him. He packed away his easel and his brushes. He cleaned up the studio of its wrecked paintings. He felt no further incentive to work.

In the afternoon, he went down to Headquarters to see Evans. The weekend had been uneventful. Dana's exhibition had been called off, and although the newspaper made much of Lotti Higgins' spectacular murder, there was no official connection made between the model's death and the vandalism in Dana's studio.

Evans looked tired, as if he had gone too long without sleep, but he nodded to Dana and pushed cigarettes toward him and asked what he could do.

"I want to leave town," Dana said.

"Oh?"

"I long ago decided I wouldn't stay in New York after my exhibition, anyway. Well, that's been called off. I've nothing to exhibit. There's no reason for me to stay now."

"No personal reason, you mean."

71

"I don't see how I can help you," Dana said. "I'll never get started working again as long as I stay here. I own a little cottage on Kettle Island—that's at Stone Cove, Connecticut—and it's not too far from town. That's where I want to go."

Evans looked thoughtful.

"You realize that you'll be removing yourself from my jurisdiction if I let you go?"

"That's why I'm asking you about it first."

"On the other hand," Evans mused, "you'll also get away from your murderer. But if he's the kind of bird I think he is, he'll follow you wherever you go."

"I don't want to leave town because of that," Dana insisted. "But if he follows me, then I'll know him. If he's one of the people you've questioned in regard to Lotti Higgins, his presence in Stone Cove will tip me off."

Evans said, "If you see him first."

"I'll make a point of it," Dana grinned.

"This lad is smart," Evans warned. "Lots of things have turned up, but there's not enough on anybody to warrant an arrest. I've been seriously thinking of just waiting and using you again."

"As bait?"

"Something like that. The case won't be finished until the killer's had another try at you." He stared at his hands. "Well, as I said, I can't keep you here indefinitely. I don't like it, but I won't stop you, either. When do you want to go to this island of yours?"

"As soon as possible. Tonight, or tomorrow morning."

"Have you told your friends about your plans?"

"No."

"Then don't tell anyone," Evans advised sharply. "You're a man under sentence of death, Mr. Dana. The only difference is that you don't know who your executioner is, or when the date is set for that execution. Your nerves have stood up pretty well so far; but I can see that a nice, quiet cottage some place on the Sound will do you good. However, it will only do you good if you disappear without advance notice to any of the people involved in this thing. That includes all of them."

"I don't intend to tell anyone," Dana agreed. "On the other hand, I don't like the idea of running away."

"Sometimes you have to retreat for strategic purposes," Evans pointed out. "Don't fool yourself that you'll be safe. You won't be. And I won't be around to help you, up there."

"I'll be all right," Dana said. "Nobody will know."

There was a note in his mailbox when he returned to his studio that afternoon. The note was from Preston Marquiss, on the stationery of a mid-town hotel, and, while reading it, Dana felt the threads of the past knotting inexorably around him. There was a strong pull to most of these threads, but this particular one was repellent. The note from Marquiss suggested a meeting, at Dana's convenience. He decided to ignore the message. Then he thought of Shea Mason and Kettle Island, and his decision to return there. At eight that evening he met Marquiss in the bar of the Carlton.

Neither of them chose to shake hands. Their rivalry continued, by mutual consent, from long years in the past. It was at least five years, Dana thought, since he had last seen Marquiss, and the man seemed untouched by time. His red hair and craggy face gave no hint of what he thought as he gestured Dana to a seat at his remote corner table. It was quiet in the bar, and dimly lighted. If anything, Dana thought, Marquiss looked more prosperous than ever. Marquiss represented the canning industry in Stone Cove, and by the same token, that meant all the industry in the little Village. A big frog in a little pond, Dana thought grimly.

He ordered rye and soda and waited for Marquiss to begin with whatever he had on his mind. The red-haired man played with his drink, an onyx ring glittering smoothly on his right hand.

"It's been a long time, Hank. Longer than I ever thought you would stay away from Kettle Island."

"I haven't said anything about going back."

Marquiss smiled. "But you will, won't you? You're thinking about it. I know you, Hank. I know better, perhaps, what's in your mind than you do, yourself. I've had a lot of time to think about you and learn what makes you tick. I also happen to know that my wife wrote to you and put the idea of coming home into your head."

"Do you always read Shea's mail?" Dana asked.

The man's pale eyes measured Dana critically. "Whatever Shea may have written about our personal relations really doesn't matter. What is important, however, is that I don't want you back in Stone Cove."

Dana asked bluntly, "And why not?"

"It took Shea a long time to forget you. I don't want you around to recall the so called good old days."

"She hasn't forgotten me."

"Shea belongs to me, Dana. Your presence will only make things more difficult for her."

"That's for Shea to decide," Dana said. He found the conversation distasteful, and the man's arbitrary attitude was rankling. "What I may or may not do about coming home is of no real concern to you."

"But it might be better if you went somewhere else, don't you think—in view of what's been happening?"

"What do you mean by that?"

Marquiss smiled again. "I read the newspapers. I can put two and two together. I don't know what you're mixed up in, but someone is after your hide. Your statements to the press after your first accident, in the subway, gave that away. I don't think it will be particularly heathful for you to return to Kettle Island at this time."

"If you're trying to warn me off," Dana said, "you're wasting your time. Unless, of course, you know more than you pretend. It never occurred to me to add you to the list of suspects who might have killed Lotti Higgins."

The big man grinned. "You think I'm the lad who tried to kill you?"

"Why not?" Dana asked. "It's a definite possibility, isn't it?"

Dana finished his drink. He wondered if Marquiss was bluffing. The man was shrewd—and dangerous. He'd had opportunity in all cases, too, to qualify for the man Evans was searching for. There was a streak of vindictive brutality in Marquiss that made his candidacy as the killer perfectly fitting. Dana gave himself a mental shrug. In any case, his mind was made up; and with that decision, the insecurity of the past few days was gone.

He was going home.

He got to his feet. Marquiss sat, waiting.

"If you're after my scalp, Pres," Dana said, "then I can only thank you for the warning. But if you're just bluffing, then you're a fool."

He took a taxi downtown to his studio. He felt good, through and through. Charley wasn't in his rooms when he got home. He used half an hour to complete his packing and checked on the railroad schedules. There was no reason to stay in New York a moment longer. His mind was already full of the sea wind and the sand dunes and the memory of Shea Mason...

KAY NORCROSS paced her living room and came to a halt before the fireplace. Her fingers interlocked and clung together as she faced Petey. The little man stood stiffly near the window. It was almost evening and the room was in deep shadow.

"I'm going," Kay said. "Willi's schooner is all ready, and he's already invited us to go along."

"*You* want to go," Petey pointed out softly. "Not I."

"I'll go without you, if necessary."

"Wherever Hank Dana is, eh?"

"We need the rest," she said. "All these police, all the questions about you, Peter. I'm still not sure..."

"The point is," Peter said, "Hank is leaving town and you're going to chase him up there."

"It will be a vacation for all of us," she persisted.

Petey said, "How did you know Hank is going back to this Kettle Island place?"

"I—why, you told me so, just after lunch."

"Did I?"

"It's his home, isn't it?"

"So I've heard."

"Willi Tempel wants an answer," Kay went on. "He wants to sail by tomorrow noon, at the latest. It's only a few hours up the Sound, in any case. He and Charley Powell are coming up for dinner tonight to talk it over. I've already told Charley we would go along."

"You won't change your mind?" Petey asked.

"No."

PEACE and quiet.

Sunlight sparked on the water and the pebbly beach. The harbor was calm. The morning air was clear, alive with all the tints of New England's summer. The breeze came from the Connecticut mainland and danced in errant spirals over the calm Sound. From beyond the cove came the sound of caulking hammers in the Stone Cove boatyard, and he could see the ribs of a new fishing boat being built across the harbor. The blue of the water reflected the serenity of the sky, the tumbled white masses of cloud, and the grey and green of rocks and trees, solid and eternal, sure of themselves and of their existence.

Home, Dana thought.

He walked slowly along the beach. Two days and two nights on Kettle Island had slipped through his fingers like quicksilver, a time of renewing old sensations, of quietly existing without thought or care for the next day. He hadn't seen Shea yet. He had scarcely spoken more than a dozen words to old Abel and Sarah Mason. They let him alone, instinctively allowing him to choose his own approach to the past.

A seine boat came around the seaward point of the harbor, skirting the breakwater and the white lighthouse. The sound of the seiner's engine drifted rhythmically over the water and provided an adequate counterpoint to the noise of the gulls. The clattering of the fish cannery, hidden within a bend of the inner harbor, added the one incongruous note to the scene.

They were right, Dana thought. *It's better here.*

He looked at his dory, freshly painted, tipped on its side on the beach nearby. Mossy pilings, overgrown with barnacles, thrust stumpy fingers out of the slack water of ebb tide. Summer heat and summer silence brooded over Kettle Island.

He wondered what business could have taken Shea Mason to Boston the day he arrived. She was due back this morning. He wondered at his impatience to see her, this girl who had married someone else. Scowling, he paused and almost turned back to his cottage, then changed his mind again and trudged over the dunes toward the southern end of the island.

Shea Mason was seated on the windward side of a giant wave of sand, an easel propped firmly in the yielding dune under her canvas chair. This end of the island was bleak and exposed, pointing a finger into the wide, empty Sound. The wind was stronger and cooler here. The girl had a scarlet ribbon tied around her hair, but the wind tugged at stray curls and blew them playfully.

Dana walked silently over the dune toward her, thinking of the dream he had once dreamed. Shea Mason looked up, waved a paint-daubed hand, and returned to her easel. She had difficulty keeping the canvas from blowing away. The memory of Dana's dream came back to him more strongly, and he felt his pulse quicken. He thought he had never seen a lovelier sight.

Her painting was that of an amateur, without discipline or training or professional knowledge of line and color. He leaned over her shoulder and said, "In a few more years, you might get so that people could recognize it, Shea."

"I paint for fun, Hank, and I like it. Welcome home."

Her fingers were cool and firm in his. Dana sat down on the sand beside her. It was as if he had never been away, as if all the years had been wiped clean between them and they were starting afresh. He knew it wasn't so. Too much had happened for either of them to forget completely; but the opportunity was here to begin anew, if they wanted it that way. He wasn't sure about anything, suddenly. He looked at her impersonally. She was wearing white duck slacks and a plain cotton blouse and Greek sandals. Her figure was clean and firmly molded by the wind-rippled cotton of her blouse. She looked as if she were thoroughly enjoying the task she had set before her on the canvas. Dana folded his hands about his knee and said,

"It's as if I never left, Shea. Thank you, for keeping everything as it was."

"I thought about you," Shea said.

"Did you?"

"Hank Dana, the football star. The sea-bronzed fisherman. Captain Courageous. And you jilted me when you left to see the world. What did you see, Hank?"

"I was a fool. Everything that's good in this world is right here."

He saw the pink flush on her throat.

"I always thought so, too," she said calmly.

"I keep imagining things are as they used to be," Dana said quietly. "But they can never be that way again, can they?"

"No," Shea said.

He said bluntly, "How is Pres Marquiss?"

"I don't see him very often. No more than I have to."

Surprise was evident on Dana's face. Shea put down her brush and twisted about to face him, her eyes wide.

"Hank. Hank, didn't you know?"

"Know what?"

Shea's eyes were now enormous, full of wonder. "I left Pres Marquiss some time ago. I've been divorced. He's no longer my husband, Hank…I thought you knew all about it."

He was silent in his confusion. It was his turn to be surprised, but in this case there was more than just the emotion of unexpected news. After the first moment, the horizon seemed to stretch wider, and the sky assumed a deeper blue.

"I thought you knew," Shea said again.

"No one told me."

Silence grew between them, and he looked at her with new eyes, wondering if this was why he had returned to the island. Something grew inside him that the past had never known. He knew he was deliberately opening deep wounds, but he felt he had no choice. He had to be certain.

"You were very much in love with Pres when you married him, Shea. What went wrong?"

She said, "How would you know how much in love with him I might have been?" There was a bitter undertone in her words. "You weren't here, Hank."

"Because I was a fool," he said again.

"Do you really think so, now?"

"I'm sure of it."

"Hank, you're disturbing me. I don't want you to talk like this unless you know what you're saying. I married Preston because— well, I thought I loved him. Maybe I was just lonely, here on the island with Abel and Sarah. It's true that I wasn't here all the time. I went away to school, but somehow I came back, intending just a visit before going out to carve my career out of this conniving old world. And, somehow, I never left. I married Preston Marquiss instead."

"Didn't you think I'd ever come back?"

"You were gone," she said. "You never wrote."

"Sometimes I couldn't," he said. "And other times, I didn't think you wanted to hear from me."

"That's no excuse," she said.

"I know that, now."

"Once I thought I could never forgive you, Hank. But I waited for you to come back. I left Preston before we'd been married a year. I don't want to talk about it—it was an unhappy experience. He—he isn't quite normal, Hank. Perhaps I should never have majored in psychiatry when I went to medical school; but I did, and I knew I couldn't go on living with his abnormalities. I got a divorce, and that's all. I don't want to talk about it anymore now."

Her mood changed quickly, and her blue eyes were frank and amused, her voice light and bantering.

"Anyway, here you are again, my dream come true, and here am I, not at all glamorous. I had freckles when you last saw me."

"You still have freckles. They're cute now, as then."

It was soothing to sit here with her. There was no sense of estrangement, and he knew that was because of Shea's own natural poise, her refusal to hide behind a polite screen of amenities. He looked over his shoulder suddenly, searching the beach, but he saw nothing except the dunes and the trees beyond. He thought of Shea Mason, who was named after a great-grandfather who'd captained a Stonington Whaler. He thought of her father, whose death he could remember from childhood, drowning in the wreck of his schooner just off the point, on Dog Bar. Abel and Sarah had brought her up and educated her. Dana watched her daub paint on her canvas, and wondered if he should kiss her. He wanted to, but he didn't. He said,

"You majored in psychiatry."

Shea nodded. "You could use me, you know."

"Does it show?" He grinned.

"It certainly does. Why do you always look back over your shoulder? You did it just now."

"I don't know why I do it."

"Are you looking for someone?"

"I suppose so."

"You act as if you thought you were being followed."

He picked up her brush and adjusted a line in the surf scene she was trying to capture. But the trembling of his hand betrayed him and he dropped the brush in the sand.

"What's the matter, Hank?" she asked quickly.

"I'm not sure." Then he said, "Well, yes, I do know what is the matter. I suppose you know why I'm here. You must have read about it in the papers. And I'm sure that Marquiss told you all about it. He looked me up in New York."

"I know," Shea said. "He told me about you."

"What was he doing in New York at that time?"

"He didn't say. I didn't ask him. He knew I was writing to you, but he'd gone into town the day before that, too, so I don't think it was because of you that he went to New York. Don't think such things, Hank. He isn't fond of you, of course, because he knows I—he knows how I feel about you. But you mustn't think he's the cause of your difficulties."

"He hates my guts, doesn't he?"

"I suppose he does."

"And you say he's—abnormal?"

"Not that way," she said quickly.

"All right, Shea. Forget it."

"No. I don't want to forget it, and I don't want you to forget about it, either. I want you to tell me what happened in New York—all of it, as much as you can remember."

The quiet touch of her hand made him quiet, too, although his words were jerked out of him in erratic sentences. He told her a little of it, not all of it, but some of it, resting quietly on the warm sand beside her. He told her of the subway and his paintings and the death of Lotti Higgins. The sunlight on Shea's hair made a soft halo around her face. She wasn't really beautiful, but Dana thought she was—lovely and quiet, controlled and sympathetic.

When he finished talking, she was silent for a long moment, the wind stirring her chestnut hair. Presently, then, she said,

"So you think someone is trying to kill you. You are fairly certain of that, aren't you?"

"Yes; I'm sure of it," he said.

"But you don't know who?"

"No. Nor why."

"And you left town to come back here?"

"I thought I could fight it out better in this environment. In the city I couldn't see that I had much chance. I'm not a coward, Shea. But it's the not knowing the who and the why of it that gets me down. When I found all my paintings slashed to ribbons that night, I was thrown a little haywire. The place looked as if a madman had been let loose to run amok in it. There just doesn't seem to be anything rational about these attacks on me."

He was shivering a little. Shea kept her hand on his. "This was after the subway attack?"

"Yes, it followed directly afterward."

"This Lotti Higgins. Did you know her well?"

"No." Dana's face was tight-lipped. "She was one of Charley Powell's models. He had quite a harem. She seemed interested in me though—this sounds funny, doesn't it?—and she thought she could use her knowledge of the vandal's identity to get me to pay some attention to her. That's the only way I can figure it out. But the killer reached her before I could, that night."

Shea said, "But you think it's one of your close friends, don't you? You have it narrowed down to that. You're pretty sure of it, aren't you?"

"I don't know. No. Yes."

Suddenly he didn't care to discuss it any more. Something trembled to life inside him and drove all other thoughts from his mind. The nightmare that pursued him was forgotten.

"Shea…"

"Yes, Hank. I understand."

"But you can't—"

"I feel the same way."

She was in his arms, soft, yet firm; yielding, yet demanding in her right. For the moment, when he kissed her, it seemed as if the tides stopped flowing and the sun stood still…

It was some time later when Shea pointed to the harbor beyond the beach. A white schooner, as trim and graceful as a gull, had tacked around the breakwater from the Sound and was making its approach to Kettle Island. It sailed quite close to where they were sitting.

"We're having summer visitors," Shea said.

Dana said nothing. The color drained from his face. There was no mistaking that squat, massive figure in the stern of the yacht, starkly outlined against the clean blue of the harbor, contaminating the scene.

It was Willi Tempel.

CHAPTER SEVEN

THE WALLS began to tremble.

Dana looked at the brush in his hand, and that was trembling, too, like his hands and the rest of his body. The whole world shook and danced a macabre jig around him, the light vibrating, splintering, shivering in the air that enveloped him.

It was the following morning. He was alone in his cottage. He put down the brush and stepped back from the easel and carefully dried his hands on a handkerchief. His palms were moist and cold. He closed his eyes, but that didn't help at all. Color burned and roared behind his shut lids. The vibrations turned into nausea, deep in the pit of his stomach. He opened his eyes quickly and turned his back on the easel and looked out through the cottage window.

Peace and quiet. And the danger like hidden snakes, all around him.

Last night, after the newcomers had been settled in the Mason house—Willi Tempel, the Norcrosses, and Charley Powell—the silent midnight had been punctuated by a single shot. The bullet had gone through Shea's bedroom window, harming no one, just shattering one small pane of glass.

Dana leaned on the windowsill and that was solid enough, good and solid, supporting his weight staunchly. The world outside was the same. The sand dunes were a warm yellow under the hot sun, the harbor sparkled, the gray and green of rocks and trees stood stolidly on the opposite shore. A gull perched on his dory down the beach. Silence blanketed the island.

"If anything happens to Shea," he thought.

Under his outstretched hands, the oak of the windowsill became warm and friendly, as if alive. He leaned his weight on his hands and looked back into the sunny silence of the studio.

I shouldn't have come here. I've brought the danger to her.

No one knew anything about the shot last night. Everyone looked sleepy and startled, roused out of their beds. There was no point in a midnight search. The shot had come out of the night, a warning not to Shea, but to Dana.

The walls of the room shook, the easel danced a jig again. He licked perspiration from his upper lip and tasted salt on his tongue. He noticed that he had dropped the brush in front of his easel, and a daub of siena marred the polished oak planks of the floor. The big windows on the north side admitted an aching light, and the light vibrated. Everything joined the universal shimmering and dancing.

"Relax," he said aloud. "It will go away."

It became worse. He snatched his hand from the windowsill, from the wood that was alive, and turned to face the empty room. His dark blue eyes were unnaturally bright. A film of perspiration made his face shine.

"Stop it," he whispered. "Stop it!"

The crazy jig became a ballet. He walked carefully over the tilting floor, one shoulder hunched upward to ward off the wall that seemed about to topple on him. The bunk felt secure and solid for a moment. He sat down on it. He wiped his hands on the handkerchief again. He leaned back, then rolled over on his stomach and closed his eyes.

Nausea came quickly, gleefully. The vibrations had a sound now, a trembling roar, a mechanical clatter that rushed down on him like a wave, and then he was falling again from the subway platform and the world dissolved in a shrieking pinwheel of light, of ripped and torn paintings, of the pink and white body of Lotti Higgins. From a great distance, he heard a knocking, someone calling his name. He didn't reply. He clung to the cot and fought off his illness. The knocking sounded on the door again, and then the door opened.

Abel Mason came in.

Dana sat up. Memories churned in his mind. It took a moment to accept the existence of the cottage again. His clothes were drenched with sweat as he looked at Abel in the doorway. A cool, salty breeze came into the studio with the old man.

"You all right, Henry?" Abel asked.

Everything was the same. The bright, aching light poured in through the north windows. Dana planted his feet with care on the floor. The floor felt solid. The walls didn't move. It was over, for the time being.

Abel watched him stand up. Abel was solid, crowding seventy, but he was tall and sturdy like the spars of his beloved Grand Banks schooners. A fisherman of the old school, Dana thought, and in that moment decided to do Abel Mason's portrait some day, to capture the salt and spray and howling winds of the North Atlantic. The sea had carved a record of its stormy years on the old man's gaunt, leathery face.

"You all right, Henry?" Abel repeated.

"Yes. Yes, fine. Thanks," Dana said.

"You're looking kind of peaked."

Dana didn't answer. He lit a cigarette and his hands didn't shake. He narrowed his eyes against the glare of summer light outside. From the doorway he could see a brief stretch of shingle, the dory, and a rickety wharf fifty yards to the right. Abel's open lobster boat was tied up to the wharf. A whistle blew faintly from the cannery across the harbor. A trim white yacht, graceful as a gull, heeled to the wind beyond the stone breakwater at the harbor entrance. On the backbone of the island beyond the graciously carved sand dunes, the pine trees stood silent under the blaze of the sun. The red roof of the Mason house was just visible beyond a rocky promontory to the north.

Peace and quiet.

Abel touched his shoulder with a gnarled, horny hand. He didn't jump.

"Good thing you come up here when you did, Henry. You look better, anyway, than you did."

"I came for a rest," Dana said.

"Don't seem to me it would be such heavy work paintin' pictures. You worked a lot harder when you were a youngster here in Stone Cove, takin' summer sites on Earl's oyster boat."

"Those were the good days," Dana said.

Abel said glumly, "Don't know if it pays to get famous if it costs you your health." He squinted across the harbor. "Goin' lobstering with me today? I'm pulling traps around the new lighthouse."

"I'd better see about my guests. But we'll go tomorrow, Abel, sure thing."

"Suit yourself." The old man shrugged and searched in his cotton shirt pocket with a thick, rope-hardened finger and produced a crumpled letter. "Picked this up in town—letter for you from New York."

Dana took it without looking at it. "Thanks."

"No trouble. If you happen to go looking for Shea, you might find her over on Sandy Hill."

Dana grinned. "Thanks again."

"It still ain't any trouble."

He leaned in the doorway and watched the tall old man walk down to the wharf and clamber into his lobster boat. The name on the open forty-footer, painted in bright red letters, was *Shea,* after his grandniece. He was tempted to go with Abel. He knew he ought to, if he wanted to rest and relax. He turned and went back into the cottage.

A battered coffee pot stood on the oil stove, and he lit the flame under it and brewed himself a thick, muddy cup of coffee. He felt quieter now. The coffee was hot and steaming. It felt good in his stomach. He thought about his work and went back into the studio and pulled out half a dozen new canvases from under the bunk and propped them against the walls, around the room. Not bad. Not good. Local studies of the New England coast, a dime a dozen. The color was right, the air transparent, but they seemed empty and shallow, without life or emotion. There was nothing of himself in the oils. He picked up the brush he had dropped in front of the easel, but a queer feeling came over him and he put it down again. The canvas wasn't worth working on. He remembered the letter Abel Mason had given him, and he went to the doorway and slit the envelope with his thumbnail.

The letter was from Lieutenant Evans, written on personal stationery, and it was about Willi Tempel. The detective had covered a lot of ground, Dana realized. The information contained in the brief note sent a dull shock through him. He stuffed the letter into his pocket and trudged over the dunes in a search for Shea.

He found her along the water's edge, hunting for shells. She wore a thin cotton frock, and her figure was lithe and proud and exciting in the sunlight and the wind. With her hand in his, they turned away from the water and sat in the shade of an old, gnarled elm that grew on the edge of the woods.

"I didn't know I'd be in competition with a glamour girl like Kay Norcross," Shea said.

"Oh, that," Dana said.

"All she does is talk about you."

Dana said, "Forget it. Are you all right?"

"Of course. Why shouldn't I be?"

"Somebody shot at you last night."

Shea shook her head. "It was an accident."

"No. It was meant to hurt me, by threatening you. I'm sorry I came back, Shea. I've brought danger to you."

"Are you really sorry?"

Her face was uptilted to his, and he leaned over and kissed her, feeling the warm pressure of her body against his, the hungry embrace of her, arms about him. She pushed away from him at last with a small laugh.

"I'm a wanton woman," she said.

Their eyes met and understood each other. The sea wind whispered in the leafy crown of the elm tree overhead. Dana shook his head, his eyes perturbed.

"You see what happens, Shea. My so-called friends arrive, become Abel's guests at regular tourist rates, and within eight hours someone takes a shot at you. A warning. Next time it may not be so wide of its mark. I'm scared, now."

Shea said, "Why did you allow all your New York friends to follow you here?"

"I didn't invite them," Dana said. "They just came."

"All four of them? The Norcrosses, and Powell, and that fat man— what's his name?"

"Willi Temple. He's the one who owns the schooner. They just thought it would be fun to visit me—they say."

"You didn't encourage them, did you?"

"On the contrary. I didn't tell anyone I was coming here. But one of them found out, somehow. I've talked about this island, often enough."

Shea said, "Then you think that one of them will try to kill you here? Is that it, Hank?"

"Yes."

She was thoughtful for a moment.

"It's really quite simple," she said. "You can find out who it is, easily enough. All you have to do is ask them. Tactfully, of course—and separately."

Dana's head came up sharply and he stared at her. "Ask them what?" he demanded.

"Find out which one first suggested they come here to visit you. If you can pin down the original idea to one of the four, I think you'll know which one is anxious to be near you. You'll be all right then. You'll know, you see, and then you will be able to face it and do something about it. It's fighting the unknown that's so difficult to endure."

"It hasn't been easy," Dana nodded.

HE FELT good as he walked back toward the big house. He kicked up the sand in little spurts, in an excess of animal spirits. The sun was warm, the sea wind cool. Now it was simple. Now he knew what he had to do.

He followed the path that began at the end of the pine woods. Even with his thoughts on other matters, he noted how Abel and Sarah Mason had performed their painstaking chores on the island. The big Mason house had been given a fresh coat of red paint, from the square widow's walk perched among the gables to the big veranda that faced the glittering expanse of the Sound. A wooden stairway led down the face of the bluff to Stone Cove Harbor and the little inlet where Willi Tempel's schooner was moored. In the sunlight, there seemed to be nothing to worry about.

A clattering of pots and pans came from the kitchen as Sarah prepared lunch. Dana walked along the shell-bordered path to the lawn overlooking the bluff. Charley Powell was sprawled on the grass, sunbathing, and Dana paused, studying the big man's Herculean physique. Charley's smooth, sun-bronzed skin rippled with latent strength. He was clad only in gaily-flowered shorts that made the tan of his legs look darker than it really was.

Charley raised his head and blinked at him.

"Hi, Henry."

His square face was friendly, the planes and angles breaking up with his smile. Dana sat on the edge of a deck chair and looked down over the bluff at the schooner.

"Where are all the others?" he asked.

"Petey and Willi are playing gin. Kay's gone swimming."

The big man stretched luxuriously. "It's been a long time since you were back here, hasn't it?"

Dana said, "Only about half the island belongs to me, with my cottage. But the Masons are only too glad to take in summer people."

He looked involuntarily at Charley's hands. They would have been good hands, after the smooth, powerful perfection of the rest of Charley's physique, except for the stiff and awkward manner in which the fingers bent.

He said, "How are they today. Charley?"

"As usual. Forget them."

"I wish I could."

Charley said, "Look, will you stop worrying about them? We were all high that night. You couldn't help it if that damned fool swung out of the intersection ahead of us—you couldn't avoid going into that ditch. I've told you that a hundred times, Hank. If I was stupid enough to shove my mitts through the windshield, that's my fault."

"You haven't tried any decent painting since," Dana said quietly. "Yet you go on with your commercial stuff."

"Because I like to eat, my boy." Charley rolled over on his back and scowled at the hot sun. "I'm trying something new, though.

Experimental stuff. By the way, that schoolgirl flame of yours was snooping up in my room and looked at my work. I had to give her hell."

"Shea Mason? What for?"

There was a fine film of shiny perspiration on Charley's naked torso. "I'm a little too sensitive about this stuff I'm doing. I haven't much confidence in myself as a real artist, you know. And I didn't want that girl peeking."

"I'm sure she meant no harm," Dana said.

"She must have picked the lock on my room. Swell studio, by the way. Anyway, I caught her in there, looking over my stuff. Amateur! I lost my temper."

"Shea will understand," Dana said. "I'm glad the Masons are making you comfortable. Staying on the schooner would have been somewhat cramped."

"You can say that again," Charley grunted.

"Anyway, it's good to have you up here," Dana said. "I'm glad you thought of joining me on Kettle Island."

"It wasn't my idea," Charley shrugged. He rolled over on his stomach again. His voice was muffled under his arm. "I'm a city boy at heart. This is the last place I expected to visit this summer. Ordinarily, I'd stay away from Kay, but when she told me the rest of the gang was coming, I tagged along."

"Then you didn't suggest that Kay and Petey and Willi join me here?"

"No," Charley said bluntly.

"I see," said Dana. "Thanks."

"For nothing," Charley said.

He stood on the float and watched Kay Norcross swim toward him. She chose the schooner instead of the float, hauling her long curved body out of the water with a single, graceful movement. He thought of Aphrodite—in a white sharkskin bathing suit. She took off her cap and smiled at him. Dana stepped from the float to the deck of the schooner and walked toward her.

"It's about time you came to visit me, Henry."

There was a proud boldness about her figure and face that made him think of Charley Powell. They would have gone well together—and probably would have continued to do so, except that Charley had introduced Kay to him.

She turned toward the cabin door. "I didn't come up here just to see you at dinner, with all the others around. You know why I'm here, darling."

"Forget it," he said.

"I'm in love with you, Henry."

He followed her down the narrow ladder into the galley. A bottle of rye stood on the shining, compact sink. He leaned in the doorway; his head lowered to clear the overhead, watching her towel herself and then take ice cubes from the little refrigerator.

"None for me, thanks," he said.

"But this is to celebrate."

"Celebrate what?"

"Our being alone at last."

Dana grinned. "You're incorrigible."

"I intend to be. I never give up." Her eyes looked shadowy in the dimness of the little cabin. The outside world seemed very remote. He felt the schooner roll a little in the lapping wake of a dragger that went by in the harbor beyond the cove entrance. He heard a gull scream overhead. He looked at Kay's long, firm legs. She said abruptly, "I'm jealous, you know."

"Of what?"

"Your lady friend, Shea Mason. She's cute."

"I've known Shea since we were kids," Dana smiled. "We went to school together."

"But you're not children now," Kay said, unamused. "I suppose you even carried her books."

"Sometimes," Dana nodded. It was warm in the cabin, and the glittering water beyond the portholes made the ceiling ripple with reflected light. He watched an emerald ring sparkle on her finger. He regretted having come here, and then he thought of what he had to ask her. He said, "Shea is a smart girl. She can take care of herself."

"That doesn't make me less jealous." Kay got up and crossed the tiny cabin to where he stood. She was tall, but he was a head taller than she. "I don't like competition, especially when you haven't decided about me yet. Have you kissed her lately?"

"Yes. I've kissed her."

"Are you in love with her, Henry?"

"I think so," he said.

Kay said, "And she's in love with you. Touching. You are just too busy to notice it. She thinks you're a little tin god; that's why she tried to hide her adoration for you. But I'm different. I like my gods made out of flesh and blood."

He didn't know how she managed the kiss. He wasn't adept at countering Kay's strategems. It just happened, although he didn't want it to happen, and he regretted it instantly. She was in his arms. She was close to him, warm and vibrant and yielding. Her lips tasted of the salt sea. They were fierce and possessive, and he reached up and forced her hands from around his neck and then forced her away from him. She smiled. Her green eyes were happy.

"Henry," she said. "What is troubling you?"

"Lotti Higgins," he said flatly.

"But darling, why should you feel as if it is your responsibility? The police are taking care of it. That's what the police are for, to handle matters like that. You always take on all the woes and worries of the world, loading them on your own shoulders. They're nice shoulders, dear, and I hate to see you burden them with things that don't concern you."

Dana said harshly, "She was murdered because of me."

"There was nothing you could do about it."

"I know that. Yet I feel responsible, in a way."

"But what can you do?"

Dana said, "Petey never did explain what he was doing in that bar the night Lotti was killed."

"Do you really think he needs to explain?"

"Does he have anything to hide?"

"Petey didn't kill that girl," Kay said. Her voice for the moment was harsh and adamant, and for the same moment her carefully groomed beauty had all the appearance of a meticulously lacquered mask. Then she laughed and turned back to Dana, her hand sliding up to his shoulders. "Why are we discussing such morbid things, with all this sunshine around us? Henry, I love you."

"Is that really why you came up here?"

"You know why I'm here."

"Was it your idea?" he asked.

"Naturally."

"Listen," he said. "I mean this, it's important. Was it your idea to come up here with all the others?"

"The others? No."

"Then who suggested that you and Petey and Charley and Willi make this unexpected cruise up the Sound?"

"I don't know what you mean."

"Yes, you do," he insisted. "Answer me."

She said, "Why, Petey suggested it. He thought it would be good for all of us to get out of the city for a few days."

She swayed toward him again. He felt a sudden fierce exultation, like an explosion inside him. Now he knew. Now he was free. Kay was smiling, her green eyes brilliant, feminine. Her arms were around his neck again when he heard a sound in the doorway behind him, and Peter Norcross said,

"Don't believe her, Henry. She's lying to you."

The man's voice was soft and amused. Dana took Kay's arms from the back of his neck and turned to face Petey. Sunlight struck behind the little man and left his round, intellectual face in shadow. As always, he wore his thick, horn-rimmed glasses, the wide bars poked back into his sandy hair. He looked rather like an ineffectual chicken, and Dana felt struck suddenly by an enormous pity for the man.

"I'm sorry about this, Petey," he said.

"Don't apologize. I'm the one who should apologize, Henry, because my wife is such a congenital liar, and because I must contradict the lie she told you. I didn't suggest that we all come up here to see you. You know I'd be the last person in the world to want that."

"I'm not so sure," Dana said.

"No, you wouldn't be. You can't be sure of anything these days, can you?" The little man sighed and looked at his wife. "You can't even be sure of Kay, because she is such liar. Oddly enough, she always tells me the truth, Henry. That may surprise you, but it is so."

"Shut up, Peter," Kay said. Her mouth was ugly. "Nobody told you to interrupt us."

"I'm sorry about that, my dear. I would willingly spare myself the sight of your indiscretions. I did not intend to eavesdrop. But I had to correct the impression you were giving Henry that I am responsible for this junket."

"If you didn't suggest it," Dana said, "who did?"

"I know why you want to know," Petey said. He smiled. "I am not stupid. Tell him the truth, Kay."

She had returned to her drink, swallowing the last of it calmly. "Willi Tempel mentioned it at dinner, the night you left New York. I thought it was a wonderful idea."

"Willi Tempel?" Dana repeated.

Peter Norcross said, "That is correct, Henry. I did not have much choice in the matter, naturally. As a matter of fact, I was rather afraid to come up here."

"Why?" Dana asked angrily.

"I don't want to see you or to be near you, simply because it would give me so much pleasure to kill you."

Kay laughed. "You sound like a line from one of those plays you're always reviewing, Peter. Why kill Henry? Why not me? I'm the one who's chasing him. Don't blame Henry. Blame me."

"I know that. You know why I won't ever hurt you."

Dana didn't say anything. He felt angry and confused. He was embarrassed by Peter Norcross' obvious shortcomings as a man, and he felt guilty for himself, although he told himself he was not to blame. At least he knew where Petey stood, and that was a help. He knew something else, too, and with the thought he was reminded of Willi Tempel, and he remembered the letter that Evans had sent him. He touched the crumpled envelope in his pocket and straightened suddenly.

"If you will excuse me," he said.

Petey stepped aside from the doorway.

"You'll find Willi in the house," he said quietly.

The bed was old-fashioned, with a massively carved walnut headboard and sturdy iron springs. Willi Tempel lay on the damp white sheets, flat on his back, his head turned to avoid the sharp, hot sunlight that poured through the curtained windows. The man's enormous belly moved rhythmically up and down, and his round features were plump and shiny, dark with beard along the jowls. He was naked except for a pair of red silk shorts. The shorts were delicately printed with giant white tulips.

Dana paused in the bedroom doorway and rapped lightly. Willi turned his round head to look at him. He had not been asleep. His dark little eyes were like merry marbles set in the deep folds of his flesh. He looked at Dana and sighed. He saw what he had been looking for in Dana's hard, tight-mouthed face.

"So you have some information at last." Willi said heavily. "Something about me, eh?"

"Yes," Dana said. "I've heard from New York."

"I knew that detective was snooping in my affairs. That little gray man—Evans, no?" Willi sighed. "I had no time to put my things in order for him. But now you know."

"Yes," Dana said again. "You're a crook, Willi."

"A crook." Willi remained flat on his back on the large bed. He nodded, his chins folding over his fat neck. "Like that, eh?"

Dana said, "Aside from Lieutenant Evans, I am the only one who knows. None of your other clients suspects you of cheating them on the sales you made for them."

"Quite so."

Dana tapped the letter on the knuckles of his left hand. "Not even the accountant Evans hired for me knows what it's all about, except that your books and figures are screwy, Willi. You owe me six thousand dollars. You owe Charley Powell eight thousand. I don't know how many others of your clients have been fleeced this way."

"All of them," Willi admitted blandly.

"Why did you do it? We were friends!"

"I did it for money. I like money."

Dana just looked at him. The fat man sighed and stared at the ceiling. He lay still for a moment, as if he had forgotten Dana was there. Then Willi sat up ponderously. His stomach sagged over the elastic of his red silk shorts. The tulips looked ridiculous. Willi leaned sidewise and groped with a pudgy hand under the crushed damp pillow. He came up with a revolver in his fat, white fingers. The barrel was blue, the muzzle a dark, round eye staring at Dana.

Dana looked at the revolver. Willi Tempel made a chuckling sound in his fat throat.

"Really. I ought to kill myself," he said finally. "Imagine the disgrace, the scandal, when I am exposed as a thief and a swindler, an exploiter of poor, young struggling artists like yourself. I should kill myself."

Dana said, "Or kill me."

"Yes, that is a thought."

"Well?"

Willi looked at him.

"Now?" Dana asked.

"No," Willi said. "After dinner. Mrs. Mason is a fabulous cook. Exquisite. Her talents are wasted on this miserable island, I understand we are having lobster tonight."

Dana looked at the gun.

"Put it away," he said quietly. "Better still, give it to me."

"No."

"Give it to me."

Willi looked at the gun in his hand and shrugged his fat, hairy shoulders. Beads of perspiration glistened on his bald scalp. He leaned forward and reversed the gun, grunting a little as he handed it to Dana. Dana took it and put it away in his trouser pocket. It felt heavy, sagging in the cloth against his leg. Somehow, he didn't think he had won a victory over the fat man.

"Did you try to kill me other times, Willi?"

"Why should I? You knew nothing about me then."

"But I suspected."

"Suspicion is far from proof."

"And Lotti Higgins? You had nothing to do with her?"

Willi Tempel's small, dark eyes swept beyond Dana's figure to the bright rectangle of the sunlit window.

"I never knew her," he said briefly.

"You met her in Kolevici's, remember?"

"A chance meeting. Nothing in it."

"Then why did you come here, Willi?"

"To enjoy life. Now the enjoyment is gone."

"Why did you inveigle the others into coming up here on the schooner with you?"

Willi Tempel raised his heavy brows. "But I did no such thing, Henry."

"Then whose idea was it?"

"I'm sure I don't know. Was it Charley's?"

"I'm asking you."

"I cannot recall. It just happened. The suggestion came spontaneously from all of us. Is it so important, Henry?"

"Who first suggested it, in so many words?"

"I do not remember."

Dana said, "You're a liar, Willi."

"A crook and a liar."

"I want you to tell me."

"But I don't know! Why should I lie about a trivial thing like that?"

"All right," Dana said. He turned toward the bedroom door. Willi Tempel remained seated on the bed. The mattress sagged painfully under his weight. Dana halted as Willi spoke again, quietly, "Henry?"

"Yes?"

"What are you planning to do? Expose me? Ruin me? If I should promise to pay you back, and all the others, too, would that change what you have in mind?"

Dana wanted to get out of the room.

"What are you going to do?" Willi persisted.

"Nothing," Dana said. Nothing—just yet."

CHAPTER EIGHT

SHEA FOUND HIM late that afternoon, staring at the sea. The setting sun tinged the clouds a bright red, and in turn the clouds reflected bloodily in the quiet sea. There was no breeze from over the Sound. The surf was quiet. Dana had been sitting there for an hour, not doing anything, not thinking, just watching the sea.

He heard her footsteps and turned his head to watch her approach. Her head was held high and proud. He liked the way she walked, the way she held her shoulders straight, the lift of her bosom and the swing of her hips. It was a warm evening, but she looked cool and comfortable. She smiled at him and sat down on the ledge beside him, and he moved over to give her more room.

"Well?" she asked.

He shrugged. "I didn't learn anything. They all had a different story to tell. One of them certainly originated the idea of this visit, but they claim they don't remember. Their stories conflict. But I'm more convinced than ever that one of them wants my life."

She said, "I'm inclined to agree with you. You're dealing with a person who has covered his tracks carefully, piling confusion upon confusion. Quite clever, too, bringing the others with him to avoid sole suspicion. A black sheep losing himself among other black sheep."

Her face was serious. Her eyes searched his, and when he looked at her he remembered what Kay had said about her, that she was in love with him, that she adored him as a tin god. It didn't seem plausible. That business belonged back in their high school days.

"I don't like it," Shea frowned. "I hate to admit it, but I'm frightened."

"You?"

"There's too much tension here, Hank. Too much emotional ill-balance. I don't think it's safe for you."

He felt the weight of Willi's gun in his pocket.

"I'll be all right now," he said.

She was still concerned. "But you won't get any painting done here. Do you plan to do new ones for the paintings that were destroyed in New York?"

"I've done some so far," he said, and saw that she was pleased. "But I'm not satisfied with them."

She stood up quietly, slim and graceful. She was smiling at him, amused by something. She said abruptly, "Hank, did Kay tell you I'm in love with you?"

He felt oddly embarrassed. "Don't let her annoy you."

"Why should Kay annoy me?" she smiled. "It's quite true, you know."

She turned to the path that led down to the beach. He didn't follow. He watched her free stride, the tilt of her head. He felt good. He felt wonderful. He knew she didn't want him to follow her now, and he remained standing there on the ledge of rock, watching her until she was out of sight.

He sat down again and quietly watched the sunset. His fingers itched for a brush; there was that sense of impatience in the flesh and muscles of his hands, a wellspring of enthusiasm to do some new work. But he just sat there, watching the sun go down over the mainland. He felt at peace. He didn't think about Shea. A plan formed slowly in the back of his mind...

The sun was gone. A cool night wind swept in from the darkening expanse of the sea, whispering in the pine woods. Dana felt the sudden chill of the wind and shivered a little as he became aware of the time. He looked at his watch and was surprised that more than an hour had gone by since Shea had left him. The thought of Shea made him feel good once more. He stood up and stretched and watched a seagull winging purposefully homeward in the dusk. From somewhere behind him, in the pines, a bird suddenly burst into warbling song and then was quiet as abruptly as it had begun.

Dana's steps were long and springy as he leaped down from the rocks to the sandy beach that stretched away toward the woods. His body felt light and strong. He wondered if Abel Mason had had much luck with his lobster traps during the day, and then he realized he was far too late to join the others for dinner. He didn't much care. When he thought of the way his nerves had shattered this morning, he grimaced; there would be no more of that. From somewhere—perhaps from Shea—he had gained a new sense of strength and security.

Maybe that cop, Evans, had been right. Maybe it had all been a coincidence. His conscious mind knew it was not coincidental, but there was nothing to fear now. Things were coming out in the open, like the attack in his studio and the murder of Lotti Higgins. Up to that point, he had been fighting shadows.

The urge to work with brush and palette came back to him once more. He walked faster, his shoes gritting on the path through the woods. Dusk came over the island, and through the trees he glimpsed occasional lights from Stone Cove, winking cheerily across the harbor. The heat of the day was already gone, swept away by the evening's sea breeze. Enormous dark clouds towered high in the southeastern horizon. He felt impatient to get back to his cottage, where he could be alone with his painting, away from all the others.

He could see, where the path skirted the woods near the Mason house, that the others were all sitting about and resting after dinner. Their voices murmured in the shadows of the big veranda, and glowing cigarettes moved in tiny arcs through the darkness. The lighted kitchen windows, where Sarah and Abel Mason worked at the dishes, cast cheery rectangles of yellow light on the lawn. He stepped through them and kept going.

It was almost completely dark when he reached his cottage on the other side of the island. The shift in wind had kicked up a surf on the rocky beach. He paused in the gloom and frowned toward the water.

A sleek little cabin cruiser was tied up to the rickety pier that jutted into the surf before the cottage. It was Preston Marquiss' boat, Dana knew, but there was no one aboard. He walked down to where his own dory was tilted on the sand, watching the white line of combers come racing out of the night. He wondered what Marquiss was doing on Kettle Island, and with the thought came a vision of Shea Mason; she had said nothing about expecting a visit from Marquiss. Perhaps the man was on the island without an invitation. The thought made Dana uneasy as he turned across the beach toward his cottage.

The door stood open, swinging on its hinges in the wind. He noted it absently as he stepped up on the porch and paused to light a cigarette, cupping the match in his hand. The wind had blown a little wave of sand across the porch floor directly in front of the doorway, and in the faint, flickering light of the match, he saw the soft outline of a woman's high-heeled shoe. Dana kept the match alight while he went inside, groping for the oil lamp on the table just inside the threshold. He found the lamp and turned the little brass wheel and touched the match to the wick.

The room leaped and screamed at him.

This time it was more than just hacking his new work into torn ribbons of canvas. There was more, this time. And worse. Someone had taken his tubes of pigment and squeezed them dry in wild, giggling blobs and lines all over the walls, the floor, the furniture. Giant daubs of permanent green and cadmium yellow and red oxides jeered and bellowed an insane message to him from the shattered interior of the cottage.

He stood in the doorway and trembled. Something was screaming an answer in his throat to the paranoiac disorder before his eyes. The trembling grew worse. He stepped backward carefully, out of the doorway to the wind-swept porch again. He couldn't take his eyes from the nightmare of childish colors squeezed into the room. Nothing moved in there, yet everything was movement, wild and irrational, dangerous and insane. He shuddered. He felt for the narrow porch rail, then backed down the three steps to the sandy path.

He ran without thinking, perhaps fifty frantic steps into the darkness of the pine woods, along the path that led across the island to the main house. Then he thought of Willi's gun in his pocket, and he stopped running. He stood still. He listened to the rising crash of the surf an around the island. The wind made a whimpering sound in the pines. The night was completely dark, tasting of rain and the sea. He put his hand in his pocket and felt for the gun. He thought of Preston Marquiss' boat tied up to the pier in front of his cottage, and an anger coiled inside him. He turned and started back to the cottage, and someone came running behind him along the path through the woods.

"Hank!"

It was Shea Mason. She came running with quick steps, a flashlight bobbing in her hand to light the way ahead of her. Her chestnut hair looked lighter in the gloom. Her face was pale and anxious, searching for him, and she had changed into a white linen dress that clung to her figure as the wind pressed against it. Her hair was kept in place now by a broad band of blue ribbon. Her hands touched his gratefully as she caught up to him. She struggled for breath.

His voice was rough. "What's the matter?"

"Nothing. That is—I was worried about you. You didn't—you weren't at dinner with the rest of us."

"Has anything happened?"

"No. Yes. No. I don't think so. Hank, where have you been?"

He didn't reply. He was looking at a dark, ugly bruise along the soft line of her jaw. He hadn't noticed it at first; he hadn't been able to see her face clearly in the darkness. Now he took the flashlight from her hand and shone it directly at her. She shrank back and started to lift her fingers to her face, to cover the bruise, but she knew it was too late and that he had already seen it. Her eyes were enormous, watching him.

Dana's voice was strangled. "How did that happen?"

"It was an accident," she said quickly.

"What kind of an accident?" he insisted.

"I can't tell you."

He said, "Preston Marquiss is on the island, isn't he? His boat is tied up by my cottage. You've seen him, haven't you?"

"Yes," she said.

"Did he hit you?"

She hesitated. "Hank, I don't want you involved in this. He's half out of his mind, since you came back. He's insane with jealousy. That's one of the reasons why we broke up. I couldn't stand the constant torment of his suspicions."

Dana's face was white. "Answer me," he said. "Did he hit you?"

"Yes," Shea said.

He felt a murderous rage. He wanted to tear something, anything, into little shreds and pieces. He could have wept. He reached out and touched Shea's face. His fingers were gentle.

"We'll straighten it out."

"It's my affair!" she said. "You keep out of it."

"I'm making it mine, too, Shea."

"Hank…"

He said, "Have you seen my cottage, Shea?"

She looked at him.

"Have you?" he repeated.

She nodded. "Yes. I saw it. Those crazy daubs! I was here less than an hour ago."

"With Marquiss?"

"That's when I saw him."

"Was the cottage torn up then?"

She nodded, swallowed, and looked worried. "I don't know if Pres did it or not. I met him on the beach. He was walking away from your place. He told me he had just arrived and had gone into your cottage to look for you, but that you weren't there. He showed me what had happened in there, but he said he knew nothing about it. Then he started to talk to me about you, like a madman. We quarreled and—that's about all."

"Almost all," Dana corrected quietly. "Where is Marquiss, now?"

"I have no idea. I thought he'd left the island. But I was concerned about you, after seeing your torn paintings. Are you sure you're all right, Hank? When you and Kay Norcross didn't come to dinner—"

"Kay?" he asked sharply.

"Yes. Isn't she with you?"

"Of course not."

She looked at him again. Dana sent the flashlight beam wandering aimlessly through the underbrush that thrashed in the wind. The island suddenly seemed a wild and uncivilized place.

"Where is Kay, then?" Dana asked.

"I don't know. She didn't come to dinner, as I said, and everyone assumed that she was with you."

"Did you assume that, too?"

"I—no."

"You're a poor liar," Dana smiled. "Don't ever lie to me. You thought I was with her."

"Yes, I did. But if you haven't seen her, then—Hank, I've simply got to talk to you. I'm truly worried."

He thought of the woman's high-heeled footprint in the sand that was blown over his cottage porch. She was wearing flat-heeled sandals. She hadn't made those prints. He took her arm and looked at the bruise on her jaw, briefly.

"I'm worried, too," he said.

IT WAS going to rain. Thunder crashed and shook the air over the island, and lightning made a sheet of blue beyond the curved window. Dana looked at his watch. It was just nine-thirty. He sat back in the barrel chair and watched Shea put a pot of coffee on the oil stove. She looked good in the soft light of the oil lamp. He didn't talk about the bruise on her jaw any more. She wanted to ignore it. He had no intention of ignoring it, but this was not the moment for discussing it further. She moved about, quiet and competent, under his gaze. Everything about her gave him a deep sense of reassurance.

They were in the little lighthouse on the northern tip of Kettle Island. Long ago, Kettle Island Light had been abandoned when the new harbor breakwater was built for Stone Cove. Abel Mason had built and restored the old tower, even to repairing the oil-fuel mechanism of the old beacon and hand operated shutters. Shea had transformed the lower floor into a comfortable little apartment, to be used as a spare room whenever the island was overcrowded with summer tourists. She had taken it over now, when Dana's friends arrived from New York. Kay Norcross was using Shea's room in the main house.

"Comfortable?" Shea smiled. "Coffee will be ready in a minute. Or would you rather have a drink?"

"Coffee. I don't need a drink when I'm with you."

"Are you getting gallant, Hank?"

"Just smart," he said.

"It's about time."

Her smile was frank and happy, touching her eyes. She didn't say any more. She turned to a phonograph and put on a record, winding the old-fashioned crank. It was an antiquated machine, but it played remarkably well. Schubert's Seventh Symphony flooded the old lighthouse. The girl's shadow crossed the iron circular stairway leading up through the ceiling to the tower above.

"Pres fixed the gramaphone for me," she said. "Those were in better days. The good old days. Remember, Pres was a senior and played right end on the football team? You and Charley and Pres Marquiss—the Galloping Ghosts of Stone Cove."

Dana grinned. "Charley pretends he never came from here, but I remember when he was nuts about you, too. Now he behaves as if he'd never met you before."

"Poor Charley," Shea said. "He wanted to be captain, and you were elected. He wanted to be class president, and you got it. He wanted me, and I—" She bit her lip.

"In that respect, I used to think he was off his trolley," Dana smiled. "Of course, I never assumed I had a chance with you."

"Flatterer, I was eating out of your hand."

Dana said, "I guess no one ever recognizes the good things of life while he has them. Trite but true. I must have been an extremely backward youth."

Shea said, "It's not too late."

Shea crossed the room and sat down beside him. Her body was soft and pliant against his. Neither said anything. He kissed her. Outside, thunder crashed explosively, and lightning crackled across the sky. Shea moved out of his arms and stood up. Her face was pale. She crossed her arms as if she were chilled suddenly, and walked to the phonograph and turned the record over on the other side. The music of the symphony swelled and was lost in another rumbling mutter of thunder, and then returned to fill the circular, white-walled room. Shea turned to face Dana, her eyes suddenly sober.

"Hank, what are you going to do?"

"I don't know yet," he said. He was thinking of her kiss. "I haven't decided."

She scrubbed her cheek with the palm of her hand. There was fear behind her sober eyes. "It's someone on the island, one of your friends. That's fairly evident. You were right about it, all along. Someone here has it in for you, actually wants to kill you. Someone who has killed once before."

"Yes," he said.

"Do you know why?"

Dana said, "I'm beginning to understand it a little better. The why of it, however, is not the pressing point at the moment. Shea, we could waltz around that forever, I suspect. The point is, we must stick to the tangibles, to what has already been done in fact. What happened down in my cottage just now is important. You saw those crazy blobs of paint someone threw around in there.

She shuddered. "Crazy, yes."

"Did you actually go inside my cottage?"

"No. I was—I was looking for you. I wanted to be near you. After I told you about—how I feel about you, Hank—I came to the cottage, just to be near your place. I looked in through the north windows and saw what had happened."

"Then you didn't go up on the porch?"

"No."

"And Preston Marquiss?"

"He was on the beach when I first saw him."

"Near his boat?"

"He said he'd just arrived."

"He wasn't on the porch, either, at any time you were with him?"

"No."

"Then it was Kay," he said. His voice was suddenly decisive. "She was there, too. I saw her footprints in the sand. She's seen it, too."

"Or perhaps she did it herself?"

"Perhaps," he nodded. "I don't know about that yet. The thing is, what happened was no coincidence. None of it has been a coincidence, though attempts have been made to explain it as such. I mean, the way my paintings were similarly ruined in New York. The timing of each one of these incidents is important."

"The timing?"

He felt excited, on the verge of grasping something very elusive.

"Look here, I was telling you about the New York thing earlier today. Did you discuss it with anyone on the island after I mentioned it to you?" He saw her frown. "Think carefully, Shea. You were painting on the dunes when I talked to you about it. It has to be after I left you, then; between that time and the time I finally returned to my cottage."

She seemed to be listening to the music instead of to him. Turning, she switched off the phonograph and lifted the needle arm. Lightning turned the windows into dazzling sheets of blue for an instant. Dana became aware of the slow, heavy spatter of rain against the lighthouse walls.

Shea said, "You were down on the boat with Kay, I think. When I came back to the main house, you were upstairs, talking to Willi Tempel. Kay and Petey Norcross then came up the cliff stairs, quarreling rather loudly. They broke it up when they saw me, and Kay came into the kitchen with me and just hung around for a while. I don't know where her husband, went. Kay wanted to know all about your boyhood days. Then she mentioned the fact that you had lost a chance to exhibit your work, because your paintings had been destroyed, and I said you had just been telling me about it."

"So you mentioned it to Kay, and she knew it was on my mind at the time. Did you talk to anyone else about it?"

"No, no one else. Do you think it was Kay?"

"I don't know. Kay might have told someone else, any of the others." Dana frowned. "Or perhaps she acted on the assumption that whatever she did would be blamed on the man who killed Lotti Higgins. It might have been an act of spite on her part. On the other hand, she might have repeated the conversation to the others, and it gave the killer the idea to pull the stunt again, to further torment me."

"Then the thing to do is to question Kay."

"But no one knows where she is."

"We'll have to find her." Shea's eyes reflected sudden fear. "As soon as we can."

The rain was just starting. They ran together down the path from the lighthouse. Shea's flashlight guiding them through the woods. They reached the house before the summer downpour really began.

Abel and Sarah Mason were in the kitchen, reading the evening newspapers. The old lobsterman had changed his clothes; he wore a brushed blue suit and a bright silk necktie knotted an inch below his gold collar button. His big gnarled hands stuck out awkwardly from his coat sleeves. Sarah Mason, large and stout, had the weathered face and quiet fortitude of a fisherman's wife.

The sound of Charley Powell's voice in hot argument with Willi Tempel came down the back stairs. Sarah Mason got up and lighted the stove under a pot of coffee. Abel rattled the *Stone Cove Times* and cleared his throat. The kitchen was spotless, shining with white paint, and the polished copper kettles on the wall would have made any Fifth Avenue antique dealer envious.

Dana nodded toward the sound of voices that came from the upper floor. "What's going on?"

"Mr. Tempel wants to see Mr. Powell's new paintings," Abel said quietly. "Powell is doing some objecting. Don't see why, unless he's ashamed of the stuff." His eyes regarded Dana and then Shea with objective curiosity. He settled on Shea, on the bruise on her jaw, and his weather-beaten face went tight. "You all right, honey?"

"Of course, Abel."

"You ain't seen Pres since?"

"No."

Dana said, "He's still on the island. I'll find him."

Abel said, "That's for me to take care of, Hank."

Shea spoke desperately, "Stop that, you two. He won't bother me again. He went too far this time, and he'll stay away from me from now on."

"I intend to make sure of that," Abel said quietly.

Rain hissed against the windows. With a quick change of expression, Abel Mason looked at Dana, and his voice was casual and no longer strained.

"There was good lobstering today, Henry. I'm going down to Needle Neck tomorrow morning, first thing. Got more traps to pull down there. You want to go?"

"Yes, I'd like to," Dana said. "I'll go, too," Shea added.

Dana looked at Abel. "Have you seen Mrs. Norcross?"

"Nope. I reckon she's down on the schooner. Don't see what everybody is making such a fuss about. It's her loss if she missed out on Sarah's cooking—and yours, too, Henry."

"I wasn't with her," Dana said.

Footsteps thumped on the back stairs and Charley Powell came into the kitchen. His big figure bulged in his tan, open collared sport shirt. His thick, straight eyebrows were angry. He looked back over his shoulder as Willi Tempel puffed down the steps after him; then he looked at Dana.

"I thought Kay was with you, Henry," he said.

"No. Haven't you seen her, either?"

"I make a point of seeing as little of her as possible." He looked at Willi Tempel. Willi was wearing a gaily-flowered yellow silk dressing gown. His fat face bore traces of talcum powder, and he smelled of lilac after-shave lotion. He looked better than he had earlier in the afternoon. Charley said, "Well, that's settled, anyway. Poker, Willi?"

Willi said, "Not now. Hasn't Kay returned yet?"

"No. Henry's here, but he was with Miss Mason."

Willi said, "I'd like to talk to you, Henry—alone."

Dana said, "Stay here, Shea."

He followed the fat man toward the front of the house. Several lamps were lighted in the big paneled living room. Rain slammed with increasing fury against the long casement windows that faced the cove. A fire crackled in the big fieldstone fireplace, and someone had left a tray of cocktails untouched on the coffee table, before the copper fire screen. The big room looked warm and comfortable, with its heavy oak ceiling timbers and oriental rugs.

Willi picked up one of the cocktails and drank it with two furious gulps. His round face was flushed.

"Have you made up your mind yet, Henry?"

"About what?"

"Me," Willi said.

Dana watched the fat man drain another cocktail glass. "I haven't been thinking about you, Willi."

Willi said heavily, "But I must know, Henry. I'm your friend. I've helped you in your career, guided you and introduced you to clients, sold your paintings—"

"And stole from me," Dana concluded. "In my books, you're still a crook."

"I'm willing to make it good," the fat man said. "If you expose me, I'll be ruined. My life is in your hands."

Dana said, "I'm not ready to discuss it with you yet, Willi. I'm worried about Kay. I want to find her."

Willi said, "Oh, her. We all thought she was with you." He winked lasciviously, then sobered as he saw the look on Dana's face. "I don't know what's happened to her. She never cared to play the part of a hermit before."

"That's why I'm worried," Dana said.

"Worried, Henry?"

"I think something has happened to her." Dana was aware of Charley Powell and Shea entering the room, but he didn't take his gaze from Willi's fat face. "I think we all ought to get out and look for her."

Charley said, "We could organize a search of the island, if you think she's had an accident."

"No accident," Dana said abruptly. "Where is Petey?"

Willi said, "He went down to the boat to look for her. You're not serious, are you, Henry?"

"Yes, I'm serious," Dana said.

"You won't do anything about me, without letting me know first, will you, Henry?"

"No. I can promise you that." Dana turned up his coat collar and started for the front door. Shea crossed the room with him. He said, "You'd better stay here, Shea. Those steps are dangerous in this weather."

"I want to go with you."

He hesitated, and knew she wouldn't be easily swayed. "I'd rather you stayed here, Shea. Please. All I want is your flashlight."

She got it for him and he went out into the rain alone. The wind slammed across the harbor and drove the rain across the lip of the bluff in wild sheets of water. The lighted windows guided him down the flagstone walk across the lawn toward the wooden stairs that went down the face of the cliff. He bent his head into the wind, his eyes half closed. He was drenched to the skin in a moment. No one followed him from the house. At the edge of the cliff he paused and squinted down into the dark hollow of the cove. The schooner's lights danced on the black water below. He gripped the wet, slippery rail and started down the zigzag steps. The rain and wind pounded at him, pushing him against the rough face of the cliff. Lightning scratched at the sky. In the momentary glare he saw the white, tossing hull of the yacht and the canvas-covered length of Abel's lobster boat. At the bottom of the stairs he turned his flashlight on the float, streaming with dark water. There was a little surf in the cove, pounding at the pebbled beach. The schooner's manila fenders bumped heavily against the raft. He went down the float's swaying length and leaped nimbly aboard.

"Kay!" he called.

The wind snatched the words from his mouth. He found the cabin hatch and slid it aside and went down the narrow ladder into the hull of the boat. A dim bulb burned in the companionway, and the main cabin door was open, admitting more light from in there. Dana turned off his flash and went inside.

"Hello, Petey," he said.

Peter Norcross crouched on the edge of a bunk across the room. He was alone. He was drunk. His thin cotton pajamas were plastered wetly to his scrawny frame. His glasses dangled from one ear. He held a bottle of rye in both hands, between his bony knees, and he looked up with a blank stare as Dana opened the door.

Rain drummed on the deck overhead.

"I'm looking for Kay," Dana said bluntly. "Where is she, Petey?"

Petey giggled. "Are you asking me, Henry?"

"Yes. You."

"To hell with you, Henry."

Petey raised the bottle to his lips. Dana crossed the cabin and took the bottle from him. Petey's fingers clung tightly for a moment, then let go. He giggled, and the giggle turned into a strangled sob. Dana didn't touch the little man. He was afraid of what might happen if he did.

"I must see her, Petey," he said quietly. "There is something I must ask her. When did you see her last?"

"Not long ago."

"Where?"

Petey fumbled for his glasses and made an effort to put them on straight. His hands were shaking. His face was wet, but Dana didn't know whether it was from tears or the rain. The little man was risking pneumonia, sitting there in his wet pajamas. He controlled his angry impatience.

"Petey, is she all right?"

"Sure. Just fine. Worried about her, Henry?"

"We're all worried."

"But *you?*"

"Of course."

"Gimme back my bottle, Henry."

"Later," Dana said. "Answer my question first."

Petey said, "I ought to kill you. Maybe I will. But I want a drink first. That's my whole trouble. I always want a drink first."

"Is Kay aboard?" Dana asked.

"She's at your place," Petey said, and his face twitched. "She's waiting for you there, Henry."

"Did you see her there?"

"She's at your place, don't worry."

"When were you at my cottage, Petey?"

The little man looked at him, his mouth open, and then he suddenly burst into sobs. Dana stared at him with shocked eyes. He hesitated. Petey was in no condition to answer anything coherently. He crossed the cabin and put the bottle down where Petey could reach it, and went out.

Rain drove into his face as he reached the deck. The schooner pitched and bumped irregularly against the float. Dana looked across the harbor at the lights of Stone Cove, then up at the dark, bulking mass of the bluff. He made his way with careful steps to the flight of stairs going up the cliff.

Someone was waiting for him at the top of the steps. He stiffened for a moment, until he saw who it was. Preston Marquiss' face swam out of the darkness. The man looked half-wild. His clothing was disheveled, drenched with rain, and his face was scratched and torn as if he had spent hours staggering through the island's underbrush.

"Dana!"

"I've been looking for you," Dana said grimly.

The wind came between them, garbling the man's next words. His hands came out in a curious gesture of appeal. "Lost my head...sorry I hit her...I'm all through, Dana, all through..."

Dana fought down an impulse to swing at him. All his rage against the man vanished. Only contempt was left inside him as the man weaved forward.

"What happened to you?" Dana asked.

"My boat—it's been wrecked."

"How?" Dana asked sharply.

"I don't know. It's on the beach. Somebody cut the lines and let it drift on the rocks. I can't get off the island, and I'm being framed, I tell you!"

"Framed?"

The man's face went cunning. "Abel Mason is after me—he'll kill me—I have nothing to defend myself with! All I want is to get off this cursed island."

"There are other boats," Dana said. "Why don't you go?"

The big man wiped rain from his face. In the light of the torch, Dana saw a dark smear on the back of Marquiss' hand. It looked like blood, but he couldn't be sure. He moved forward suddenly, but the big man retreated, backing away from him over the dark, rain-swept lawn.

"I didn't have anything to do with it!" Marquiss shouted.

"What are you talking about?"

Without warning, the big man whirled, his feet slipping in the wet grass. Dana lunged after him, but Marquiss ducked backward, swinging wildly, and struck the flashlight from Dana's hand. Darkness folded in, heavy with rain. In the dim light from the house windows, the man was all but invisible. Dana dived for him, but Marquiss was already running, skirting the edge the lawn and fleeing for the dark shelter of the pine woods. Dana pursued him for only a few steps. In the night and the rain, the man could lose himself easily. It would be like looking for the proverbial needle in a haystack. He gave up the idea and walked back to retrieve his flashlight.

Shea came running toward him from the veranda. Her voice called to him, high and anxious.

"Hank, who was it?"

"Marquiss," he said. He turned to meet her and took her arm. She was trembling. "It's all right, Shea. Nothing much happened. He ran away."

Her eyes searched his face for a moment.

"Did you find Kay on the schooner?"

"She's not there," he said. "I'm going back to my place to look for her."

"Now? In all this?"

"She talked to someone about my paintings. I've got to find out who she talked to."

He walked toward the house with her. She was wearing a transparent plastic raincoat, with a hood over her head. She paused

THE ART STUDIO MURDERS

after a few steps and then ran up on the porch and searched on the chairs there. She came back and handed him a yellow fisherman's slicker."

"I wish you wouldn't go."

"I have to."

"Then put this on. You're soaking wet."

Dana took the slicker from her cold hands. He couldn't see much of her face in the dark rain. They went on, along the path to the woods.

Shea said, "Hank, can you take care of yourself, alone? I mean, you need something to protect—"

"I've got a gun." He touched Willi's revolver in his pocket. "Are the others still in the house?"

"No." Shea's voice sounded strained. "They decided to help you in the search. How was Mr. Norcross?"

"Drunk... Are they all gone? Abel too?"

She nodded. "All but Sarah. I want to go with you, Hank. I don't want to stay here."

He shook his head. "You'll be better off with Sarah. I don't want to have your safety on my mind."

He left her at the edge of the woods and waited until she regained the house. He didn't like to leave her just now, but he liked the thought of Shea meeting Kay at his cottage even less.

A flashlight flickered through the trees far to one side of the path, near the lighthouse, but aside from that there was no sign of the other searchers. He trudged on alone through the woods, rain beating coldly on his head and shoulders. The darkness drew a circle around him.

He was halfway across the island before he first got the impression that someone was following him. He turned his head sharply and looked back across the narrow path, but there was nothing to see. The rain hissed in the underbrush and smothered all other sounds except the muttering of the surf. His flashlight turned the tree trunks silvery against the darkness. He kept one hand in his pocket, on Willi Tempel's gun. He hoped he wouldn't have to use it. He didn't want to use it. No one was following him.

From the right, in the underbrush, came a quick crackling noise, as if an animal prowled there.

He turned and sent the flashlight beam sharply into the brush. There was nothing there. It was the rain. He took two steps off the path, and still he saw nothing, heard nothing but the rain and the thrashing of wind. He wondered if it could have been Marquiss; but it could be anyone; they were all wandering around loose on the island. He went on, descending through the woods to the opposite shore of the island.

He didn't turn around again. He heard more sounds, vague little cracklings and hissings in the darkness. He knew if he turned around, he would start to run; or he would fire blindly into the bushes. He kept the gun in his pocket.

Sand gritted under his shoes. The wind pressed the slicker flat against his body, flapping it out behind his legs. Long lines of white surf raced out of the night and thundered on the beach. At the rickety little wharf, lashed in a smother of foam, he paused and looked back again.

The shadows moved and swayed in the wind, but no one appeared. He turned up the path to the cottage.

The windows were dark. The doorway was open again, and rain lashed across the threshold on the oak floor inside. He put the flashlight in his left hand and looked on the porch, where the sand had been. There were no more footprints. He sent the light dancing around the nightmare of colors splashed on his walls and his tattered paintings.

"Kay?" he called.

The surf bellowed behind him. He turned and looked along the beach, and again he thought he saw a shadow stop when he turned his head.

"Kay?"

There was no answer. He went inside, and the quality of sounds changed, grew muted. Rain drummed and tinkled on the windows, and a damp sea wind blew steadily all through the little house. He shivered and avoided looking at the silently screaming blobs of paint on the walls. The house had an empty sound and empty tone to it. Kay wasn't here. He stood frowning, using his flashlight to check the closet, looking for something he didn't want to find.

The back kitchen door was also open. He tried to remember whether he had left the oil lamp burning in the studio when he last left here. He couldn't remember. He took the gun from his pocket and stepped outside.

There was a small cleared space of sand-blown grass behind the cottage, and then the underbrush began, rising on a dune topped by woods. The pine trees seemed to tower over him like a dark wall, weaving in the wind. To the right of the back steps was a rectangular shadow, echoing hollowly as the rain beat upon it. He had to struggle to remember and identify it. The wood box. His flashlight touched the bin, swung away, and came back to it again. He felt a quick ache in his throat. He stepped off the small back porch into the sand, keeping the light on the wood box.

A woman's pale gray snakeskin shoe lay on its side in the wet sand, soggy with rain. A bare foot, with toenails painted a garish crimson, was just visible around the edge of the box. Kay's shoe. Kay's foot. He walked around to look at her. Kay Norcross was huddled in the corner made by the bin and wall of the house. Her head leaned back, resting against the stone foundation. She had been strangled.

There was nothing violent about her figure, except for that. She sat there with her naked shoulders against the wall, one leg drawn up so that the knee shone smoothly white in the light of the flash; the other leg was extended straight out beyond the bin, the shoe off. Rain had ruined her elaborate dark coiffure. Rain pattered all over her tanned body, on her cheeks, her mouth, and on her eyes. Her eyes were wide open, glistening in the rain. Her mouth was open, too, and her tongue stuck out between her lips. Great mottled bruises showed dark and ugly on her slim neck.

She looked lonely and far away, sitting there in the rain.

Dana's knees felt weak. The flashlight drooped in his hand. The gun seemed senseless now. He leaned on the wet edge of the woodbin and turned off the flashlight so that Kay Norcross wouldn't be there. Darkness took her away and brought the trees closer, made the sound of the wind and surf louder, made him smaller and almost as lonely as the dead girl. He turned and walked back into the cottage kitchen.

Halfway across the kitchen he stopped and remembered Petey Norcross, giggling and sobbing on the schooner; he thought of Willi Tempel—Willi on Fifth Avenue with his gold-knobbed staff, and Willi sprawled, bearded and sweating on the bed in a stifling bedroom; he thought of Charley Powell's crippled hands and the anger in Charley's voice when he mentioned Shea snooping in his room.

He thought of himself last. He thought of himself too late. He didn't hear anything; he had no warning; he sensed a sudden rush of air behind him, but he had no chance to turn. Something crashed down on the back of his head and he was on his knees, not knowing how he had gotten there, aware only of a blinding pain in his head and down through his spine and a complete loss of strength. He was on his knees and crawling through the darkness of the kitchen toward the door. He heard a footstep behind him and a voice spoke to him from far away, from high above his head, thick with satisfaction.

"So now you're dead!"

Again something crashed down on his head, but this time he didn't feel it. Darkness folded wings around him and took him back to where Kay Norcross waited for him…

CHAPTER NINE

COLOR MOVED OUT of the darkness and swam across his consciousness. A gaudy orange amoeba took shape and wiggled and squirmed before his eyes, and then it swam away. It was replaced by a shower of elongated gray raindrops that changed to yellow and then to green. The drops of color splashed on lichened rocks like miniature bombs.

More color, without shape and without reason, ranging the entire spectrum, followed the gray slanting rain, wriggling about with an ugly crawling motion. The pigments bellowed and shrieked at him.

His head ached. His back ached. His body was full of furies. Dana gritted his teeth. He groaned, but made no sound. He groaned again, this time aloud.

Shea's voice spoke soothingly to him, "You're coming along fine, Hank."

He opened his eyes suddenly, opened them wide, and the gaudy blobs of color became the mad splashes of pigment on his cottage walls. He lay on his bunk, a pillow under his head, his coat and shirt off, his shoes off. Shea was bending anxiously over the bunk.

Pain hammered through his head. Shea's face withdrew and he looked sidewise and saw her trimming the oil lamp on the table. The sound of rain on the windows scratched and plucked at his nerves. His ribs ached. He listened to the friendly clicking of Shea's heels as she moved about the room, and everything slid into place with that safe, comfortable sound. He raised his wrist with a tremendous effort and saw that it was almost midnight. He touched his head and found a neat, professional bandage over his scalp. He looked at Shea again and wondered that he was still alive. By all odds, he should have been dead now. This time, for keeps. But he wasn't. He waited until Shea turned to face him again.

"What are you doing here?" he asked quietly.

Her words came gently. "I couldn't stay in the house with Sarah—not when I knew you were alone here. I decided to walk over. Just as I got here, I heard a noise in the kitchen. You were sprawled over the threshold of the back door." Her smile was twisted, full of tears. "Lying in your own gore, as they say. Whoever attacked you beat it out the back door as I came in. I was just as pleased."

"Did you see who it was?"

"No. I couldn't even glimpse him. He was gone as soon as I stepped on the porch. Now be quiet, Hank. You've had a close call."

"Have you been outside?" he asked. "In the back?"

"Yes."

"Did you see Kay?"

"Yes. I saw her. Be quiet."

"I can't be quiet. Listen, Shea, Petey knew she was dead. He was here, and he told me she was waiting for me here. He acted half-crazy when I saw him on the schooner. He must have known Kay was dead."

Shea said, "I wish I had a little morphine for you. That's what you really need. You were hit with a fireplace poker, did you know that? From your fireplace here."

"I thought it was a battleship." It hurt him to smile. His face felt stiff; his legs felt stiff. He looked at the fireplace, turning his head very carefully to lull the sudden explosions of pain in the back of his neck, and he saw that she had built a fire there. The cottage was warm and cozy, soft with mellow light, comfortable and sane—except for the presence of the paint daubs on all the walls. He looked into Shea's solicitous eyes and said, "Where are all the others?"

"I don't know. I left Sarah alone—with a shotgun."

"Marquiss didn't come back?"

"No."

"What really made you follow me here?"

"I was worried about you. Do I need any other reason?" She came back to him and sat down carefully on the edge of the bunk. He reached out and took her hand and she said, "The power is off, by the way. The telephone and lights all went dead. So I followed you here, and none too soon, as I see it. Don't complain."

"I'm not complaining. Was it the storm?"

"No, not the storm. I checked the wires from the house. They were cut."

"Deliberately?"

Shea said, "Our man means business, I guess."

"We can always use the boats."

"Not anymore," Shea said. "They're both sitting in the mud, both Abel's and Willi Tempel's schooner. Someone scuttled them. The schooner's deck is awash."

Dana cursed tiredly. "Petey was aboard the schooner."

"I doubt if he was aboard when the boat went down."

"Then we're cut off from town?"

"Not necessarily. Our man may think so—that's undoubtedly why he went to all that trouble—but there's still your dory here, and in a pinch, I could even swim it."

"In this weather?"

"The tide is coming in. There wouldn't be any real danger."

The pain came back for a moment, and with it the bright pinwheels of color. Shea's hand on his face wiped it all away. "Drink this, Hank."

Brandy burned in his throat. He began to feel a little better. He wanted to get up; he felt he was wasting precious time. He lay still and looked up at Shea's calm face and wondered just how badly damaged he was. *So now you're dead,* he remembered. The voice was just a voice. It didn't connect with anything he could remember. It could have been anybody's voice, glutted with hate. Even his own. Or just a last glimmer of conscious thought in his own mind as he went down under that brutal slugging. He shivered and looked sidewise and saw the gun he had taken from Willi Tempel. It lay on the table beside the oil lamp.

He grimaced. "That little gadget didn't do me much good."

"It wouldn't have helped you anyway," Shea said. "It wasn't loaded."

"That Willi," Dana said. "He pretended he was going to commit suicide with it."

"Not that specimen. He loves life too much," Shea smiled.

He tried to sit up. His head swam. Shea pushed him gently backward, and he closed his eyes and rested on his elbows. Then he sat up again. Nausea squirmed inside him. He fought it off. Shea didn't try to push him back again. He got his feet on the floor and sat there. He felt perspiration break out all over his body. His breathing came in long, ragged gasps. Every nerve jittered inside him.

Shea said, "Relax, Hank."

"I can't."

"Look, pretend I'm your doctor. I *am* a doctor, you know."

He nodded. He was shivering. He tried to gather strength with which to stand up, but nothing happened. He willed himself to stand up. Nothing happened. A great, dark fear welled up inside him as he looked down at his legs. He ran his hands up and down his thighs, feeling the quiver of muscles. He stared at Shea. He stood up.

Shea said, "Oh, Hank."

"I'll be all right," he said, and sat down again.

"You'll go to pieces this way."

The walls swam. He looked at the blobs of color splashed on them. He looked at Shea, and the girl smiled and touched his hand.

"Willi was lying to you about the gun," she said.

"Yes."

"Do you think Willi Tempel wants to kill you?"

"Yes."

"Just Willi?"

"No. The others, too."

"Why, Hank? What have you done?"

"Nothing," he said. "That is—nothing. I learned that Willi is a thief. He's been stealing money from the sales of paintings he handles. I found out about it. I told him I knew about it. I don't care about my own losses so much, but I don't like the idea of his cheating all the others. I'm the only one who knows about Willi. If his thefts become public knowledge, it will ruin him, of course."

"Would you ruin him, Hank?"

"No, of course not. I want him to make good the losses."

"And will he?"

"I don't know."

"Would he prefer to murder you, instead?"

"I don't know."

"And Charley Powell?"

He looked at her. "Charley?"

"Yes. Does he want to kill you, too?"

"No. I don't think so... Yes."

She prodded him. "Make up your mind, Hank."

"Yes."

"Why."

"I crippled him. We were driving home from a party one night, last winter. That is, I was driving. We had an accident—I tried to avoid it, but the car turned over and Charley's hands were badly damaged. You know he's a painter, too. At the time, we were both working on material in the hope that we would get exhibitions. But Charley gave it up. He's able to paint, of course, and he does his commercial illustrations without any effort, but he seems to have lost all confidence in any serious work he might do. I'm afraid he'll never try it again, and it's my fault."

"Does he blame you for it?" Shea asked quietly. "Has he ever said anything about it?"

"No, but I feel guilty about it just the same. The blame is mine. It seems that ever since we were kids, I always got the things he wanted very badly—and got them without making too much effort about it. It was just luck, the way the cards fell, but that rivalry was always there. Sometimes I think he hates me for it. I never paid much attention to his attitude, though, until all this began."

She was silent for a moment, her eyes introspective, wondering and calculating. The logs hissed in the fireplace. The rain was a lulling sound on the roof.

"And Petey Norcross?" she asked quietly.

Her questions were like soft hammers tapping on his conscience. He said,

"You know about Kay."

"Yes. Have you ever really given him cause…?"

"No."

"Please tell me frankly. I love you, darling."

"I love you, too, Shea. There was never anything between Kay and me—on my part, at any rate. Nothing that Petey could use as evidence, I'm sure. But of course, I don't know what Kay might have told him. She liked to torment him. She seemed to derive a sadistic pleasure out of flaunting other men over Petey."

"Would he kill you because of her? Out of jealousy? To remove you from the scene?"

"I don't know."

"But he was on the scene the night that girl, Lotti Higgins, was murdered, wasn't he? Do you suppose…?"

"I'm not sure. He might have managed to get to her apartment before I did. It would be nip and tuck, though. Lotti was already dead when I arrived, and I moved as fast as I possibly could."

"Would Petey kill Kay?"

"No, I don't think so. He'd take any kind of vicious treatment she cared to dish out to him, but he wouldn't exploit it into a motive for murdering her. But he would kill me, if he dared." A log rolled over in the fireplace, and Shea glanced at the screen, then at the dark, wet windows. Dana stood up again. He remained standing, swaying, until she looked at him. Then he sank back once more. He was feeling better. Shea's voice had a soothing quality, and her questions no longer made him writhe inside.

"Which one of those men do you really believe wants to kill you?" she asked.

"I don't know, Shea."

"Yes, you do. You do know."

"No. I think—no. My head hurts."

"What do you think?" she asked quietly.

"Nothing. I think of Kay out there. We've got to move her."

"Not until the sheriff comes," Shea said.

"But it isn't decent to leave her like that."

"Don't think about Kay. We can't do anything for her now. Think of the man who wants to kill you, and why he wants to kill you, and think of his name."

"I don't know who he is," Dana said.

"But you do. You do know. Think about it. All of them may want to kill you, but only one of them would really do it. You know them better than I do, Hank. They're your friends. You know them. Which one is it?"

He stared at her helplessly.

She said, "I'm your doctor now, Hank."

"I know. It's no good."

She said, "Why don't you paint anymore?"

"But I do," he replied quickly.

"Not really. You've been pretending, just dabbling. You admitted you didn't consider your work as good as it was before. Is it because you've been upset over all this?"

"I suppose so."

She said, "Hank, do you love me?"

"Yes," he said, "You know I do."

"Would you paint for me?"

"Yes," he said.

"Now?"

"No."

She said earnestly, "It will help you. You need it. Get your brush, Hank."

"Shea, this is silly," he said.

"No, it's not. Paint for me, now."

"But—"

He looked at her and didn't seem to see her. Her voice soothed and quieted him. She had something in her mind, a scheme to help him. She needed his cooperation. She wanted him to paint. Now. With Kay out there in the rain. And strangely, he did want to paint. The thought appealed to him, offered an escape, a means of easing the tension inside him.

"What shall I paint?" he asked. "Is it anything in particular that you want?"

"Whatever is in your mind."

"All I'm thinking of is death," he said.

"Then paint it."

He looked at his palette and brushes and saw that she had stretched a new canvas on the easel and had prepared everything for him—prepared him for this, from the moment he came to. He looked at her, and she nodded quietly, acknowledging her awareness of his thought.

"What do you have in mind?" he asked.

"I just want you to paint. Paint it, or draw it—use the symbols and the language you know best, darling! Try!"

He walked to the easel and picked up one of the red sable brushes, feeling the softness of it with his fingertips. His legs were still trembling. He looked at the bunk and he wanted to sit down again beside Shea. He picked up the palette and stared at the canvas on the easel. It was blank. Kay returned to his thoughts for a moment.

"I don't paint abstracts," he said. "I can't paint death."

"Have you ever tried?"

He nodded. "Once, during the war, I was in a field hospital, then. I tried to do an abstract of death, and I could only paint a Nazi swastika. That's all."

"That was an abstract of death for you, at the time," Shea said. "There was nothing wrong with that. But paint whatever you like, Hank."

The rain beat with less violence on the windows. He started to mix pigments on the palette, then picked up a piece of charcoal instead. He looked at the walls. She said sharply, "Don't pay any attention to what's around here. Empty your mind on that canvas, Hank. Sketch it, if you prefer. You must find out who the murderer is—to save me, as well as yourself. That's what I want you to do."

"It won't work," he said dubiously.

"We'll see," she told him. "But I don't want you to worry about what's going on here on the island while you sketch. I'll see to it that you're not interrupted. Please begin."

He turned to his work. He had heard of men losing themselves in furious exertions at a time of emotional stress.

"I get it now," he said. "You want me to do the same as Szezak did."

"Who was he?"

"A friend of mine, a musician. He stayed up all night, composing a new symphony, the night his wife died. He kept pounding and crashing out chords until he dropped from exhaustion. Is that your remedy for me, Shea?"

"Sketch," she said. "Go ahead, draw it."

Now he didn't mind the idea of working. He found he wanted to use his hands. He looked at the blank canvas on the easel and touched his charcoal to it. The studio and Shea's bright head fell away from him, together with the flickering of the firelight and the sound of the rain. His first strokes were unsure, without decision. He didn't know where he was going, or what he was about to portray. The quiet crackling of the fireplace and the tapping of rain on the windows slowly faded...

THE murderer stood in the center of a howling maelstrom and shuddered and shook in tempo with the storm. His fingers held tight to the wet iron railing that curved before him. On every hand, there was nothing but a waste of dark water and black wind, streaked with flying streamers of white. There was a roaring in his ears and voices in the wind, and he shouted a bitter, futile defiance to the elements.

He could go no farther. And anyway, this was not the direction in which he wanted to go. Back there, behind him, was his objective, and when he thought of it, a dark red hate seeped through his mind and he turned away abruptly, away from the howling storm, and went through the doorway and slammed the door shut behind him.

The silence was abrupt, stunning. Below him, curving and sweeping downward beside the curvature of the rail, were the iron stairs, going down and down into the darkness. He felt momentarily dizzy, and for a brief instant he forgot his own identity in the wonder of the place and the time. He went on down and across the room below, opened another door, and stepped out again into the rain and wind.

Now he experienced another change within himself, with the cold slash of the rain on his face. He felt a unity with the storm, a fierce exultation. He laughed softly as he started forward, walking with that light strength that filled him so that he felt omnipotent, above all tangible things. The thought of murder filled his mind and made light of his difficulties. The night was dark. He walked without looking for the path through the woods, and somehow he knew he would not lose his way. He walked a little faster, until he was almost running.

Someone was floundering through the woods nearby.

He halted, half crouching under the swaying brush, waiting, the breath stopped in his throat. Anger filled him. He would brook no interference now.

The thrashing continued through the brush, over and above the noise of the wind. He waited. A shape stumbled toward the path. He felt around on the wet, sandy ground underfoot. A pebble, too small. A larger rock, fitting neatly into the palm of his hand, as if it were made for him. He strained to see through the gloom, the rain blinding him for a moment. Even the elements were against him again, he thought savagely.

Someone halted before him, slipped around and across the path to where he crouched.

"Hey!"

The other's voice was whipped away by the wind. He didn't recognize the man's figure. He lunged upward suddenly, and the other man stumbled backward, startled.

"I thought you were—hurt—don't—!"

He lifted his hand with the rock in it and brought it down on the other's head with stunning force. The strength of giants was in him. The other man went down without a whimper. He sprawled there, just off the path, satisfactorily concealed in wind-whipped bushes.

The murderer dropped the rock and breathed deeply of the wet, stinging air. He laughed, and then he started forward along the path once more...

For the first time in hours, Dana thought of Shea.

He lifted his gaze from the charcoal sketch and turned to look for her. The room was empty.

The cottage was silent. It was still raining, only a light drizzle, and the thunder of the surf mingled in a single voice to protest against the night. But there was just the faintest lightening of the darkness outside that hinted of dawn. He looked at his watch and then stood up, all at once, alarm tingling along his nerves. The fire was out in the fireplace. The big studio room felt cold. Gray tendrils of fog crept against the windowpanes, overcoming the drizzly rain. Dawn would be delayed, he thought. He had completely forgotten time and place while he sketched.

"Shea?" he called.

There was no answer. He glimpsed himself in the maple-framed wall mirror and was surprised at the bandage on his head. His shirt, stained with blood, lay in a crumpled heap on one of the kitchen chairs. He felt all right, though.

He wondered where Shea had gone, and he felt a gnawing worry over her. He turned back to his bunk, slid a suitcase out from under it, and rummaged inside for a fresh shirt. He had packed everything he owned when he quit the studio in New York; he had cleaned out the closet and the chest of drawers, and even packed his old laundry. Some of his soiled shirts and socks were in this suitcase, along with old handkerchiefs, and he impatiently pulled them aside to get at his fresh clothing.

Something fell from among the folds of a crumpled hand-kerchief and made a faint clattering on the floor. Dana looked down for it, reached the shirt he had uncovered, and then suddenly stooped and picked up the object that had been entangled with his laundry.

It was a little rubber shoe lift.

Abruptly he remembered a man's desk in New York, and a pathetic red-leather, high-heeled pump that had the rubber lift missing from one heel. Lotti Higgin's shoe. The one that had troubled Lieutenant Evans and Sullivan so much. It seemed a long time ago. It didn't make sense, turning up here on Kettle Island, in his own suitcase. No sense at all.

He pocketed the rubber wedge and shrugged into a fresh shirt and then turned back to the kitchen. The door was closed, and he did not go out to see if Kay's body was still there. He returned to the studio, his steps sliding silently on the floor.

Fear worked inside him. He called again.

"Shea!"

He went to the front door. He was walking all right now. The weakness was gone. He looked out at the dark, foggy beach. It would take a long time for daylight to come. The fog was everywhere, curling thickly around the little island.

"Shea?"

A shadow moved on the porch and stepped into the yellow light of the doorway. It was Abel Mason. The old lobsterman was wearing his sou'wester and yellow slicker. His face, weathered and gaunt, was calm. He had been standing quietly near one end of the porch, and now he turned to face Dana.

"She's gone," he said.

Dana stared at him. "Gone where?"

"Back to the house."

"How long have you been here, Abel?"

"All the time. I came over here with her, but Shea didn't want me to come in. She said she didn't want you to know I was hanging around on guard. She told me to watch you and see that you weren't disturbed by anybody."

Dana said, "You shouldn't have let her go. When did she leave?"

"Mebbe ten minutes ago, or thereabouts. She said it was important, Henry. I ain't never been able to argue with her much. She has a mind of her own."

"Where are Mr. Tempel and Mr. Powell?"

Abel shrugged. "I ain't seen 'em."

"Or Preston Marquiss?"

Abel said grimly, "You'd know it, if I caught up with him. You'd have heard about it, Henry."

"I'll take care of Marquiss, Abel."

"We'll see," Abel said.

Dana looked beyond him to the dark beach, then turned back into the cottage. The need for haste made his legs tremble. He wanted to run. He picked up the gun from the table, remembered that it was empty, and that Willi Tempel had used it only as a bluff. He dropped it into his pocket, anyway. He found his slicker and threw it impatiently over his shoulders and then paused before returning to his easel and canvas.

The charcoal looked dull, absorbing the glow of the dying firelight. The sketch was full of dark, somber tones that were unusual in Dana's style. Staring at it, Dana swore softly.

He had sketched a portrait of Charley Powell.

Abel Mason leaned in the doorway and said, "What now, Henry?"

He looked at Abel without seeing him. He didn't see anything for a moment. Abel said something else, and he didn't hear. He looked at the studio walls and toward the back window, thinking of Kay Norcross out there in the rain.

"Let's find Shea," he said.

He went out on the porch with a long stride and squeezed a beam of yellow light from his torch. "Did you come here with Shea in the first place, Abel?"

"Sure, we both found you on the kitchen floor. Found Mrs. Norcross, too. Shea chased me outside while she fixed you up."

"Why outside?"

"Said she was going to try an experiment. Told me to keep everybody out if they showed up, like I said. But nobody came around."

"And she went back to the house alone?"

Abel's face was worried. "You think she's in trouble?"

"Let's hurry," Dana said.

CHAPTER TEN

SARAH WAS ALONE in the big, shining kitchen when they came in out of the rain. Her face looked drawn. She looked at Dana and then at Abel. Her mouth grew tight. The kitchen felt warm and cozy after stumbling along the dark path across the island. Dana shook rain from his slicker. Sarah's eyes touched him with disapproval.

"I don't pretend to know what's going on here," she said. "Have you found Mrs. Norcross yet?"

"Yes," Dana said. "Are you alone, Sarah?"

She shook her head. "No."

"Where is Shea?" he asked. "Didn't she come back?"

"Yes, she was here. What happened to you, Henry? Shea said you'd hurt yourself—"

The sound of footsteps upstairs interrupted her. Dana went up the back stairway two steps at a time, his slicker flapping around his legs. He pushed open the door at the top of the steps and went down the upper corridor. A lamp near the head, of the front stairs cast a soft glow on the gray carpet. The walls were lined with framed marine oils and line drawings, the swords of swordfish, glass net floats, and mementos of a past that had lived by the sea. Some of the marine paintings were his own, which he had refused to sell. All the bedroom doors were closed but one. A shaft of light came from the open door. It was Charley Powell's room. Dana started for it, and Willi Tempel appeared in the doorway.

The fat man's jowls were dark with beard, although he had shaved once for dinner. He started to shut the door.

"Hold it," Dana said.

Willi said, "Don't go in there, Henry."

"Why not?"

"Just don't, that's all."

"Get out of my way," Dana ordered.

The fat man looked surprised at the tone of his voice. He looked at the bandage on Dana's head and then squeezed heavily to one side to let Dana into Charley's room.

There was a bed and tall windows and a bureau and an overstuffed chair. The windows were open and rain drove in on the floor. Paintings stood against the walls, and Dana felt a quick stab in his stomach as he looked at them. They weren't like Charley's usual work, what he could gather of them. The canvases were tormented, distorted expressions of things he couldn't understand

And like his own recently, every one of them was slashed and tattered to mad ribbons.

He looked at the rumpled bed. Petey Norcross sprawled on the sheets, fully clothed now, his little body flung in a grotesquely relaxed position. His big head lolled on the pillow. He was snoring, with light fluttery noises, and an empty bottle of rye lay near his out-flung hand.

Dana turned to Willi. The fat man pursed his little mouth and shrugged. He was wearing a lavender shirt and white flannels, evidently having changed his clothes from those worn in the rain. His shoes were muddy. His belt sagged far below his bulging belly.

Dana pointed to the slashed paintings. "Who did that?"

"I don't know," Willi muttered. "Charley will raise absolute hell, though."

"Where is Charley?"

"He's gone after Shea."

"Where?"

"I don't know."

"Are those the paintings Charley was working on since he came here?"

"Yes," Willi nodded. "Shea saw them and said some rather pointless things about them. Anyway, I thought they were pointless." Willi's face looked gray. He looked at Petey's limp, sprawled figure on the bed. "Maybe Petey tore them up. Or Shea. The only thing I'm sure of is that I didn't do it."

Dana looked at Petey, too. "Is he really drunk?"

"Try to wake him," Willi said.

Dana took the gun from his pocket and thumbed out the empty magazine clip. He looked at Willi.

"Let's have the slugs, Willi."

"Henry, I—"

"Give them to me!"

"What's the matter with you, Henry? You look—what's wrong now, anyway?"

"Nothing. Everything. The slugs, Willi."

Willi looked at Dana's face and dug deep into his huge trousers and came up with an extra clip of cartridges in his soft hand. He gave them to Dana silently. Dana snapped the bullets into the gun and tossed the empty magazine to the bed. It landed on Petey Norcross's scrawny chest. Petey didn't move. His breathing didn't change.

Dana went downstairs fast. Abel and Sarah were just coming down the hall toward the front of the house. He didn't wait for them. He yanked open the front door and ran out into the dark dawn, turning north toward the lighthouse.

It seemed even darker than before, the fog misting everything with vague outlines. He ran with all his strength, staggering and stumbling. The darkness held no terrors for him now. Anger twisted his brain and his stomach, wrenching his body forward across the shadowed sand dunes. Rain hissed softly around him. His head began to throb again. His pace slowed, his legs weakening in the sticky, clinging sand. He staggered to the top of a high dune and paused, drawing his lungs full of cold wet air. His heart hammered against his ribs. He wanted to sit down and rest. He looked out across the harbor and saw that Stone Cove was still asleep across the dark water, with just a dim light or two twinkling here and there. Kettle Island Light was cut off from his view by the intervening woods and a rise in the land. He slid down the opposite slope of the dune and stumbled across a drainage inlet whose stream poured toward the beach. He followed it, his flash-light sending a bobbing beam of light ahead of him. He reached the beach and turned north again. The way was easier here, the sand packed hard by the night's rain. He sprinted. A rock tripped him and he went sprawling, flying through the air. He landed on all fours, skinning his hands on the pebbles. His flashlight rolled ahead of him, tinkling as the lens and bulb shattered. Surf thundered in his ears. He couldn't get up for a moment. He felt warm wetness under the bandage on his scalp. He got one leg flexed under him and tried to rise. He couldn't. He got the other leg bent and rose to his knees. He stood up. He had no light now, but he didn't need one; his boyhood had been spent on this island. He went on until a rock jetty barred his way, dark against the night sky. He swung inland at this point, running slower now through the fog, along the edge of the woods. His footsteps thudded more heavily with each new moment—and found an echo in his ears.

He halted abruptly.

A shadow stopped its gliding motion about fifty paces to the left of him and was lost against the somber walls of the pine trees. He could see the light on the harbor breakwater now, but not the tower on the island itself. Kettle Light. The little white tower was still obscured by the trees and the fog that fought the dawn. The harbor light sent its powerful beam out to sea, revolving in a complete circle, its radiance fuzzy and diminished by the mist. Dana watched it swing away from him, and then the darkness crept nearer as it pointed south. He waited for the momentary flash of brightness as it touched Kettle Island once again in its slow revolution. When it came, he saw the shadow move. It slid quickly into the other shadows of the woods, melting away in there.

He lifted his gun. Anger pounded through him—and fear, but not for himself.

He thought: This time I'm not running away.

He thought: If anything has happened to Shea!

Turning, he plunged toward the shadow in the woods. The underbrush thrashed and crackled as a heavy body in there tried to scramble away. Dana drove deeper into the dense foliage, saw something flicker and vanish in a corner of his eye. He halted again and stood still, listening.

The leaves dripped all around him. A bell buoy tolled solemnly, with sonorous notes, out in the fairway of Stone Cove Harbor. From far off he heard a church bell on the mainland. Around him, the fog moved sinuously through the pines and the brush.

A twig snapped with the sound of a miniature pistol report.

Dana swung that way, and then again stood still. High up in the pine tops, a squirrel chattered angrily; a blue jay screamed; and all around was the steady, monotonous drip of water from the foliage. There was movement to his left, slow and stealthy. Dana swallowed, dried his palm on his thigh, and took a fresh grip on the gun. He darted forward suddenly, diving between two clumps of undergrowth. A heavy body twisted, lashed out in sudden panic. The man's voice was a high, short-lived scream of tenor.

"Don't—"

Dana used his left hand, fingers open, to slap across the man's face. His knuckles made a sharp cracking sound.

"Marquiss! What are you following me for?"

"I wasn't—I—I didn't know—"

The big man swayed before him, shoulders sagging. His eyes were white crescents in the pre-dawn gloom. There was a heavy crusted smear of blood on his left temple, and his clothing was even more tattered than it had been before.

"What the devil are you doing, wandering around on the island?" Dana rasped.

"I just wanted off, that's all," the man breathed. "Off!"

"What happened to your head?"

"I don't know."

"Didn't you see who hit you?"

"No, he came at me so suddenly—I don't remember anything at all about it. I thought it was you—"

"It wasn't me," Dana said grimly. "You're lucky to be alive."

"I don't know. I don't know," the man muttered. "What are you doing with that gun?"

Dana ignored his question. "You'd better get back to the house and have your head attended to."

"Abel will kill me!"

"No, he won't. Not this time. You're getting away with it, this time, because there are other things to be done. But you won't be so lucky again."

"I don't ever want to see Shea again," the man muttered. "I know when I'm licked."

"Then get back to the house."

The man looked at Dana's gun and licked his lips. His shoulders moved in a shrug of resignation, and then he turned and shuffled off toward the path that led toward the Mason house. Dana watched him until he was swallowed up by the darkness; and then listened to sound of his footsteps until he could hear them no longer.

Turning, he went in the opposite direction. He came out of the woods after a moment, and there was nothing but a short stretch of dunes separating him from the restored lighthouse tower on the rocky point of land there. He didn't believe what he saw. He stopped and looked and dragged air deep into his struggling lungs. He dashed moisture from his eyes and hair. What he saw was still there.

Kettle Island Light was working again.

The old beacon was brilliant with light.

THE big reflectors, carefully tended and polished by Abel Mason for all these years, shot the beam far out over the harbor waters, magnifying the little flicker of flame thousands of times. Then, as Dana watched, the shutters closed laboriously in the glass dome and the light was snuffed out.

He started across the sand toward the lighthouse. The shutters opened and closed again, and a wink of light darted through the fog. He looked across the harbor. The beam was directed toward the sleeping village of Stone Cove. Twice more the heavy shutters swung aside and closed, then the light went out for good as he stumbled up the brick steps.

The curved, oaken door wasn't locked. He stood on the threshold, out of the rain. His eyes were wary. The circular room was empty. Heat radiated from the oil stove, and the lamps, modeled from the running lights of old fishing schooners, shed a soft glow on Shea's furniture, on the table and the deep, comfortable chairs and the old-fashioned phonograph. He looked toward the spiral iron steps that wound up through the trapdoor in the ceiling. Silence filled the place, but it was not an empty silence.

"Shea!" he called.

There was no answer. Then:

"Hank?"

It was Shea's voice. It come from up above, in the tower, and it was strangely muffled. But there was a glad note to it, and he plunged across the room and up the stairs three at a time. She was waiting for him on the narrow platform that encircled the beacon. An empty oil can stood to one side, attesting to her efforts to get the light burning again. With the shutters drawn, the only illumination came from below. She stepped back a little as he came up, and her face was alive with soft shadows, her eyes touching him tenderly. She had thrown off her rain cape and hood; the heat generated by the reflectors more than offset the chill of the foggy dawn.

"Shea," he said. "Are you all right?"

"Yes. What did you do—run all the way?"

"It doesn't matter."

"Your scalp is bleeding again."

"Never mind," he said. He looked at the shuttered light. "You were signaling, weren't you?"

"Morse. It's the easiest way of contacting the mainland. Kettle Light hasn't been in use for ages. Someone will notice it in Stone Cove and come to investigate. They'll know something is wrong out here."

He wanted to take her in his arms and hold her tight and never let her go. Relief made him feel weak all over. She was all right. He had reached her in time. There was nothing else to be afraid of.

He said, "Where is Charley?"

"Somewhere around."

"Have you seen him?"

"Not yet. But he's here. I know he's here, and not far off. He'll show up soon." Her voice was calm. She touched his arm, and the movement cast long shadows on the little balcony. "You understand what has happened, don't you, Hank?"

"Yes," he said.

"You painted death."

"Yes."

"And you were right. You really knew which one was trying to kill you, all along. You just didn't want to bring it out where you could face it. You buried it in your subconscious because it was an ugly knowledge and you didn't want to believe it. But you know, now."

"I'm all right now," he said. "I found this."

He took the rubber lift he had found in his laundry and showed it to her. Shea eyed it dubiously.

"What is it?"

"This came from Lotti Higgins' shoe, just before she was murdered. She lost it and the murderer stuffed it in his pocket. Later, when he got rid of the rest of the shoe, this rubber heel was caught in his handkerchief. He didn't know about it. I found it in my laundry just a little while ago."

She frowned. "I don't understand."

"It wasn't planted in my clothes deliberately," Dana said. "If it was designed to frame me, the police would have been tipped off about it. So it got into my laundry by pure accident. It could only get there in one way. Charley's clothes were often mixed up with mine—we wear the same sizes, generally. It proves Charley killed Lotti Higgins—and by the same token, Kay Norcross."

Shea's eyes were wide, searching his face. "Now that you know who it is—now that it's out in the open and clear in your mind—how do you feel about it, Hank?"

"I hate it. I'm not afraid of it anymore," he said. "I'm just angry. Every little bit of me is shocked and angry."

"That's good," she said.

She started for the circular stairway and paused. He stood still beside her. The sound of rain suddenly grew louder as the door downstairs was opened. Footsteps moved across the floor below, paused, and moved again. Dana looked at Shea. Her face was white. He felt her arm against his. She was trembling. He listened to the footsteps moving around in Shea's room, and a furious anger rose up inside him at the thought of an intruder down there.

Music, soft and muted from the old phonograph, suddenly swept up to him in a sweet flood. Schubert's Seventh. Dana started for the stairs; Shea's hand drew him back. He shook her off and went to the trapdoor. He could see a square patch of the carpet and an edge of a chair and the polished old phonograph machine. A hand gripped the edge of the machine and then was withdrawn from sight.

"Charley?" he called softly.

The machine clicked off.

"Come on down, Henry." It was Charley Powell's voice, queer and garbled in the echoing tower. "Come down."

"I'm coming," Dana said.

Shea's hand touched him again. Her fingers were cold.

"Hank—"

"I must!" he said harshly.

"Let me. He's not—"

Charley's voice gobbled at him. "Come down, Henry!"

Dana gripped the iron rail.

"Why do you want to kill me?" he called.

"You know why!"

"Tell me!"

"My hands," Charley said. "You wrecked that car deliberately, to end my painting. To stop me from showing you I'm better than you."

"That's not so, Charley. It was an accident. It could have happened to anybody."

"I hate your guts, Henry. Because of you, I can't paint any more. You smashed my hands. You took everything from me. For years! Since we were in school together. You took Kay away from me, and Lotti, too."

"No," Dana said.

"I'm going to kill you, Henry. Don't run away this time."

"I'm coming down," Dana said. "I'm through running away from you."

He went downstairs on swift, careful feet, aware of Shea behind him, motionless. He didn't look back at her. His legs came through the trapdoor and he ducked under the floor and the floor became the ceiling of the lower room. He went down to the bottom of the stairs and looked at Charley Powell.

The big man was across the room from him. His striped singlet and duck trousers were plastered tight to his muscular frame. His wet hair dripped in dark strands over his forehead. He was standing on the balls of his feet, his heels slightly raised off the floor. His shoulders hunched forward, and the flat planes of his face moved and twitched and squirmed.

Charley's voice still had that queer, gobbling effect. "We haven't much time, Henry."

"No."

"I know Shea signaled to town. I'm glad you're being sensible. I'm glad you came down to me."

"Why did you kill Kay?"

"Kay? She was a snooper, like Lotti. She saw me in your place. I'm glad I killed her. She said I was a failure, she said you were always the better man. But when I kill you, Henry—I'll be the better man, after all these years."

"No, you won't," Dana said.

"You're not going to paint any more, you understand?" Charley whispered "I can't paint any more, and neither will you."

Dana looked at the man's odd eyes. "That's not so. You can paint. You can use your hands."

"I can't!"

"You used them to strangle Kay. You used them to cut the power line. You used them to rip up your paintings and mine, Charley. You're just kidding yourself. Your failings are all in your head, not your hands."

The big man just looked at him.

Dana went on, "Your hands are all right. They're not useless. You've done plenty with them. You've done too much."

The muscles continued their movement in the big man's face, distorting and convulsing the square, flat planes. He looked down at his twisted hands. Rain beat through the silence in the room. Dana heard Shea's footsteps on the stairs behind him, coming down. He looked at Charley Powell and anger shook him.

"You've been trying to kill me for a long time, haven't you?"

Charley said, "It ends here."

They stared at each other across the width of the room. Dana thought of the gun in his pocket. He didn't need it. He leaned on the back of a wooden chair, and Charley took a step toward him. Dana didn't move. He waited. He felt as if he had been waiting for this moment forever. He looked at Charley's strange face. He waited for Charley to kill him.

Shea's voice tore the fabric of silence.

"Stop it. Stop it, both of you!"

Charley looked up at her and grinned. It was a crooked grimace that twisted his mouth queerly.

"You, too," he said. "You looked at my new paintings."

Shea's voice was quiet, professional. "You need help, Charley. You're not thinking right. Something's happened to you and it's distorted all the world for you. You've become afraid to compete. You can paint with your hands, but not with your heart."

"That's right," Charley said

"The shock of having your hands injured was the last straw, wasn't it? But Dana isn't your real enemy. You've identified Dana with yourself, with your own failures, which you want to wipe out. Let me help you, Charley."

Charley laughed. "You think I'm insane."

"No, I don't."

"That's what you said about my new paintings," His voice jeered at her. "You told Willi they expressed a severe emotional disturbance."

Shea nodded. She came down another step.

"Charley, listen to me. I know. We give little tests, like drawing simply human figures, to people every day. People who come to us for help. The drawings tell us more than the patient realizes. I saw your new paintings. And I know you need help."

"You think I'm crazy, all right."

Dana said harshly, "Get back, Shea—"

Charley moved the instant his attention was diverted. He moved fast, lunging toward Dana. His hand came out of his pocket. He had a gun. He held it as a club in his twisted fingers. Dana picked up the chair he was leaning on and threw it. He used all his strength. The chair was of heavy oak. He saw at once that he had missed. Time seemed to stop as he watched it twist through the air. Charley put up one hand to beat it farther aside. The heavy oak legs smashed into his hand. The chair crashed to the floor. A queer animal screaming filled the room.

Dana started forward, then stopped. Charley had halted, too. He had dropped the gun. He was staring at the hand struck by the chair. His mouth was open and the queer screams came from him again and again.

Dana moved toward him. The big man stepped back. His eyes jerked from side to side. The scream became a moan. Dana said, "I never did anything just to do it better than you, Charley. I didn't want Kay. I didn't take her from you—no more than I wanted to take anything else from you."

"You're not afraid of me now, Henry?"

"No."

Charley seemed to crumple before his eyes. Dana felt his anger turn to sick pity. He started to follow as Charley suddenly turned and plunged for the doorway. The fog and the trees swallowed him. Dana ran after him. White spray burst around the rocky base of the lighthouse.

Shea's voice came from far away! "Let him go, Hank!"

He continued to run after the other man. He glimpsed Charley clambering on the rocks on the seaward side of the tower. He scrambled after him. He couldn't stop.

"Come back!" he shouted. "Charley!"

He hauled himself up on a wet ledge of granite, careless of his own danger as more spray burst around him in a white smother of foam. Charley was moving out to the last point of rock. A great white comber came racing out of the mist, growing to furious size. It broke with a clap of thunder over the stone ledges, over the flat rock where Charley Powell stood facing the dark sea. The comber smashed Dana flat, washed him sidewise, slamming him cruelly against the base of the lighthouse. He clung to a jagged rock and let the cold sea wash over him. He couldn't breathe. He fought against the demoniac pull of the water, and then it was gone and he stood up and looked toward the distant point where Charley had been.

The rock was empty and barren. There was nothing but the fog and the dark ocean. Dana stood there for a long moment. Another comber smashed out of the darkness, battering and dragging at his body. He heard Shea calling to him. Turning, he climbed slowly back off the ledge. She was standing near the door of the lighthouse. She started toward him and then stopped and pointed wordlessly over the harbor.

Dana felt drained of all strength, exhausted.

"It's over now," Shea said. "Please, Hank."

"It's not that," Dana said.

"I know…he was your friend."

"I never knew how he felt. He was ill. I could have helped him—"

"No, there was nothing you could ever have done about it. Please don't talk about it now."

The fog moved coldly across his face. He turned away from the girl and looked out over the harbor to where she had pointed. A pier was blazing with light over in Stone Cove. Two boat lights were bobbing toward the island. The sound of urgently drumming motors came over the water.

"That will be the police," Shea said. "They must have received my message."

He watched the lights draw closer. To the east, a long glimmer of radiance showed along the horizon as the mists thinned. He looked at Shea's dim face beside him. He thought of his paintings, of Willi Tempel's thefts. He had never intended to do more than frighten the truth out of Willi. He thought of many other things. There was a great emptiness inside him.

"None of it was your fault," Shea said gently. "Don't ever blame yourself."

"Stay with me, Shea," he said.

"I intend to," she said. "I'll never leave you."

He walked with her, with long strides, over the dark beach, away from the lighthouse. She kept pace with him. Her hand crept into his, and gradually the emptiness inside him was filled.

Together, they turned to the beach and waited for the approaching boats.

THE END

If you've enjoyed this book, you will not want to miss these terrific titles…

ARMCHAIR SCI-FI & HORROR DOUBLE NOVELS, $12.95 each

D-141 **ALL HEROES ARE HATED** by Milton Lesser
       AND THE STARS REMAIN by Bryan Berry

D-142 **LAST CALL FOR DOOMSDAY** by Edmond Hamilton
       HUNTRESS OF AKKAN by Robert Moore Williams

D-143 **THE MOON PIRATES** by Neil R. Jones
       CALLISTO AT WAR by Harl Vincent

D-144 **THUNDER IN THE DAWN** by Henry Kuttner
       THE UNCANNY EXPERIMENTS OF DR. VARSAG by David V. Reed

D-145 **A PATTERN FOR MONSTERS** by Randall Garrett
       STAR SURGEON by Alan E Nourse

D-146 **THE ATOM CURTAIN** by Nick Boddie Williams
       WARLOCK OF SHARRADOR by Gardner F. Fox

D-148 **SECRET OF THE LOST PLANET** by David Wright O'Brien
       TELEVISION HILL by George McLociard

D-147 **INTO THE GREEN PRISM** by A Hyatt Verrill
       WANDERERS OF THE WOLF-MOON by Nelson S. Bond

D-149 **MINIONS OF THE TIGER** by Chester S. Geier
       FOUNDING FATHER by J. F. Bone

D-150 **THE INVISIBLE MAN** by H. G. Wells
       THE ISLAND OF DR. MOREAU by H. G. Wells

ARMCHAIR SCIENCE FICTION CLASSICS, $12.95 each

C-61   **THE SHAVER MYSTERY, Book Six**
       by Richard S. Shaver

C-62   **CADUCEUS WILD**
       by Ward Moore & Robert Bradford

B-5   **ATLANTIDA** (Lost World-Lost Race Classics #1)
       by Pierre Benoit

ARMCHAIR MYSTERY-CRIME DOUBLE NOVELS, $12.95 each

B-1   **THE DEADLY PICK-UP** by Milton Ozaki
       KILLER TAKE ALL by James O. Causey

B-2   **THE VIOLENT ONES** by E. Howard Hunt
       HIGH HEEL HOMICIDE by Frederick C. Davis

B-3   **FURY ON SUNDAY** by Richard Matheson
       THE AGONY COLUMN by Earl Derr Biggers

If you've enjoyed this book, you will not want to miss these terrific titles…

ARMCHAIR SCI-FI & HORROR DOUBLE NOVELS, $12.95 each

D-151   **MAGNANTHROPUS** by Manly Banister
BEYOND THE FEARFUL FOREST by Geoff St. Reynard

D-152   **IN CAVERNS BELOW** by Stanton A. Coblentz
DYNASTY OF THE LOST hy George O. Smith

D-153   **NO MORE STARS** by Lester del Rey & Frederick Pohl
THE MAN WHO LIVED FOREVER R. De Witt Miller & Anna Hunger

D-154   **THE CORIANIS DISASTER** by Murray Leinster
DEATHWORLD by Harry Harrison

D-155   **HE FELL AMONG THIEVES** by Milton Lesser
PRINCESS OF ARELLI, THE by Aladra Septama

D-156   **THE SECRET KINGDOM** by Otis Adelbert Kline & Allen S. Kilne
SCRATCH ONE ASTEROID by Willard Hawkins

D-157   **ENSLAVED BRAINS** by Eando Binder
CONCEPTION: ZERO by E. K. Jarvis

D-158   **VICTIMS OF THE VORTEX** by Rog Phillips
THE COSMIC COMPUTER by H. Beam Piper

D-159   **THE GOLDEN GODS** by S. J. Byrne
RETURN OF MICHAEL FLANIGAN by S. J. Byrne

D-160   **BATTLE OUT OF TIME** by Dwight V. Swain
THE PEOPLE THAT TIME FORGOT by Edgar Rice Burroughs

ARMCHAIR SCIENCE FICTION CLASSICS, $12.95 each

C-63   **THE OMEGA POINT TRILOGY**
by George Zebrowski

C-64   **THE UNIVERSE WRECKERS**
by Edmond Hamilton

C-65   **KING OF THE DINOSAURS**
by Raymond A. Palmer

ARMCHAIR SCI-FI & HORROR GEMS SERIES, $12.95 each

G-17   **SCIENCE FICTION GEMS, Vol. Nine**
Ben Bova and others

G-18   **HORROR GEMS, Vol. Nine**
Emil Petaja and others

If you've enjoyed this book, you will not want to miss these terrific titles…

ARMCHAIR SCI-FI & HORROR DOUBLE NOVELS, $12.95 each

D-161 **THE TIME-RAIDER** by Edmond Hamilton
WHISPER OF DEATH, THE by Harl Vincent

D-162 **SONS OF THE DELUGE** by Nelson S. Bond
THE COUNTRY BEYOND THE CURVE by Walt Sheldon

D-163 **HIS TOUCH TURNED STONE TO FLESH** by Milton Lesser
ULLR UPRISING by H. Beam Piper

D-164 **WOLFBANE** by C. M. Kornbluth & Frederick Pohl
THE LAST TWO ALIVE! by Alfred Coppel

D-165 **LET FREEDOM RING** by Fritz Leiber
THE MACHINE THAT FLOATS by Joe Gibson

D-166 **EXILES OF THE MOON** by Nat Schachner & Arthur Leo Zagut
DEATH PLAYS A GAME by David V. Reed

D-167 **DAWN OF THE DEMIGODS** by Raymond Z. Gallun
EMPIRE by Clifford D. Simak

D-168 **ARMAGEDDON** by Rog Phillips aka Craig Browning
THE LOVE MACHINE, THE by James Cooke Brown

D-169 **THREE AGAINST THE ROUM** by Robert Moore Williams
OUT OF TIME'S ABYSS by Edgar Rice Burroughs

D-170 **BEYOND THE GREEN PRISM** by A. Hyatt Verrill
ALCATRAZ OF THE STARWAYS by Henry Hasse & Albert dePina

ARMCHAIR SCIENCE FICTION CLASSICS, $12.95 each

C-67 **POWER METAL**
by S. J. Byrne

C-64 **THE PROFESSOR JAMESON SAGA, Book One**
by Neil R. Jones

C-64 **THE PROFESSOR JAMESON SAGA, Book Two**
by Neil R. Jones

ARMCHAIR SCI-FI & HORROR GEMS SERIES, $12.95 each

G-19 **SCIENCE FICTION GEMS, Vol. Ten**
Robert Sheckley and others

G-20 **HORROR GEMS, Vol. Ten**
Manly Wade Wellman and others

If you've enjoyed this book, you will not want to miss these terrific titles…

ARMCHAIR SCI-FI & HORROR DOUBLE NOVELS, $12.95 each

D-171   **REGAN'S PLANET** by Robert Silverberg
        SOMEONE TO WATCH OVER ME by H. L. Gold and Floyd Gale

D-172   **PEOPLE MINUS X** by Raymond Z. Gallun
        THE SAVAGE MACHINE by Randall Garrett

D-173   **THE FACE BEYOND THE VEIL** by Rog Phillips
        REST IN AGONY by Paul W. Fairman

D-174   **VIRGIN OF VALKARION** by Poul Anderson
        EARTH ALERT by Kris Neville

D-175   **WHEN THE ATOMS FAILED** by John W. Campbell, Jr.
        DRAGONS OF SPACE by Aladra Septama

D-176   **THE TATTOOED MAN** by Edmond Hamilton
        A RESCUE FROM JUPITER by Gawain Edwards

D-177   **THE FLYING THREAT** by David H. Keller, M. D.
        THE FIFTH-DIMENSION TUBE by Murray Leinster

D-178   **LAST DAYS OF THRONAS** by S. J. Byrne
        GODDESS OF WORLD 21 by Henry Slesar

D-179   **THE MOTHER WORLD** by B. Wallis & George C. Wallis
        BEYOND THE VANISHING POINT by Ray Cummings

D-180   **DARK DESTINY** by Dwight V. Swain
        SECRET OF PLANETOID 88 by Ed Earl Repp

ARMCHAIR SCIENCE FICTION CLASSICS, $12.95 each

C-69   **EXILES OF THE MOON**
       by Nathan Schachner & Arthur Leo Zagut

C-70   **SKYLARK OF SPACE**
       by E. E. "Doc' Smith

ARMCHAIR MYSTERY-CRIME DOUBLE NOVELS, $12.95 each

B-11   **THE BABY DOLL MURDERS** by James O. Causey
       DEATH HITCHES A RIDE by Martin L. Weiss

B-12   **THE DOVE** by Milton Ozaki
       THE GLASS LADDER by Paul W. Fairman

B-13   **THE NAKED STORM** by C. M. Kornbluth
       THE MAN OUTSIDE by Alexander Blade

If you've enjoyed this book, you will not want to miss these terrific titles…

ARMCHAIR MYSTERY-CRIME DOUBLE NOVELS, $12.95 each

B-16   **KISS AND KILL** by Richard Demlng
THE DEAD STAND-IN by Frank Kane

B-17   **DANGEROUS LADY** by Octavus Roy Cohen
ONE HOUR LATE by William O'Farrell

B-18   **LOVE ME AND DIE!** by Day Keene
YOU'LL GET YOURS by Thomas Wills

B-19   **EVERYBODY'S WATCHING ME** by Mickey Spillane
A BULLET FOR CINDERELLA by John D. MacDonald

B-20   **WILD OATS** by Harry Whittington
MAKE WAY FOR MURDER by A. A. Marcus

B-21   **THE ART STUDIO MURDERS** by Edward Ronns
THE CASE OF JENNIE BRICE by Mary Roberts Rinehart

B-22   **THE LUSTFUL APE** by Bruno Fisher
KISS THE BABE GOODBYE by Bob McKnight

B-23   **SARATOGA MANTRAP** by Dexter St. Claire
CLASSIFICATION: HOMICIDE by Jonathan Craig

ARMCHAIR SCI-FI & HORROR DOUBLE NOVELS, $12.95 each

E-5   **THE IDOLS OF WULD** by Milton Lesser
PLANET OF THE DAMNED by Harry Harrison

E-6   **BETWEEN WORLDS** by Garret Smith
PLANET OF THE DEAD by Rog Phillips

E-7   **DAUGHTER OF THOR** by Edmond Hamilton
TALENTS, INCORPORATED by Murray Leinster

E-8   **ALL ABOARD FOR THE MOON** by Harold M. Sherman
THE METAL EMPEROR by Raymond A. Palmer

E-9   **DEATH HUNT** by Robert Gilbert
THE BEST MADE PLANS by Everett B. Cole

E-10   **GIANT KILLER** by Dwight V. Swain
GOLDEN AMAZONS OF VENUS by John Murray Reynolds

ARMCHAIR SCI-FI & HORROR GEMS SERIES, $12.95 each

G-21   **SCIENCE FICTION GEMS, Vol. Eleven**
Gordon R. Dickson and others

G-22   **HORROR GEMS, Vol. Eleven**
Thorp McClusky and others

WOULDN'T YOU LIKE TO KNOW...

Why a man on trial for his life appeared so cool, calm, and amused at the proceedings?

How a little teetotaler came to sudden grief when he tried to act out the part of a suspected killer?

What happened to a missing onyx clock and where it was finally found?

Why a poor and lonely widow didn't reveal her identity to her ever so wealthy niece?

The identity of the mysterious woman who crossed the bridge in the early hours of dawn?

A deluge of starling answers awaits you this gripping story of a most grisly killing. The police are baffled, but an amateur criminologist and his landlady set out to solve this amazing crime in a flood-ravaged city.

POLICE LINEUP:

ELIZABETH PITMAN
The middle-aged keeper of a cheap boardinghouse. Life had made her hard, but underneath she was still a gentle, kind soul.

MR. HOLCOMBE
A small, alert, be-spectacled man who liked stray cats and dogs. What kinds of notes was he always jotting down in his notebook?

ELLIS HOWELL
This struggling young newspaperman was always long on smiles, but always a bit short on cash.

LIDA HARVEY
She was the beautiful daughter of Elizabeth Pitman's wealthy sister, but her life of luxury hadn't spoiled her—yet.

JENNIE BRICE
This attractive blonde actress played lots of small parts in a small stock company, but had a hard time making ends meet.

PHILIP LADLEY
A stout actor and Jennie Brice's husband, he'd recently turned playwright, with a new work he was sure would be produced.

ZACHARIAH REYNOLDS
One of Mrs. Pitman's lodgers who worked in the silk department of a large store—but his real love was reading detective stories.

TEMPLE HOPE
Unlike Jennie Brice, this tall, beautiful actress had achieved top-billing status with the local stock company.

MR. GRAVES
He was a local detective and a familiar figure around the Allegheny flood district.

THE CASE OF
JENNIE BRICE

By
MARY ROBERTS RINEHART

ARMCHAIR FICTION
PO Box 4369, Medford, Oregon 97504

*For more information about Armchair Books and products, visit our
website at…*

www.armchairfiction.com

Or email us at…

armchairfiction@yahoo.com

CHAPTER ONE
The Rising Waters

We have just had another flood, bad enough, but only a foot or two of water on the first floor. Yesterday we got the mud shoveled out of the cellar and found Peter, the spaniel that Mr. Ladley left when he "went away". The flood, and the fact that it was Mr. Ladley's dog whose body was found half buried in the basement fruit closet, brought back to me the strange events of the other flood five years ago, when the water reached more than half way to the second story, and brought with it, to some, mystery and sudden death, and to me the worst case of "shingles" I have ever seen.

My name is Pitman—in this narrative. It is not really Pitman, but that does well enough. I belong to an old Pittsburgh family. I was born on Penn Avenue, when that was the best part of town, and I lived, until I was fifteen, very close to what is now the Pittsburgh Club. It was a dwelling then; I have forgotten who lived there.

I was a girl in seventy-seven, during the railroad riots, and I recall our driving in the family carriage over to one of the Allegheny hills, and seeing the yards burning, and a great noise of shooting from across the river. It was the next year that I ran away from school to marry Mr. Pitman, and I have not known my family since. We were never reconciled, although I came back to Pittsburgh after twenty years of wandering. Mr. Pitman was dead; the old city called me, and I came. I had a hundred dollars or so, and I took a house in lower Allegheny, where, because they are partly inundated every spring, rents are cheap, and I kept boarders. My house was always orderly and clean, and although the neighborhood had a bad name, a good many theatrical people stopped with me. Five minutes across the bridge, and they were in the theater district. Allegheny at that time, I believe, was still an independent city. But since then it has allied itself with Pittsburgh; it is now the North Side.

I was glad to get back. I worked hard, but I made my rent and my living, and a little over. Now and then on summer evenings I went to one of the parks, and sitting on a bench, watched the children playing around, and looked at my sister's house, closed for the summer. It is a very large house: her butler once had his wife boarding with me—a nice little woman.

It is curious to recall that, at that time, five years ago, I had never seen my niece, Lida Harvey, and then to think that only the day before yesterday she came in her automobile as far as she dared, and then sat there, waving to me, while the police patrol brought across in a skiff a basket of provisions she had sent me.

I wonder what she would have thought had she known that the elderly woman in a calico wrapper with an old overcoat over it, and a pair of rubber boots, was her full aunt!

The flood and the sight of Lida both brought back the case of Jennie Brice. For even then, Lida and Mr. Howell were interested in each other.

This is April. The flood of 1907 was earlier, in March. It had been a long hard winter, with ice gorges in all the upper valley. Then, in early March, there came a thaw. The gorges broke up and began to come down, filling the rivers with crushing grinding ice.

There are three rivers at Pittsburgh, the Allegheny and the Monongahela uniting there at the Point to form the Ohio. And all three were covered with broken ice, logs, and all sorts of debris from the upper valleys.

A warning was sent out from the weather bureau, and I got my carpets ready to lift that morning. That was on the fourth of March, a Sunday. Mr. Ladley and his wife, Jennie Brice, had the parlor bedroom and the room behind it. Mrs. Ladley, or Miss Brice, as she preferred to be known, had a small part at a local theater that kept a permanent company. Her husband was in that business, too, but he had nothing to do. It was the wife who paid the bills, and a lot of quarreling they did about it.

I knocked at the door at ten o'clock, and Mr. Ladley opened it. He was a short man, rather stout and getting bald, and he always had a cigarette. Even yet, the parlor carpet smells of them.

"What do you want?" he asked sharply, holding the door open about an inch.

"The water's coming up very fast, Mr. Ladley," I said. "It's up to the swinging-shelf in the cellar now. I'd like to take up the carpet and move the piano."

"Come back in an hour or so," he snapped, and tried to close the door. But I had got my toe in the crack.

"I'll have to have the piano moved, Mr. Ladley," I said. "You'd better put off what you are doing."

I thought he was probably writing. He spent most of the day writing, using the wash-stand as a desk, and it kept me busy with oxalic acid taking ink-spots out of the splasher and the towels. He was writing a play, and talked a lot about the Shuberts having promised to star him in it when it was finished.

"Hell!" he said, and turning, spoke to somebody in the room.

"We can go into the back room," I heard him say, and he closed the door. When he opened it again, the room was empty. I called in Terry, the Irishman who does odd jobs for me now and then, and we both got to work at the tacks in the carpet, Terry working by the window, and I by the door into the back parlor, which the Ladleys used as a bedroom.

That was how I happened to hear what I afterward told the police.

Some one—a man, but not Mr. Ladley—was talking. Mrs. Ladley broke in: "I won't do it!" she said flatly. "Why should I help him? He doesn't help me. He loafs here all day, smoking and sleeping, and sits up all night, drinking and keeping me awake."

The voice went on again, as if in reply to this, and I heard a rattle of glasses, as if they were pouring drinks. They always had whisky, even when they were behind with their board.

"That's all very well," Mrs. Ladley said. I could always hear her, she having a theatrical sort of voice—one that carries. "But what about the prying she-devil that runs the house?"

"Hush, for God's sake!" broke in Mr. Ladley, and after that they spoke in whispers. Even with my ear against the panel, I could not catch a word.

The men came just then to move the piano, and by the time we had taken it and the furniture up-stairs, the water was over the kitchen floor, and creeping forward into the hall. I had never seen the river come up so fast. By noon the yard was full of floating ice, and at three that afternoon the police skiff was on the front street, and I was wading around in rubber boots, taking the pictures off the walls.

I was too busy to see who the Ladleys' visitor was, and he had gone when I remembered him again. The Ladleys took the second-story front, which was empty, and Mr. Reynolds, who was in the silk department in a store across the river, had the room just behind.

I put up a coal stove in a back room next the bathroom, and managed to cook the dinner there. I was washing up the dishes when Mr. Reynolds came in. As it was Sunday, he was in his slippers and had the colored supplement of a morning paper in his hand.

"What's the matter with the Ladleys?" he asked. "I can't read for their quarreling."

"Booze, probably," I said. "When you've lived in the flood district as long as I have, Mr. Reynolds, you'll know that the rising of the river is a signal for every man in the vicinity to stop work and get full. The fuller the river, the fuller the male population."

"Then this flood will likely make 'em drink themselves to death!" he said. "It's a lulu."

"It's the neighborhood's annual debauch. The women are busy keeping the babies from getting drowned in the cellars, or they'd get full, too. I hope, since it's come this far, it will come farther, so the landlord will have to paper the parlor."

That was at three o'clock. At four Mr. Ladley went down the stairs, and I heard him getting into a skiff in the lower hall. There were boats going back and forth all the time, carrying crowds of curious people, and taking the flood sufferers to the corner grocery, where they were lowering groceries in a basket on a rope from an upper window.

I had been making tea when I heard Mr. Ladley go out. I fixed a tray with a cup of it and some crackers, and took it to their door. I had never liked Mrs. Ladley, but it was chilly in the house with the gas shut off and the lower floor full of ice-water. And it is hard enough to keep boarders in the flood district.

She did not answer to my knock, so I opened the door and went in. She was at the window, looking after him, and the brown valise, that figured in the case later, was opened on the floor. Over the foot of the bed was the black and white dress, with the red collar.

When I spoke to her, she turned around quickly. She was a tall woman, about twenty-eight, with very white teeth and yellow hair, which she parted a little to one side and drew down over her ears. She had a sullen face and large well-shaped hands, with her nails long and very pointed.

"The 'she-devil' has brought you some tea," I said. "Where shall she put it?"

"'She-devil'!" she repeated, raising her eyebrows. "It's a very thoughtful she-devil. Who called you that?"

But, with the sight of the valise and the fear that they might be leaving, I thought it best not to quarrel. She had left the window, and going to her dressing-table, had picked up her nail-file.

"Never mind," I said. "I hope you are not going away. These floods don't last, and they're a benefit. Plenty of the people around here rely on 'em every year to wash out their cellars."

"No, I'm not going away," she replied lazily. "I'm taking that dress to Miss Hope at the theater. She is going to wear it in *Charlie's Aunt* next week. She hasn't half enough of a wardrobe to play leads in stock. Look at this thumb-nail, broken to the quick!"

If I had only looked to see which thumb it was! But I was putting the tea-tray on the wash-stand, and moving Mr. Ladley's papers to find room for it. Peter, the spaniel, begged for a lump of sugar, and I gave it to him.

"Where is Mr. Ladley?" I asked.

"Gone out to see the river."

"I hope he'll be careful. There's a drowning or two every year in these floods."

"Then I hope he won't," she said calmly. "Do you know what I was doing when you came in? I was looking after his boat, and hoping it had a hole in it."

"You won't feel that way to-morrow, Mrs. Ladley," I protested, shocked. "You're just nervous and put out. Most men have their ugly times. Many a time I wished Mr. Pitman was gone—until he went. Then I'd have given a good bit to have him back again."

She was standing in front of the dresser, fixing her hair over her ears. She turned and looked at me over her shoulder.

"Probably Mr. Pitman was a man," she said. "My husband is a fiend, a devil."

Well, a good many women have said that to me at different times. But just let me say such a thing to *them*, or repeat their own words to them the next day, and they would fly at me in a fury. So I said nothing, and put the cream into her tea.

I never saw her again.

CHAPTER TWO
The Floating Slipper

There is not much sleeping done in the flood district during a spring flood. The gas was shut off, and I gave Mr. Reynolds and the Ladleys each a lamp. I sat in the back room that I had made into a temporary kitchen, with a candle, and with a bedquilt around my shoulders. The water rose fast in the lower hall, but by midnight, at the seventh step, it stopped rising and stood still. I always have a skiff during the flood season, and as the water rose, I tied it to one spindle of the staircase after another.

I made myself a cup of tea, and at one o'clock I stretched out on a sofa for a few hours' sleep. I think I had been sleeping only an hour or so, when some one touched me on the shoulder and I started up. It was Mr. Reynolds, partly dressed.

"Some one has been in the house, Mrs. Pitman," he said. "They went away just now in the boat."

"Perhaps it was Peter," I suggested. "That dog is always wandering around at night."

"Not unless Peter can row a boat," said Mr. Reynolds dryly.

I got up, being already fully dressed, and taking the candle, we went to the staircase. I noticed that it was a minute or so after two o'clock as we left the room. The boat was gone, not untied, but cut loose. The end of the rope was still fastened to the stair-rail. I sat down on the stairs and looked at Mr. Reynolds.

"It's gone!" I said. "If the house catches fire, we'll have to drown."

"It's rather curious, when you consider it." We both spoke softly, not to disturb the Ladleys. "I've been awake, and I heard no boat come in. And yet, if no one came in a boat, and came from the street, they would have had to swim in."

I felt queer and creepy. The street door was open, of course, and the lights going beyond. It gave me a strange feeling to sit there in the darkness on the stairs, with the arch of the front door like the entrance to a cavern, and see now and then a chunk of ice slide into view, turn around in the eddy, and pass on. It was bitter cold, too, and the wind was rising.

"I'll go through the house," said Mr. Reynolds. "There's likely nothing worse the matter than some drunken mill-hand on a vacation while the mills are under water. But I'd better look."

He left me, and I sat there alone in the darkness. I had a presentiment of something wrong, but I tried to think it was only discomfort and the cold. The water, driven in by the wind, swirled at my feet. And something dark floated in and lodged on the step below. I reached down and touched it. It was a dead kitten. I had never known a dead cat to bring me anything but bad luck, and here was one washed in at my very feet.

Mr. Reynolds came back soon, and reported the house quiet and in order.

"But I found Peter shut up in one of the third-floor rooms," he said. "Did you put him there?"

I had not, and said so; but as the dog went everywhere, and the door might have blown shut, we did not attach much importance to that at the time.

Well, the skiff was gone, and there was no use worrying about it until morning. I went back to the sofa to keep warm, but I left my candle lighted and my door open. I did not sleep: the dead cat was on my mind, and, as if it were not bad enough to have it washed in at my feet, about four in the morning Peter, prowling uneasily, discovered it and brought it in and put it on my couch, wet and stiff, poor little thing!

I looked at the clock. It was a quarter after four, and except for the occasional crunch of one ice-cake hitting another in the yard, everything was quiet. And then I heard the stealthy sound of oars in the lower hall.

I am not a brave woman. I lay there, hoping Mr. Reynolds would hear and open his door. But he was sleeping soundly. Peter snarled and ran out into the hall, and the next moment I heard Mr. Ladley speaking. "Down, Peter," he said. "Down. Go and lie down."

I took my candle and went out into the hall. Mr. Ladley was stooping over the boat, trying to tie it to the staircase. The rope was short, having been cut, and he was having trouble. Perhaps it was the candle-light, but he looked ghost-white and haggard.

"I borrowed your boat, Mrs. Pitman," he said, civilly enough. "Mrs. Ladley was not well, and I—I went to the drug store."

"You've been more than two hours going to the drug store," I said.

He muttered something about not finding any open at first, and went into his room. He closed and locked the door behind him, and although Peter whined and scratched, he did not let him in.

He looked so agitated that I thought I had been harsh, and that perhaps she was really ill. I knocked at the door, and asked if I could do anything. But he only called "No" curtly through the door, and asked me to take that infernal dog away.

I went back to bed and tried to sleep, for the water had dropped an inch or so on the stairs, and I knew the danger was over. Peter came, shivering, at dawn, and got on to the sofa with me. I put an end of the quilt over him, and he stopped shivering after a time and went to sleep.

The dog was company. I lay there, wide awake, thinking about Mr. Pitman's death, and how I had come, by degrees, to be keeping a cheap boarding-house in the flood district, and to having to take impudence from everybody who chose to rent a room from me, and to being called a she-devil. From that I got to thinking again about the Ladleys, and how she had said he was a fiend, and to doubting about his having gone out for medicine for her. I dozed off again at daylight, and being worn out, I slept heavily.

At seven o'clock Mr. Reynolds came to the door, dressed for the store. He was a tall man of about fifty, neat and orderly in his habits, and he always remembered that I had seen better days, and treated me as a lady.

"Never mind about breakfast for me this morning, Mrs. Pitman," he said. "I'll get a cup of coffee at the other end of the bridge. I'll take the boat and send it back with Terry."

He turned and went along the hall and down to the boat. I heard him push off from the stairs with an oar and row out into the street. Peter followed him to the stairs.

At a quarter after seven Mr. Ladley came out and called to me: "Just bring in a cup of coffee and some toast," he said. "Enough for one."

He went back and slammed his door, and I made his coffee. I steeped a cup of tea for Mrs. Ladley at the same time. He opened the door just wide enough for the tray, and took it without so much as a "thank you." He had a cigarette in his mouth as usual, and I could see a fire in the grate and smell something like scorching cloth.

"I hope Mrs. Ladley is better," I said, getting my foot in the crack of the door, so he could not quite close it. It smelled to me as if he had accidentally set fire to something with his cigarette, and I tried to see into the room.

"What about Mrs. Ladley?" he snapped.

"You said she was ill last night."

"Oh, yes! Well, she wasn't very sick. She's better."

"Shall I bring her some tea?"

"Take your foot away!" he ordered. "No. She doesn't want tea. She's not here."

"Not here!"

"Good heavens!" he snarled. "Is her going away anything to make such a fuss about? The Lord knows I'd be glad to get out of this infernal pig-wallow myself."

"If you mean my house—" I began.

But he had pulled himself together and was more polite when he answered. "I mean the neighborhood. Your house is all that could be desired for the money. If we do not have linen sheets and double cream, we are paying muslin and milk prices."

Either my nose was growing accustomed to the odor, or it was dying away: I took my foot away from the door. "When did Mrs. Ladley leave?" I asked.

"This morning, very early. I rowed her to Federal Street."

"You couldn't have had much sleep," I said dryly. For he looked horrible. There were lines around his eyes, which were red, and his lips looked dry and cracked.

"She's not in the piece this week at the theater," he said, licking his lips and looking past me, not at me. "She'll be back by Saturday."

I did not believe him. I do not think he imagined that I did. He shut the door in my face, and it caught poor Peter by the nose. The dog ran off howling, but although Mr. Ladley had been as fond of the animal as it was in his nature to be fond of anything, he paid no attention. As I started down the hall after him, I saw what Peter had been carrying—a slipper of Mrs. Ladley's. It was soaked with water; evidently Peter had found it floating at the foot of the stairs.

Although the idea of murder had not entered my head at that time, the slipper gave me a turn. I picked it up and looked at it—a black one with a beaded toe, short in the vamp and high-heeled, the sort most actresses wear. Then I went back and knocked at the door of the front room again.

"What the devil do you want now?" he called from beyond the door.

"Here's a slipper of Mrs. Ladley's," I said. "Peter found it floating in the lower hall."

He opened the door wide, and let me in. The room was in tolerable order, much better than when Mrs. Ladley was about. He looked at the slipper, but he did not touch it. "I don't think that is hers," he said.

"I've seen her wear it a hundred times."

"Well, she'll never wear it again." And then, seeing me stare, he added: "It's ruined with the water. Throw it out. And, by the way, I'm sorry, but I set fire to one of the pillow-slips—dropped asleep, and my cigarette did the rest. Just put it on the bill."

He pointed to the bed. One of the pillows had no slip, and the ticking cover had a scorch or two on it. I went over and looked at it.

"The pillow will have to be paid for, too, Mr. Ladley," I said. "And there's a sign nailed on the door that forbids smoking in bed. If you are going to set fire to things, I shall have to charge extra."

"Really!" he jeered, looking at me with his cold fishy eyes. "Is there any sign on the door saying that boarders are charged extra for seven feet of filthy river in the bedrooms?"

I was never a match for him, and I make it a principle never to bandy words with my boarders. I took the pillow and the slipper and went out. The telephone was ringing on the stair landing. It was the theater, asking for Miss Brice.

"She has gone away," I said.

"What do you mean? Moved away?"

"Gone for a few days' vacation," I replied. "She isn't playing this week, is she?"

"Wait a moment," said the voice. There was a hum of conversation from the other end, and then another man came to the telephone.

"Can you find out where Miss Brice has gone?"

"I'll see."

I went to Ladley's door and knocked. Mr. Ladley answered from just beyond.

"The theater is asking where Mrs. Ladley is."

"Tell them I don't know," he snarled, and shut the door. I took his message to the telephone.

Whoever it was swore and hung up the receiver.

All the morning I was uneasy—I hardly knew why. Peter felt it as I did. There was no sound from the Ladleys' room, and the house was quiet, except for the lapping water on the stairs and the police patrol going back and forth.

At eleven o'clock a boy in the neighborhood, paddling on a raft, fell into the water and was drowned. I watched the police boat go past, carrying his little cold body, and after that I was good for nothing. I went and sat with Peter on the stairs. The dog's conduct had been strange all morning. He had sat just above the water, looking at it and whimpering. Perhaps he was expecting another kitten or—

It is hard to say how ideas first enter one's mind. But the notion that Mr. Ladley had killed his wife and thrown her body into the water came to me as I sat there. All at once I seemed to see it all: the quarreling the day before, the night trip in the boat, the water-soaked slipper, his haggard face that morning—even the way the spaniel sat and stared at the flood.

Terry brought the boat back at half past eleven, towing it behind another.

"Well," I said, from the stairs, "I hope you've had a pleasant morning."

"What doing?" he asked, not looking at me.

"Rowing about the streets. You've had that boat for hours."

He tied it up without a word to me, but he spoke to the dog. "Good morning, Peter," he said. "It's nice weather—for fishes, ain't it?"

He picked out a bit of floating wood from the water, and showing it to the dog, flung it into the parlor. Peter went after it with a splash. He was pretty fat, and when he came back I heard him wheezing. But what he brought back was not the stick of wood. It was the knife I use for cutting bread. It had been on a shelf in the room where I had slept the night before, and now Peter brought it out of the flood where its wooden handle had kept it afloat. The blade was broken off short.

It is not unusual to find one's household goods floating around during flood-time. More than once I've lost a chair or two, and seen it after the water had gone down, new scrubbed and painted, in Molly Maguire's kitchen next door. And perhaps now and then a bit of luck would come to me—a dog kennel or a chicken-house, or a kitchen table, or even, as happened once, a month-old baby in a wooden cradle, that lodged against my back fence, and had come forty miles, as it turned out, with no worse mishap than a cold in its head.

But the knife was different. I had put it on the mantel over the stove I was using up-stairs the night before, and hadn't touched it since. As I sat staring at it, Terry took it from Peter and handed it to me.

"Better give me a penny, Mrs. Pitman," he said in his impudent Irish way. "I hate to give you a knife. It may cut our friendship."

I reached over to hit him a clout on the head, but I did not. The sunlight was coming in through the window at the top of the stairs, and shining on the rope that was tied to the banister. The end of the rope was covered with stains, brown, with a glint of red in them.

I got up shivering. "You can get the meat at the butcher's, Terry," I said, "and come back for me in a half-hour." Then I turned and went up-stairs, weak in the knees, to put on my hat and coat. I had made up my mind that there had been murder done.

CHAPTER THREE
The Onyx Clock

I looked at my clock as I went down-stairs. It was just twelve-thirty. I thought of telephoning for Mr. Reynolds to meet me, but it was his lunch hour, and besides I was afraid to telephone from the house while Mr. Ladley was in it.

Peter had been whining again. When I came down the stairs he had stopped whimpering and was wagging his tail. A strange boat had put into the hallway and was coming back.

"Now, old boy!" somebody was saying from the boat. "Steady, old chap! I've got something for you."

A little man, elderly and alert, was standing up in the boat, poling it along with an oar. Peter gave vent to joyful yelps. The elderly gentleman brought his boat to a stop at the foot of the stairs, and reaching down into a tub at his feet, held up a large piece of raw liver. Peter almost went crazy, and I remembered suddenly that I had forgotten to feed the poor beast for more than a day.

"Would you like it?" asked the gentleman. Peter sat up, as he had been taught to do, and barked. The gentleman reached down again, got a wooden platter from a stack of them at his feet, and placing the liver on it, put it on the step. The whole thing was so neat and businesslike that I could only gaze.

"That's a well-trained dog, madam," said the elderly man, beaming at Peter over his glasses. "You should not have neglected him."

"The flood put him out of my mind," I explained, humbly enough, for I was ashamed.

"Exactly. Do you know how many starving dogs and cats I have found this morning?" He took a note-book out of his pocket and glanced at it. "Forty-eight. Forty-eight, madam! And ninety-three cats! I have found them marooned in trees, clinging to fences, floating on barrels, and I have found them in comfortable houses where there was no excuse for their neglect. Well, I must be moving on. I have the report of a cat with a new litter in the loft of a stable near here."

He wiped his hands carefully on a fresh paper napkin, of which also a heap rested on one of the seats of the boat, and picked up an oar, smiling benevolently at Peter. Then, suddenly, he bent over and looked at the stained rope end, tied to the stair-rail.

"What's that?" he said.

"That's what I'm going to find out," I replied. I glanced up at the Ladleys' door, but it was closed.

The little man dropped his oar, and fumbling in his pockets, pulled out a small magnifying-glass. He bent over, holding to the rail, and inspected the stains with the glass. I had taken a fancy to him at once, and in spite of my excitement I had to smile a little.

"Humph!" he said, and looked up at me. "That's blood. Why did you *cut* the boat loose?"

"I didn't," I said. "If that is blood, I want to know how it got there. That was a new rope last night." I glanced at the Ladleys' door again, and he followed my eyes.

"I wonder," he said, raising his voice a little, "if I come into your kitchen, if you will allow me to fry a little of that liver. There's a wretched Maltese in a tree at the corner of Fourth Street that won't touch it, raw."

I saw that he wanted to talk to me, so I turned around and led the way to the temporary kitchen I had made.

"Now," he said briskly, when he had closed the door, "there's something wrong here. Perhaps if you tell me, I can help. If I can't, it will do you good to talk about it. My name's Holcombe, retired merchant. Apply to First National Bank for references."

"I'm not sure there *is* anything wrong," I began. "I guess I'm only nervous, and thinking little things are big ones. There's nothing to tell."

"Nonsense. I come down the street in my boat. A white-faced gentleman with a cigarette looks out from a window when I stop at the door, and ducks back when I glance up. I come in and find a pet dog, obviously overfed at ordinary times, whining with hunger on the stairs. As I prepare to feed him, a pale woman comes down, trying to put a right-hand glove on her left hand, and with her jacket wrong side out. What am I to think?"

I started and looked at my coat. He was right. And when, as I tried to take it off, he helped me, and even patted me on the shoulder—what with his kindness, and the long morning alone, worrying, and the sleepless night, I began to cry. He had a clean handkerchief in my hand before I had time to think of one.

"That's it," he said. "It will do you good, only don't make a noise about it. If it's a husband on the annual flood spree, don't worry, madam. They always come around in time to whitewash the cellars."

"It isn't a husband," I sniffled.

"Tell me about it," he said. There was something so kindly in his face, and it was so long since I had had a bit of human sympathy, that I almost broke down again.

I sat there, with a crowd of children paddling on a raft outside the window, and Molly Maguire, next door, hauling the morning's milk up in a pail fastened to a rope, her doorway being too narrow to admit the milkman's boat, and I told him the whole story.

"Humph!" he exclaimed, when I had finished. "It's curious, but—you can't prove a murder unless you can produce a body."

"When the river goes down, we'll find the body," I said, shivering. "It's in the parlor."

"Then why doesn't he try to get away?"

"He is ready to go now. He only went back when your boat came in."

Mr. Holcombe ran to the door, and flinging it open, peered into the lower hall. He was too late. His boat was gone, tub of liver, pile of wooden platters and all!

We hurried to the room the Ladleys had occupied. It was empty. From the window, as we looked out, we could see the boat, almost a square away. It had stopped where, the street being higher, a door-step rose above the flood. On the step was sitting a forlorn yellow puppy. As we stared, Mr. Ladley stopped the boat, looked back at us, bent over, placed a piece of liver on a platter, and reached it over to the dog. Then, rising in the boat, he bowed, with his hat over his heart, in our direction, sat down calmly, and rowed around the corner out of sight.

Mr. Holcombe was in a frenzy of rage. He jumped up and down, shaking his fist out the window after the retreating boat. He ran down the staircase, only to come back and look out the window again. The police boat was not in sight, but the Maguire children had worked their raft around to the street and were under the window. He leaned out and called to them

"A quarter each, boys," he said, "if you'll take me on that raft to the nearest pavement."

"Money first," said the oldest boy, holding his cap.

But Mr. Holcombe did not wait. He swung out over the window-sill, holding by his hands, and lit fairly in the center of the raft.

"Don't touch anything in that room until I come back," he called to me, and jerking the pole from one of the boys, propelled the raft with amazing speed down the street.

The liver on the stove was burning. There was a smell of scorching through the rooms and a sort of bluish haze of smoke. I hurried back and took it off. By the time I had cleaned the pan, Mr. Holcombe was back again, in his own boat. He had found it at the end of the next street, where the flood ceased, but no sign of Ladley anywhere. He had not seen the police boat.

"Perhaps that is just as well," he said philosophically. "We can't go to the police with a wet slipper and a blood-stained rope and accuse a man of murder. We have to have a body."

"He killed her," I said obstinately. "She told me yesterday he was a fiend. He killed her and threw the body in the water."

"Very likely. But he didn't throw it here."

But in spite of that, he went over all the lower hall with his boat, feeling every foot of the floor with an oar, and finally, at the back end, he looked up at me as I stood on the stairs.

"There's something here," he said.

I went cold all over, and had to clutch the railing. But when Terry had come, and the two of them brought the thing to the surface, it was only the dining-room rug, which I had rolled up and forgotten to carry up-stairs!

At half past one Mr. Holcombe wrote a note, and sent it off with Terry, and borrowing my boots, which had been Mr. Pitman's, investigated the dining-room and kitchen from a floating plank; the doors were too narrow to admit the boat. But he found nothing more important than a rolling-pin. He was not at all depressed by his failure. He came back, drenched to the skin, about three, and asked permission to search the Ladleys' bedroom.

"I have a friend coming pretty soon, Mrs. Pitman," he said, "a young newspaper man, named Howell. He's a nice boy, and if there is anything to this, I'd like him to have it for his paper. He and I have been having some arguments about circumstantial evidence, too, and I know he'd like to work on this."

I gave him a pair of Mr. Pitman's socks, for his own were saturated, and while he was changing them the telephone rang. It was the theater again, asking for Jennie Brice.

"You are certain she is out of the city?" some one asked, the same voice as in the morning.

"Her husband says so."

"Ask him to come to the phone."

"He is not here."

"When do you expect him back?"

"I'm not sure he is coming back."

"Look here," said the voice angrily, "can't you give me any satisfaction? Or don't you care to?"

"I've told you all I know."

"You don't know where she is?"

"No, sir."

"She didn't say she was coming back to rehearse for next week's piece?"

"Her husband said she went away for a few days' rest. He went away about noon and hasn't come back. That's all I know, except that they owe me three weeks' rent that I'd like to get hold of."

The owner of the voice hung up the receiver with a snap, and left me pondering. It seemed to me that Mr. Ladley had been very reckless. Did he expect any one to believe that Jennie Brice had gone for a vacation without notifying the theater? Especially when she was to rehearse that week? I thought it curious, to say the least. I went back and told Mr. Holcombe, who put it down in his note-book, and together we went to the Ladleys' room.

The room was in better order than usual, as I have said. The bed was made—which was out of the ordinary, for Jennie Brice never made a bed—but made the way a man makes one, with the blankets wrinkled and crooked beneath, and the white counterpane pulled smoothly over the top, showing every lump beneath. I showed Mr. Holcombe the splasher, dotted with ink as usual.

"I'll take it off and soak it in milk," I said. "It's his fountain pen; when the ink doesn't run, he shakes it, and—"

"Where's the clock?" said Mr. Holcombe, stopping in front of the mantel with his note-book in his hand.

"The clock?"

I turned and looked. My onyx clock was gone from the mantel-shelf.

Perhaps it seems strange, but from the moment I missed that clock my rage at Mr. Ladley increased to a fury. It was all I had had left of my former gentility. When times were hard and I got behind with the rent, as happened now and then, more than once I'd been tempted to sell the clock, or to pawn it. But I had never done it. Its ticking had kept me company on many a lonely night, and its elegance had helped me to keep my pride and to retain the respect of my neighbors. For in the flood district onyx clocks are not plentiful. Mrs. Bryan, the saloon-keeper's wife, had one, and I had another. That is, I *had* had.

I stood staring at the mark in the dust of the mantel-shelf, which Mr. Holcombe was measuring with a pocket tape-measure.

"You are sure you didn't take it away yourself, Mrs. Pitman?" he asked.

"Sure? Why, I could hardly lift it," I said.

He was looking carefully at the oblong of dust where the clock had stood. "The key is gone, too," he said, busily making entries in his note-book. "What was the maker's name?"

"Why, I don't think I ever noticed."

He turned to me angrily. "Why didn't you notice?" he snapped. "Good God, woman, do you only use your eyes to cry with? How can you wind a clock, time after time, and not know the maker's name? It proves my contention: the average witness is totally unreliable."

"Not at all," I snapped, "I am ordinarily both accurate and observing."

"Indeed!" he said, putting his hands behind him. "Then perhaps you can tell me the color of the pencil I have been writing with."

"Certainly. Red." Most pencils are red, and I thought this was safe.

But he held his right hand out with a flourish. "I've been writing with a fountain pen," he said in deep disgust, and turned his back on me.

But the next moment he had run to the wash stand and pulled it out from the wall. Behind it, where it had fallen, lay a towel covered with stains, as if some one had wiped bloody hands on it. He held it up, his face working with excitement. I could only cover my eyes.

"This looks better," he said, and began making a quick search of the room, running from one piece of furniture to another, pulling out bureau drawers, drawing the bed out from the wall, and crawling along the base-board with a lighted match in his hand. He gave a shout of triumph finally, and reappeared from behind the bed with the broken end of my knife in his hand.

"Very clumsy," he said. "*Very* clumsy. Peter the dog could have done better."

I had been examining the wall-paper about the wash-stand. Among the ink-spots were one or two reddish ones that made me shiver. And seeing a scrap of note-paper stuck between the base-board and the wall, I dug it out with a hairpin, and threw it into the grate, to be burned later. It was by the merest chance there was no fire there. The next moment Mr. Holcombe was on his knees by the fireplace reaching for the scrap.

"*Never* do that, under such circumstances," he snapped, fishing among the ashes. "You might throw away valuable—Hello, Howell!"

I turned and saw a young man in the doorway, smiling, his hat in his hand. Even at that first glance, I liked Mr. Howell, and later, when every one was against him, and many curious things were developing, I stood by him through everything, and even helped him to the thing he wanted more than anything else in the world. But that, of course, was later.

"What's the trouble, Holcombe?" he asked. "Hitting the trail again?"

"A very curious thing that I just happened on," said Mr. Holcombe. "Mrs. Pitman, this is Mr. Howell, of whom I spoke. Sit down, Howell, and let me read you something."

With the crumpled paper still unopened in his hand, Mr. Holcombe took his note-book and read aloud what he had written. I have it before me now:

"'Dog meat, two dollars, boat hire'—that's not it. Here. 'Yesterday, Sunday, March the 4th, Mrs. Pitman, landlady at 42 Union Street, heard two of her boarders quarreling, a man and his wife. Man's name, Philip Ladley. Wife's name, Jennie Ladley, known as Jennie Brice at the Liberty Stock Company, where she has been playing small parts.'"

Mr. Howell nodded. "I've heard of her," he said. "Not much of an actress, I believe."

"'The husband was also an actor, out of work, and employing his leisure time in writing a play.'"

"Everybody's doing it," said Mr. Howell idly.

"The Shuberts were to star him in this," I put in. "He said that the climax at the end of the second act—"

Mr. Holcombe shut his note-book with a snap. "After we have finished gossiping," he said, "I'll go on."

"'Employing his leisure time in writing a play—'" quoted Mr. Howell.

"Exactly. 'The husband and wife were not on good terms. They quarreled frequently. On Sunday they fought all day, and Mrs. Ladley told Mrs. Pitman she was married to a fiend. At four o'clock Sunday afternoon, Philip Ladley went out, returning about five. Mrs. Pitman carried their supper to them at six, and both ate heartily. She did not see Mrs. Ladley at the time, but heard her in the next room. They were apparently reconciled: Mrs. Pitman reports Mr. Ladley in high good humor. If the quarrel recommenced during the night, the other boarder, named Reynolds, in the next room, heard nothing. Mrs. Pitman was up and down until one o'clock, when she dozed off. She heard no unusual sound.

"'At approximately two o'clock in the morning, however, this Reynolds came to the room, and said he had heard some one in a boat in the lower hall. He and Mrs. Pitman investigated. The boat which Mrs. Pitman uses during a flood, and which she had tied to the stair-rail, was gone, having been cut loose, not untied. Everything else was quiet, except that Mrs Ladley's dog had been shut in a third-story room.

"'At a quarter after four that morning Mrs. Pitman, thoroughly awake, heard the boat returning, and going to the stairs, met Ladley coming in. He muttered something about having gone for medicine for his wife and went to his room, shutting the dog out. This is worth attention, for the dog ordinarily slept in their room.'"

"What sort of a dog?" asked Mr. Howell. He had been listening attentively.

"A water-spaniel. 'The rest of the night, or early morning, was quiet. At a quarter after seven, Ladley asked for coffee and toast for one, and on Mrs. Pitman remarking this, said that his wife was not playing this week, and had gone for a few days' vacation, having left early in the morning.' Remember, during the night he had been out for medicine for her. Now she was able to travel, and, in fact, had started."

Mr. Howell was frowning at the floor. "If he was doing anything wrong, he was doing it very badly," he said.

"This is where I entered the case," said Mr. Holcombe, "I rowed into the lower hall this morning, to feed the dog, Peter, who was whining on the staircase. Mrs. Pitman was coming down, pale and agitated over the fact that the dog, shortly before, had found floating in the parlor down-stairs a slipper belonging to Mrs. Ladley, and, later, a knife with a broken blade. She maintains that she had the knife last night up-stairs, that it was not broken, and that it was taken from a shelf in her room while she dozed. The question is, then: Why was the knife taken? Who took it? And why? Has this man made away with his wife, or has he not?"

Mr. Howell looked at me and smiled. "Mr. Holcombe and I are old enemies," he said. "Mr. Holcombe believes that circumstantial evidence may probably hang a man; I do not." And to Mr. Holcombe: "So, having found a wet slipper and a broken knife, you are prepared for murder and sudden death!"

"I have more evidence," Mr. Holcombe said eagerly, and proceeded to tell what we had found in the room. Mr. Howell listened, smiling to himself, but at the mention of the onyx clock he got up and went to the mantel.

"By Jove!" he said, and stood looking at the mark in the dust. "Are you sure the clock was here yesterday?"

"I wound it night before last, and put the key underneath. Yesterday, before they moved up, I wound it again."

"The key is gone also. Well, what of it, Holcombe? Did he brain her with the clock? Or choke her with the key?"

Mr. Holcombe was looking at his note-book. "To summarize," he said, "we have here as clues indicating a crime, the rope, the broken knife, the slipper, the towel, and the clock. Besides, this scrap of paper may contain some information." He opened it and sat gazing at it in his palm. Then, "Is this Ladley's writing?" he asked me in a curious voice.

"Yes."

I glanced at the slip. Mr. Holcombe had just read from his note-book: "Rope, knife, slipper, towel, clock."

The slip I had found behind the wash-stand said "Rope, knife, shoe, towel. Horn—" The rest of the last word was torn off.

Mr. Howell was staring at the mantel. "Clock!" he repeated.

CHAPTER FOUR
The Memory of a Voice

It was after four when Mr. Holcombe had finished going over the room. I offered to make both the gentlemen some tea, for Mr. Pitman had been an Englishman, and I had got into the habit of having a cup in the afternoon, with a cracker or a bit of bread. But they refused. Mr. Howell said he had promised to meet a lady, and to bring her through the flooded district in a boat. He shook hands with me, and smiled at Mr. Holcombe.

"You will have to restrain his enthusiasm, Mrs. Pitman," he said. "He is a bloodhound on the scent. If his baying gets on your nerves, just send for me." He went down the stairs and stepped into the boat. "Remember, Holcombe," he called, "every well-constituted murder has two things: a motive and a corpse. You haven't either, only a mass of piffling details—"

172

"If everybody waited until he saw flames, instead of relying on the testimony of the smoke," Mr. Holcombe snapped, "what would the fire loss be?"

Mr. Howell poled his boat to the front door, and sitting down, prepared to row out.

"You are warned, Mrs. Pitman," he called to me. "If he doesn't find a body to fit the clues, he's quite capable of making one to fill the demand."

"Horn—" said Mr. Holcombe, looking at the slip again. "The tail of the 'n' is torn off—evidently only part of a word. Hornet, Horning, Horner—Mrs. Pitman, will you go with me to the police station?"

I was more than anxious to go. In fact, I could not bear the idea of staying alone in the house, with heaven only knows what concealed in the depths of that muddy flood. I got on my wraps again, and Mr. Holcombe rowed me out. Peter plunged into the water to follow, and had to be sent back. He sat on the lower step and whined. Mr. Holcombe threw him another piece of liver, but he did not touch it.

We rowed to the corner of Robinson Street and Federal—it was before Federal Street was raised above the flood level—and left the boat in charge of a boy there. And we walked to the police station. On the way Mr. Holcombe questioned me closely about the events of the morning, and I recalled the incident of the burned pillow-slip. He made a note of it at once, and grew very thoughtful.

He left me, however, at the police station. "I'd rather not appear in this, Mrs. Pitman," he said apologetically, "and I think better along my own lines. Not that I have anything against the police; they've done some splendid work. But this case takes imagination, and the police department deals with facts. We have no facts yet. What we need, of course, is to have the man detained until we are sure of our case."

He lifted his hat and turned away, and I went slowly up the steps to the police station. Living, as I had, in a neighborhood where the police, like the poor, are always with us, and where the visits of the patrol wagon are one of those familiar sights that no amount of repetition enabled any of us to treat with contempt, I was uncomfortable until I remembered that my grandfather had been one of the first mayors of the city, and that, if the patrol had been at my house more than once, the entire neighborhood would testify that my boarders were usually orderly.

At the door some one touched me on the arm. It was Mr. Holcombe again.

"I have been thinking it over," he said, "and I believe you'd better not mention the piece of paper that you found behind the wash-stand. They might say the whole thing is a hoax."

"Very well," I agreed, and went in.

The police sergeant in charge knew me at once, having stopped at my house more than once in flood-time for a cup of hot coffee.

"Sit down, Mrs. Pitman," he said. "I suppose you are still making the best coffee and doughnuts in the city of Allegheny? Well, what's the trouble in your district? Want an injunction against the river for trespass?"

"The river has brought me a good bit of trouble," I said. "I'm—I'm worried, Mr. Sergeant. I think a woman from my house has been murdered, but I don't know."

"Murdered," he said, and drew up his chair. "Tell me about it."

I told him everything, while he sat back with his eyes half closed, and his fingers beating a tattoo on the arm of his chair.

When I finished he got up and went into an inner room. He came back in a moment.

"I want you to come in and tell that to the chief," he said, and led the way.

All told, I repeated my story three times that afternoon, to the sergeant, to the chief of police, and the third time to both the others and two detectives.

The second time the chief made notes of what I said.

"Know this man Ladley?" he asked the others. None of them did, but they all knew of Jennie Brice, and some of them had seen her in the theater.

"Get the theater, Tom," the chief said to one of the detectives.

Luckily, what he learned over the telephone from the theater corroborated my story. Jennie Brice was not in the cast that week, but should have reported that morning (Monday) to rehearse the next week's piece. No message had been received from her, and a substitute had been put in her place.

The chief hung up the receiver and turned to me. "You are sure about the clock, Mrs. Pitman?" he asked. "It was there when they moved up-stairs to the room?"

"Yes, sir."

"You are certain you will not find it on the parlor mantel when the water goes down?"

"The mantels are uncovered now. It is not there."

"You think Ladley has gone for good?"

"Yes, sir."

"He'd be a fool to try to run away, unless—Graves, you'd better get hold of the fellow, and keep him until either the woman is found or a body. The river is falling. In a couple of days we will know if she is around the premises anywhere."

Before I left, I described Jennie Brice for them carefully. Asked what she probably wore, if she had gone away as her husband said, I had no idea; she had a lot of clothes, and dressed a good bit. But I recalled that I had seen, lying on the bed, the black and white dress with the red collar, and they took that down, as well as the brown valise.

The chief rose and opened the door for me himself. "If she actually left town at the time you mention," he said, "she ought not to be hard to find. There are not many trains before seven in the morning, and most of them are locals."

"And—and if she did not, if he—do you think she is in the house—or—or—the cellar?"

"Not unless Ladley is more of a fool than I think he is," he said, smiling. "Personally, I believe she has gone away, as he says she did. But if she hasn't—He probably took the body with him when he said he was getting medicine, and dropped it in the current somewhere. But we must go slow with all this. There's no use shouting 'wolf' yet."

"But—the towel?"

"He may have cut himself, shaving. It *has* been done."

"And the knife?"

He shrugged his shoulders good-naturedly.

"I've seen a perfectly good knife spoiled opening a bottle of pickles."

"But the slippers? And the clock?"

"My good woman, enough shoes and slippers are forgotten in the bottoms of cupboards year after year in flood-time, and are found floating around the streets, to make all the old-clothesmen in town happy. I have seen almost everything floating about, during one of these annual floods."

"I dare say you never saw an onyx clock floating around," I replied a little sharply. I had no sense of humor that day. He stopped smiling at once, and stood tugging at his mustache.

"No," he admitted. "An onyx clock sinks, that's true. That's a very nice little point, that onyx clock. He may be trying to sell it, or perhaps—" He did not finish.

I went back immediately, only stopping at the market to get meat for Mr. Reynolds' supper. It was after half past five and dusk was coming on. I got a boat and was rowed directly home. Peter was not at the foot of the steps. I paid the boatman and let him go, and turned to go up the stairs. Some one was speaking in the hall above.

I have read somewhere that no two voices are exactly alike, just as no two violins ever produce precisely the same sound. I think it is what they call the timbre that is different. I have, for instance, never heard a voice like Mr. Pitman's, although Mr. Harry Lauder's in a phonograph resembles it. And voices have always done for me what odors do for some people, revived forgotten scenes and old memories. But the memory that the voice at the head of the stairs brought back was not very old, although I had forgotten it. I seemed to hear again, all at once, the lapping of the water Sunday morning as it began to come in over the door-sill; the sound of Terry ripping up the parlor carpet, and Mrs. Ladley calling me a she-devil in the next room, in reply to this very voice.

But when I got to the top of the stairs, it was only Mr. Howell, who had brought his visitor to the flood district, and on getting her splashed with the muddy water, had taken her to my house for a towel and a cake of soap.

I lighted the lamp in the hall, and Mr. Howell introduced the girl. She was a pretty girl, slim and young, and she had taken her wetting good-naturedly.

"I know we are intruders, Mrs. Pitman," she said, holding out her hand. "Especially now, when you are in trouble."

"I have told Miss Harvey a little," Mr. Howell said, "and I promised to show her Peter, but he is not here."

I think I had known it was my sister's child from the moment I lighted the lamp. There was something of Alma in her, not Alma's hardness or haughtiness, but Alma's dark blue eyes with black lashes, and Alma's nose. Alma was always the beauty of the family. What with the day's excitement, and seeing Alma's child like this, in my house, I felt things going round and clutched at the stair-rail. Mr. Howell caught me.

"Why, Mrs. Pitman!" he said. "What's the matter?"

I got myself in hand in a moment and smiled at the girl.

"Nothing at all," I said. "Indigestion, most likely. Too much tea the last day or two, and not enough solid food. I've been too anxious to eat."

Lida—for she was that to me at once, although I had never seen her before—Lida was all sympathy and sweetness. She actually asked me to go with her to a restaurant and have a real dinner. I could imagine Alma, had she known! But I excused myself.

"I have to cook something for Mr. Reynolds," I said, "and I'm better now, anyhow, thank you. Mr. Howell may I speak to you?"

He followed me along the back hall, which was dusk.

"I have remembered something that I had forgotten, Mr. Howell," I said. "On Sunday morning, the Ladleys had a visitor."

"Yes?"

"They had very few visitors."

"I see."

"I did not see him, but—I heard his voice." Mr. Howell did not move, but I fancied he drew his breath in quickly. "It sounded—it was not by any chance *you*?"

"I? A newspaper man, who goes to bed at three A.M. on Sunday morning, up and about at ten!"

"I didn't say what time it was," I said sharply.

But at that moment Lida called from the front hall.

"I think I hear Peter," she said. "He is shut in somewhere, whining."

We went forward at once. She was right. Peter was scratching at the door of Mr. Ladley's room, although I had left the door closed and Peter in the hall. I let him out, and he crawled to me on three legs, whimpering. Mr. Howell bent over him and felt the fourth.

"Poor little beast!" he said. "His leg is broken!"

He made a splint for the dog, and with Lida helping, they put him to bed in a clothes-basket in my up-stairs kitchen. It was easy to see how things lay with Mr. Howell. He was all eyes for her: he made excuses to touch her hand or her arm—little caressing touches that made her color heighten. And with it all, there was a sort of hopelessness in his manner, as if he knew how far the girl was out of his reach. Knowing Alma and her pride, I knew better than they how hopeless it was.

I was not so sure about Lida. I wondered if she was in love with the boy, or only in love with love. She was very young, as I had been. God help her, if, like me, she sacrificed everything, to discover, too late, that she was only in love with love!

CHAPTER FIVE
A Sodden Fur Coat

Mr. Reynolds did not come home to dinner after all. The water had got into the basement at the store, he telephoned, one of the flood-gates in a sewer having leaked, and they were moving some of the departments to an upper floor. I had expected to have him in the house that evening, and now I was left alone again.

But, as it happened, I was not alone. Mr. Graves, one of the city detectives, came at half past six, and went carefully over the Ladleys' room. I showed him the towel and the slipper and the broken knife, and where we had found the knife-blade. He was very non-committal, and left in a half-hour, taking the articles with him in a newspaper.

At seven the door-bell rang. I went down as far as I could on the staircase, and I saw a boat outside the door, with the boatman and a woman in it. I called to them to bring the boat back along the hall, and I had a queer feeling that it might be Mrs. Ladley, and that I'd been making a fool of myself all day for nothing. But it was not Mrs. Ladley.

"Is this number forty-two?" asked the woman, as the boat came back.

"Yes."

"Does Mr. Ladley live here?"

"Yes. But he is not here now."

"Are you Mrs. Pittock?"

"Pitman, yes."

The boat bumped against the stairs, and the woman got out. She was as tall as Mrs. Ladley, and when I saw her in the light from the upper hall, I knew her instantly. It was Temple Hope, the leading woman from the Liberty Theater.

"I would like to talk to you, Mrs. Pitman," she said. "Where can we go?"

I led the way back to my room, and when she had followed me in, she turned and shut the door.

"Now then," she said without any preliminary, "where is Jennie Brice?"

"I don't know, Miss Hope," I answered.

We looked at each other for a minute, and each of us saw what the other suspected.

"He has killed her!" she exclaimed. "She was afraid he would do it, and—he has."

"Killed her and thrown her into the river," I said. "That's what I think, and he'll go free at that. It seems there isn't any murder when there isn't any corpse."

"If he has done that the river will give her up, eventually."

"The river doesn't always give them up," I retorted. "Not in flood-time, anyhow. Or when they are found it is months later, and you can't prove anything."

She had only a little time, being due at the theater soon, but she sat down and told me the story she told afterward on the stand:

She had known Jennie Brice for years, they having been together in the chorus as long before as *Nadjy*.

"She was married then to a fellow on the vaudeville circuit," Miss Hope said. "He left her about that time, and she took up with Ladley. I don't think they were ever married."

"What!" I said, jumping to my feet, "and they came to a respectable house like this! There's never been a breath of scandal about this house, Miss Hope, and if this comes out I'm ruined."

"Well, perhaps they were married," she said. "Anyhow, they were always quarreling. And when he wasn't playing, it was worse. She used to come to my hotel, and cry her eyes out."

"I knew you were friends," I said. "Almost the last thing she said to me was about the black and white dress of hers you were to borrow for the piece this week."

"Black and white dress! I borrow one of Jennie Brice's dresses!" exclaimed Miss Hope. "I should think not. I have plenty of my own."

That puzzled me; for she had said it, that was sure. And then I remembered that I had not seen the dress in the room that day, and I went in to look for it. It was gone. I came back and told Miss Hope.

"A black and white dress! Did it have a red collar?" she asked.

"Yes."

"Then I remember it. She wore a small black hat with a red quill with that dress. You might look for the hat."

She followed me back to the room and stood in the doorway while I searched. The hat was gone, too.

"Perhaps, after all, he's telling the truth," she said thoughtfully. "Her fur coat isn't in the closet, is it?"

It was gone. It is strange that, all day, I had never thought of looking over her clothes and seeing what was missing. I hadn't known all she had, of course, but I had seen her all winter in her fur coat and admired it. It was a striped fur, brown and gray, and very unusual. But with the coat missing, and a dress and hat gone, it began to look as if I had been making a fool of myself, and stirring up a tempest in a teacup. Miss Hope was as puzzled as I was.

"Anyhow, if he didn't kill her," she said, "it isn't because he did not want to. Only last week she had hysterics in my dressing-room, and said he had threatened to poison her. It was all Mr. Bronson, the business manager, and I could do to quiet her."

She looked at her watch, and exclaimed that she was late, and would have to hurry. I saw her down to her boat. The river had been falling rapidly for the last hour or two, and I heard the boat scrape as it went over the door-sill. I did not know whether to be glad that the water was going down and I could live like a Christian again, or to be sorry, for fear of what we might find in the mud that was always left.

Peter was lying where I had put him, on a folded blanket laid in a clothes-basket. I went back to him, and sat down beside the basket.

"Peter!" I said. "Poor old Peter! Who did this to you? Who hurt you?" He looked at me and whined, as if he wanted to tell me, if only he could.

"Was it Mr. Ladley?" I asked, and the poor thing cowered close to his bed and shivered. I wondered if it had been he, and, if it had, why he had come back. Perhaps he had remembered the towel. Perhaps he would come again and spend the night there. I was like Peter: I cowered and shivered at the very thought.

At nine o'clock I heard a boat at the door. It had stuck there, and its occupant was scolding furiously at the boatman. Soon after I heard splashing, and I knew that whoever it was was wading back to the stairs through the foot and a half or so of water still in the hall. I ran back to my room and locked myself in, and then stood, armed with the stove-lid-lifter, in case it should be Ladley and he should break the door in.

The steps came up the stairs, and Peter barked furiously. It seemed to me that this was to be my end, killed like a rat in a trap and thrown out the window, to float, like my kitchen chair, into Mollie Maguire's kitchen, or to be found lying in the ooze of the yard after the river had gone down.

The steps hesitated at the top of the stairs, and turned back along the hall. Peter redoubled his noise; he never barked for Mr. Reynolds or the Ladleys. I stood still, hardly able to breathe. The door was thin, and the lock loose: one good blow, and—

The door-knob turned, and I screamed. I recall that the light turned black, and that is all I *do* remember, until I came to, a half-hour later, and saw Mr. Holcombe stooping over me. The door, with the lock broken, was standing open. I tried to move, and then I saw that my feet were propped up on the edge of Peter's basket.

"Better leave them up." Mr. Holcombe said. "It sends the blood back to the head. Half the damfool people in the world stick a pillow under a fainting woman's shoulders. How are you now?"

"All right," I said feebly. "I thought you were Mr. Ladley."

He helped me up, and I sat in a chair and tried to keep my lips from shaking. And then I saw that Mr. Holcombe had brought a suit case with him, and had set it inside the door.

"Ladley is safe, until he gets bail, anyhow," he said. "They picked him up as he was boarding a Pennsylvania train bound east."

"For murder?" I asked.

"As a suspicious character," he replied grimly. "That does as well as anything for a time." He sat down opposite me, and looked at me intently.

"Mrs. Pitman," he said, "did you ever hear the story of the horse that wandered out of a village and could not be found?"

I shook my head.

"Well, the best wit of the village failed to locate the horse. But one day the village idiot walked into town, leading the missing animal by the bridle. When they asked him how he had done it, he said: 'Well, I just thought what I'd do if I was a horse, and then I went and did it.'"

"I see," I said, humoring him.

"You *don't* see. Now, what are we trying to do?"

"We're trying to find a body. Do you intend to become a corpse?"

He leaned over and tapped on the table between us. "We are trying to prove a crime. I intend for the time to be the criminal."

He looked so curious, bent forward and glaring at me from under his bushy eyebrows, with his shoes on his knee—for he had taken them off to wade to the stairs—and his trousers rolled to his knees, that I wondered if he was entirely sane. But Mr. Holcombe, eccentric as he might be, was sane enough.

"Not *really* a criminal!"

"As really as lies in me. Listen, Mrs. Pitman. I want to put myself in Ladley's place for a day or two, live as he lived, do what he did, even think as he thought, if I can. I am going to sleep in his room to-night, with your permission."

I could not see any reason for objecting, although I thought it silly and useless. I led the way to the front room, Mr. Holcombe following with his shoes and suit case. I lighted a lamp, and he stood looking around him.

"I see you have been here since we left this afternoon," he said.

"Twice," I replied. "First with Mr. Graves, and later—"

The words died on my tongue. Some one had been in the room since my last visit there.

"He has been here!" I gasped. "I left the room in tolerable order. Look at it!"

"When were you here last?"

"At seven-thirty, or thereabouts."

"Where were you between seven-thirty and eight-thirty?"

"In the kitchen with Peter." I told him then about the dog, and about finding him shut in the room.

The wash-stand was pulled out. The sheets of Mr. Ladley's manuscript, usually an orderly pile, were half on the floor. The bed coverings had been jerked off and flung over the back of a chair

Peter, imprisoned, *might* have moved the wash-stand and upset the manuscript—Peter had never put the bed-clothing over the chair, or broken his own leg.

"Humph!" he said, and getting out his note-book, he made an exact memorandum of what I had told him, and of the condition of the room. That done, he turned to me.

"Mrs. Pitman," he said, "I'll thank you to call me Mr. Ladley for the next day or so. I am an actor out of employment, forty-one years of age, short, stout, and bald, married to a woman I would like to be quit of, and I am writing myself a play in which the Shuberts intend to star me, or in which I intend the Shuberts to star me."

"Very well, Mr. Ladley," I said, trying to enter into the spirit of the thing, and, God knows, seeing no humor in it. "Then you'll like your soda from the ice-box?"

"Soda? For what?"

"For your whisky and soda, before you go to bed, sir."

"Oh, certainly, yes. Bring the soda. And—just a moment, Mrs. Pitman: Mr. Holcombe is a total abstainer, and has always been so. It is Ladley, not Holcombe, who takes this abominable stuff."

I said I quite understood, but that Mr. Ladley could skip a night, if he so wished. But the little gentleman would not hear to it, and when I brought the soda, poured himself a double portion. He stood looking at it, with his face screwed up, as if the very odor revolted him.

"The chances are," he said, "that Ladley—that I—having a nasty piece of work to do during the night, would—will take a larger drink than usual." He raised the glass, only to put it down. "Don't forget," he said, "to put a large knife where you left the one last night. I'm sorry the water has gone down, but I shall imagine it still at the seventh step. Good night, Mrs. Pitman."

"Good night, Mr. Ladley," I said, smiling, "and remember, you are three weeks in arrears with your board."

His eyes twinkled through his spectacles. "I shall imagine it paid," he said.

I went out, and I heard him close the door behind me. Then, through the door, I heard a great sputtering and coughing, and I knew he had got the whisky down somehow. I put the knife out, as he had asked me to, and went to bed. I was ready to drop. Not even the knowledge that an imaginary Mr. Ladley was about to commit an imaginary crime in the house that night could keep me awake.

Mr. Reynolds came in at eleven o'clock. I was roused when he banged his door. That was all I knew until morning. The sun on my face wakened me. Peter, in his basket, lifted his head as I moved, and thumped his tail against his pillow in greeting. I put on a wrapper, and called Mr. Reynolds by knocking at his door. Then I went on to the front room. The door was closed, and some one beyond was groaning. My heart stood still, and then raced on. I opened the door and looked in.

Mr. Holcombe was on the bed, fully dressed. He had a wet towel tied around his head, and his face looked swollen and puffy. He opened one eye and looked at me.

"What a night!" he groaned.

"What happened! What did you find?"

He groaned again. "Find!" he said. "Nothing, except that there was something wrong with that whisky. It poisoned me. I haven't been out of the house!"

So for that day, at least, Mr. Ladley became Mr. Holcombe again, and as such accepted ice in quantities, a mustard plaster over his stomach, and considerable nursing. By evening he was better, but although he clearly intended to stay on, he said nothing about changing his identity again, and I was glad enough. The very name of Ladley was horrible to me.

The river went down almost entirely that day, although there was still considerable water in the cellars. It takes time to get rid of that. The lower floors showed nothing suspicious. The papers were ruined, of course, the doors warped and sprung, and the floors coated with mud and debris. Terry came in the afternoon, and together we hung the dining-room rug out to dry in the sun.

As I was coming in, I looked over at the Maguire yard. Molly Maguire was there, and all her children around her, gaping. Molly was hanging out to dry a sodden fur coat, that had once been striped, brown and gray.

I went over after breakfast and claimed the coat as belonging to Mrs. Ladley. But she refused to give it up. There is a sort of unwritten law concerning the salvage of flood articles, and I had to leave the coat, as I had my kitchen chair. But it was Mrs. Ladley's, beyond a doubt.

I shuddered when I thought how it had probably got into the water. And yet it was curious, too, for if she had had it on, how did it get loose to go floating around Molly Maguire's yard? And if she had not worn it, how did it get in the water?

CHAPTER SIX
A Mysterious Visit

The newspapers were full of the Ladley case, with its curious solution and many surprises. It was considered unique in many ways. Mr. Pitman had always read all the murder trials, and used to talk about the *corpus delicti* and writs of *habeas corpus*—*corpus* being the legal way, I believe, of spelling corpse. But I came out of the Ladley trial—for it came to trial ultimately—with only one point of law that I was sure of: that was, that it is mighty hard to prove a man a murderer unless you can show what he killed.

And that was the weakness in the Ladley case. There was a body, but it could not be identified.

The police held Mr. Ladley for a day or two, and then, nothing appearing, they let him go. Mr. Holcombe, who was still occupying the second floor front, almost wept with rage and despair when he read the news in the papers. He was still working on the case, in his curious way, wandering along the wharves at night, and writing letters all over the country to learn about Philip Ladley's previous life, and his wife's. But he did not seem to get anywhere.

The papers had been full of the Jennie Brice disappearance. For disappearance it proved to be. So far as could be learned, she had not left the city that night, or since, and as she was a striking-looking woman, very blond, as I have said, with a full voice and a languid manner, she could hardly have taken refuge anywhere without being discovered. The morning after her disappearance a young woman, tall like Jennie Brice and fair, had been seen in the Union Station. But as she was accompanied by a young man, who bought her magazines and papers, and bade her an excited farewell, sending his love to various members of a family, and promising to feed the canary, this was not seriously considered. A sort of general alarm went over the country. When she was younger she had been pretty well known at the Broadway theaters in New York. One way or another, the Liberty Theater got a lot of free advertising from the case, and I believe Miss Hope's salary was raised.

The police communicated with Jennie Brice's people—she had a sister in Olean, New York, but she had not heard from her. The sister wrote—I heard later—that Jennie had been unhappy with Philip Ladley, and afraid he would kill her. And Miss Hope told the same story. But—there was no *corpus*, as the lawyers say, and finally the police had to free Mr. Ladley.

Beyond making an attempt to get bail, and failing, he had done nothing. Asked about his wife, he merely shrugged his shoulders and said she had left him, and would turn up all right. He was unconcerned: smoked cigarettes all day, ate and slept well, and looked better since he had had nothing to drink. And two or three days after the arrest, he sent for the manuscript of his play.

Mr. Howell came for it on the Thursday of that week.

I was on my knees scrubbing the parlor floor when he rang the bell. I let him in, and it seemed to me that he looked tired and pale.

"Well, Mrs. Pitman," he said, smiling, "what did you find in the cellar when the water went down?"

"I'm glad to say that I didn't find what I feared, Mr. Howell."

"Not even the onyx clock?"

"Not even the clock," I replied. "And I feel as if I'd lost a friend. A clock is a lot of company."

"Do you know what I think?" he said, looking at me closely. "I think you put that clock away yourself, in the excitement, and have forgotten all about it."

"Nonsense."

"Think hard." He was very much in earnest. "You knew the water was rising and the Ladleys would have to be moved up to the second floor front, where the clock stood. You went in there and looked around to see if the room was ready, and you saw the clock. And knowing that the Ladleys quarreled now and then, and were apt to throw things—"

"Nothing but a soap-dish, and that only once."

"You took the clock to the attic and put it, say, in an old trunk."

"I did nothing of the sort. I went in, as you say, and I put up an old splasher, because of the way he throws ink about. Then I wound the clock, put the key under it, and went out."

"And the key is gone, too!" he said thoughtfully. "I wish I could find that clock, Mrs. Pitman."

"So do I."

"Ladley went out Sunday afternoon about three, didn't he—and got back at five?"

I turned and looked at him. "Yes, Mr. Howell," I said. "Perhaps *you* know something about that."

"I?" He changed color. Twenty years of dunning boarders has made me pretty sharp at reading faces, and he looked as uncomfortable as if he owed me money. "I!" I knew then that I had been right about the voice. It had been his.

"You!" I cried. "You were here early Sunday and spent some time with the Ladleys. I'm the old she-devil. I notice you didn't tell your friend, Mr. Holcombe, about having been here on Sunday."

He was quick to recover. "I'll tell you all about it, Mrs. Pitman," he said smilingly. "You see, all my life, I have wished for an onyx clock. It has been my ambition, my *Great Desire*. Leaving the house that Sunday morning, and hearing the ticking of the clock up-stairs, I recognized that it was an *onyx* clock, clambered from my boat through an upper window, and so reached it. The clock showed fight, but after stunning it with a chair—"

"Exactly!" I said. "Then the thing Mrs. Ladley said she would not do was probably to wind the clock?"

He dropped his bantering manner at once. "Mrs. Pitman," he said, "I don't know what you heard or did not hear. But I want you to give me a little time before you tell anybody that I was here that Sunday morning. And, in return, I'll find your clock."

I hesitated, but however put out he was, he didn't look like a criminal. Besides, he was a friend of my niece's, and blood is thicker even than flood water.

"There was nothing wrong about my being here," he went on, "but—I don't want it known. Don't spoil a good story, Mrs. Pitman."

I did not quite understand that, although those who followed the trial carefully may do so. Poor Mr. Howell! I am sure he believed that it was only a good story. He got the description of my onyx clock and wrote it down, and I gave him the manuscript for Mr. Ladley. That was the last I saw of him for some time.

That Thursday proved to be an exciting day. For late in the afternoon Terry, digging the mud out of the cellar, came across my missing gray false front near the coal vault, and brought it up, grinning. And just before six, Mr. Graves, the detective, rang the bell and then let himself in. I found him in the lower hall, looking around.

"Well, Mrs. Pitman," he said, "has our friend come back yet?"

"She was no friend of mine."

"Not *she*. Ladley. He'll be out this evening, and he'll probably be around for his clothes."

My knees wavered, as they always did when he was spoken of.

"He may want to stay here," said Mr. Graves. "In fact, I think that's just what he *will* want."

"Not here," I said. "The very thought of him makes me quake."

"If he comes here, better take him in. I want to know where he is."

I tried to say that I wouldn't have him, but the old habit of the ward asserted itself. From taking a bottle of beer or a slice of pie, to telling one where one might or might not live, the police were autocrats in that neighborhood. And, respectable woman that I am, my neighbors' fears of the front office have infected me.

"All right, Mr. Graves," I said.

He pushed the parlor door open and looked in, whistling. "This is the place, isn't it?"

"Yes. But it was up-stairs that he—"

"I see. Tall woman, Mrs. Ladley?"

"Tall and blond. Very airy in her manner."

He nodded and still stood looking in and whistling. "Never heard her speak of a town named Homer, did you?"

"Horner? No."

"I see." He turned and wandered out again into the hall, still whistling. At the door, however, he stopped and turned. "Look anything like this?" he asked, and held out one of his hands, with a small kodak picture on the palm.

It was a snap-shot of a children's frolic in a village street, with some onlookers in the background. Around one of the heads had been drawn a circle in pencil. I took it to the gas-jet and looked at it closely. It was a tall woman with a hat on, not unlike Jennie Brice. She was looking over the crowd, and I could see only her face, and that in shadow. I shook my head.

"I thought not," he said. "We have a lot of stage pictures of her, but what with false hair and their being retouched beyond recognition, they don't amount to much." He started out, and stopped on the door-step to light a cigar.

"Take him on if he comes," he said. "And keep your eyes open. Feed him well, and he won't kill you!"

I had plenty to think of when I was cooking Mr. Reynolds' supper: the chance that I might have Mr. Ladley again, and the woman at Horner. For it had come to me like a flash, as Mr. Graves left, that the "Horn—" on the paper slip might have been "Horner."

CHAPTER SEVEN
The Periscope

After all, there was nothing sensational about Mr. Ladley's return. He came at eight o'clock that night, fresh-shaved and with his hair cut, and, although he had a latch-key, he rang the door-bell. I knew his ring, and I thought it no harm to carry an old razor of

Mr. Pitman's with the blade open and folded back on the handle, the way the colored people use them, in my left hand.

But I saw at once that he meant no mischief.

"Good evening," he said, and put out his hand. I jumped back, until I saw there was nothing in it and that he only meant to shake hands. I didn't do it; I might have to take him in, and make his bed, and cook his meals, but I did not have to shake hands with him.

"You, too!" he said, looking at me with what I suppose he meant to be a reproachful look. But he could no more put an expression of that sort in his eyes than a fish could. "I suppose, then, there is no use asking if I may have my old room? The front room. I won't need two."

I didn't want him, and he must have seen it. But I took him. "You may have it, as far as I'm concerned," I said. "But you'll have to let the paper-hanger in to-morrow."

"Assuredly." He came into the hall and stood looking around him, and I fancied he drew a breath of relief. "It isn't much yet," he said, "but it's better to look at than six feet of muddy water."

"Or than stone walls," I said.

He looked at me and smiled. "Or than stone walls," he repeated, bowing, and went into his room.

So I had him again, and if I gave him only the dull knives, and locked up the bread-knife the moment I had finished with it, who can blame me? I took all the precaution I could think of: had Terry put an extra bolt on every door, and hid the rat poison and the carbolic acid in the cellar.

Peter would not go near him. He hobbled around on his three legs, with the splint beating a sort of tattoo on the floor, but he stayed back in the kitchen with me, or in the yard.

It was Sunday night or early Monday morning that Jennie Brice disappeared. On Thursday evening, her husband came back. On Friday the body of a woman was washed ashore at Beaver, but turned out to be that of a stewardess who had fallen overboard from one of the Cincinnati packets. Mr. Ladley himself showed me the article in the morning paper, when I took in his breakfast.

"Public hysteria has killed a man before this," he said, when I had read it. "Suppose that woman had been mangled, or the screw of the steamer had cut her head off! How many people do you suppose would have been willing to swear that it was my—was Mrs. Ladley?"

"Even without a head, I should know Mrs. Ladley," I retorted.

He shrugged his shoulders. "Let's trust she's still alive, for my sake," he said. "But I'm glad, anyhow, that this woman had a head. You'll allow me to be glad, won't you?"

"You can be anything you want," I snapped, and went out.

Mr. Holcombe still retained the second-story front room. I think, although he said nothing more about it, that he was still "playing horse." He wrote a good bit at the wash-stand, and, from the loose sheets of manuscript he left, I believe actually tried to begin a play. But mostly he wandered along the water-front, or stood on one or another of the bridges, looking at the water and thinking. It is certain that he tried to keep in the part by smoking cigarettes, but he hated them, and usually ended by throwing the cigarette away and lighting an old pipe he carried.

On Thursday evening he came home and sat down to supper with Mr. Reynolds. He ate little and seemed excited. The talk ran on crime, as it always did when he was around, and Mr. Holcombe quoted Herbert Spencer a great deal. Mr. Reynolds was impressed, not knowing much beyond silks and the National League.

"Spencer," Mr. Holcombe would say, "Spencer shows that every occurrence is the inevitable result of what has gone before, and carries in its train an equally inevitable series of results. Try to interrupt this chain in the smallest degree, and what follows? Chaos, my dear sir, chaos."

"We see that at the store," Mr. Reynolds would say. "Accustom a lot of women to a silk sale on Fridays and then make it toothbrushes. That's chaos, all right."

Well, Mr. Holcombe came in that night about ten. I told him Ladley was back. He was almost wild with excitement; wanted to have the back parlor, so he could watch him through the keyhole, and was very upset when I told him there was no keyhole, that the door fastened with a thumb bolt. On learning that the room was to be papered the next morning, he grew calmer, however, and got the paper-hanger's address from me. He went out just after that.

Friday, as I say, was quiet. Mr. Ladley moved to the back parlor to let the paper-hanger in the front room, smoked and fussed with his papers all day, and Mr. Holcombe stayed in his room, which was unusual. In the afternoon Molly Maguire put on the striped fur coat and went out, strolling past the house so that I would see her. Beyond banging the window down, I gave her no satisfaction.

At four o'clock Mr. Holcombe came to my kitchen, rubbing his hands together. He had a pasteboard tube in his hand about a foot long, with an arrangement of small mirrors in it. He said it was modeled after the something or other that is used on a submarine, and that he and the paper-hanger had fixed a place for it between his floor and the ceiling of Mr. Ladley's room, so that the chandelier would hide it from below. He thought he could watch Mr. Ladley through it; and as it turned out, he could.

"I want to find his weak moment," he said excitedly. "I want to know what he does when the door is closed and he can take off his mask. And I want to know if he sleeps with a light."

"If he does," I replied, "I hope you'll let me know, Mr. Holcombe. The gas bills are a horror to me as it is. I think he kept it on all last night. I turned off all the other lights and went to the cellar. The meter was going around."

"Fine!" he said. "Every murderer fears the dark. And our friend of the parlor bedroom is a murderer, Mrs. Pitman. Whether he hangs or not, he's a murderer."

The mirror affair, which Mr. Holcombe called a periscope, was put in that day and worked amazingly well. I went with him to try it out, and I distinctly saw the paper-hanger take a cigarette from Mr. Ladley's case and put it in his pocket. Just after that, Mr. Ladley sauntered into the room and looked at the new paper. I could both see and hear him. It was rather weird.

"God, what a wall-paper!" he said.

CHAPTER EIGHT
The Veiled Woman

That was Friday afternoon. That evening, and most of Saturday and Sunday, Mr. Holcombe sat on the floor, with his eye to the reflecting mirror and his notebook beside him. I have it before me.

On the first page is the "dog meat—two dollars" entry. On the next, the description of what occurred on Sunday night, March fourth, and Monday morning, the fifth. Following that came a sketch, made with a carbon sheet, of the torn paper found behind the wash-stand:

rope
knife
shoe   towel
Horn

And then came the entries for Friday, Saturday and Sunday. Friday evening:

6:30—Eating hearty supper.

7:00—Lights cigarette and paces floor. Notice that when Mrs. P. knocks, he goes to desk and pretends to be writing.

8:00—Is examining book. Looks like a railway guide.

8:30—It is a steamship guide.

8:45—Tailor's boy brings box. Gives boy fifty cents. Query. Where does he get money, now that J.B. is gone?

9:00—Tries on new suit, brown.

9:30—Has been spending a quarter of an hour on his knees looking behind furniture and examining base-board.

10:00—He has the key to the onyx clock. Has hidden it twice, once up the chimney flue, once behind base-board.

10:15—He has just thrown key or similar small article outside window into yard.

11:00—Has gone to bed. Light burning. Shall sleep on floor.

11:30—He cannot sleep, is up walking the floor and smoking.

2:00 A.M.—Saturday. Disturbance below. He had had nightmare and was calling "Jennie!" He got up, took a drink, and is now reading.

8:00 A.M.—Must have slept. He is shaving.

12:00 M.—Nothing this morning. He wrote for four hours, sometimes reading aloud what he had written.

2:00 P.M.—He has a visitor, a man. Can not hear all—word now and then. "Llewellyn is the very man." "Devil of a risk—" "We'll see you through." "Lost the slip—" "Didn't go to the hotel. She went to a private house." "Eliza Shaeffer."

Who went to a private house? Jennie Brice?

2:30—Can not hear. Are whispering. The visitor has given Ladley roll of bills.

4:00—Followed the visitor, a tall man with a pointed beard. He went to the Liberty Theater. Found it was Bronson, business manager there. Who is Llewellyn, and who is Eliza Shaeffer?

4:15—Had Mrs. P. bring telephone book: six Llewellyns in the book; no Eliza Shaeffer. Ladley appears more cheerful since Bronson's visit. He has bought all the evening papers and is searching for something. Has not found it.

7:00—Ate well. Have asked Mrs. P. to take my place here, while I interview the six Llewellyns.

11:00—Mrs. P. reports a quiet evening. He read and smoked. Has gone to bed. Light burning. Saw five Llewellyns. None of them knew Bronson or Ladley. Sixth—a lawyer—out at revival meeting. Went to the church and walked home with him. He knows something. Acknowledged he knew Bronson. Had met Ladley. Did not believe Mrs. Ladley dead. Regretted I had not been to the meeting. Good sermon. Asked me for a dollar for missions.

9:00 A.M.—Sunday. Ladley in bad shape. Apparently been drinking all night. Can not eat. Sent out early for papers, and has searched them all. Found entry on second page, stared at it, then flung the paper away. Have sent out for same paper.

10:00 A.M.—Paper says: "Body of woman washed ashore yesterday at Sewickley. Much mutilated by flood débris." Ladley in bed, staring at ceiling. Wonder if he sees tube? He is ghastly.

That is the last entry in the note-book for that day. Mr. Holcombe called me in great excitement shortly after ten and showed me the item. Neither of us doubted for a moment that it was Jennie Brice who had been found. He started for Sewickley that same afternoon, and he probably communicated with the police before he left. For once or twice I saw Mr. Graves, the detective, sauntering past the house.

Mr. Ladley ate no dinner. He went out at four, and I had Mr. Reynolds follow him. But they were both back in a half-hour. Mr. Reynolds reported that Mr. Ladley had bought some headache tablets and some bromide powders to make him sleep.

Mr. Holcombe came back that evening. He thought the body was that of Jennie Brice, but the head was gone. He was much depressed, and did not immediately go back to the periscope. I asked if the head had been cut off or taken off by a steamer; he was afraid the latter, as a hand was gone, too.

It was about eleven o'clock that night that the door-bell rang. It was Mr. Graves, with a small man behind him. I knew the man; he lived in a shanty-boat not far from my house—a curious affair with shelves full of dishes and tinware. In the spring he would be towed up the Monongahela a hundred miles or so and float down, tying up at different landings and selling his wares. Timothy Senft was his name. We called him Tim.

Mr. Graves motioned me to be quiet. Both of us knew that behind the parlor door Ladley was probably listening.

"Sorry to get you up, Mrs. Pitman," said Mr. Graves, "but this man says he bought beer here today. That won't do, Mrs. Pitman."

"Beer! I haven't such a thing in the house. Come in and look," I snapped. And the two of them went back to the kitchen.

"Now," said Mr. Graves, when I had shut the door, "where's the dog's-meat man?"

"Up-stairs."

"Bring him quietly."

I called Mr. Holcombe, and he came eagerly, note-book and all. "Ah!" he said, when he saw Tim. "So you've turned up!"

"Yes, sir."

"It seems, Mr. Dog's—Mr. Holcombe," said Mr. Graves, "that you are right, partly, anyhow. Tim here *did* help a man with a boat that night—"

"Threw him a rope, sir," Tim broke in. "He'd got out in the current, and what with the ice, and his not knowing much about a boat, he'd have kept on to New Orleans if I hadn't caught him—or Kingdom Come."

"Exactly. And what time did you say this was?"

"Between three and four Sunday night—or Monday morning. He said he couldn't sleep and went out in a boat, meaning to keep in close to shore. But he got drawn out in the current."

"Where did you see him first?"

"By the Ninth Street bridge."

"Did you hail him?"

"He saw my light and hailed me. I was making fast to a coal barge after one of my ropes had busted."

"You threw the line to him there?"

"No, sir. He tried to work in to shore. I ran along River Avenue to below the Sixth Street bridge. He got pretty close in there and I threw him a rope. He was about done up."

"Would you know him again?"

"Yes, sir. He gave me five dollars, and said to say nothing about it. He didn't want anybody to know he had been such a fool."

They took him quietly up stairs then and let him look through the periscope. *He identified Mr. Ladley absolutely.*

When Tim and Mr. Graves had gone, Mr. Holcombe and I were left alone in the kitchen. Mr. Holcombe leaned over and patted Peter as he lay in his basket.

"We've got him, old boy," he said. "The chain is just about complete. He'll never kick you again."

But Mr. Holcombe was wrong, not about kicking Peter,—although I don't believe Mr. Ladley ever did that again,—but in thinking we had him.

I washed that next morning, Monday, but all the time I was rubbing and starching and hanging out, my mind was with Jennie Brice. The sight of Molly Maguire, next door, at the window, rubbing and brushing at the fur coat, only made things worse.

At noon when the Maguire youngsters came home from school, I bribed Tommy, the youngest, into the kitchen, with the promise of a doughnut.

"I see your mother has a new fur coat," I said, with the plate of doughnuts just beyond his reach.

"Yes'm."

"She didn't buy it?"

"She didn't buy it. Say, Mrs. Pitman, gimme that doughnut."

"Oh, so the coat washed in!"

"No'm. Pap found it, down by the Point, on a cake of ice. He thought it was a dog, and rowed out for it."

Well, I hadn't wanted the coat, as far as that goes; I'd managed well enough without furs for twenty years or more. But it was a satisfaction to know that it had not floated into Mrs. Maguire's kitchen and spread itself at her feet, as one may say. However, that was not the question, after all. The real issue was that if it was

Jennie Brice's coat, and was found across the river on a cake of ice, then one of two things was certain: either Jennie Brice's body wrapped in the coat had been thrown into the water, out in the current, or she herself, hoping to incriminate her husband, had flung her coat into the river.

I told Mr. Holcombe, and he interviewed Joe Maguire that afternoon. The upshot of it was that Tommy had been correctly informed. Joe had witnesses who had lined up to see him rescue a dog, and had beheld his return in triumph with a wet and soggy fur coat. At three o'clock Mrs. Maguire, instructed by Mr. Graves, brought the coat to me for identification, turning it about for my inspection, but refusing to take her hands off it.

"If her husband says to me that he wants it back, well and good," she said, "but I don't give it up to nobody but him. Some folks I know of would be glad enough to have it."

I was certain it was Jennie Brice's coat, but the maker's name had been ripped out. With Molly holding one arm and I the other, we took it to Mr. Ladley's door and knocked. He opened it, grumbling.

"I have asked you not to interrupt me," he said, with his pen in his hand. His eyes fell on the coat. "What's that?" he asked, changing color.

"I think it's Mrs. Ladley's fur coat," I said.

He stood there looking at it and thinking. Then: "It can't be hers," he said. "She wore hers when she went away."

"Perhaps she dropped it in the water."

He looked at me and smiled. "And why would she do that?" he asked mockingly. "Was it out of fashion?"

"That's Mrs. Ladley's coat," I persisted, but Molly Maguire jerked it from me and started away. He stood there looking at me and smiling in his nasty way.

"This excitement is telling on you, Mrs. Pitman," he said coolly. "You're too emotional for detective work." Then he went in and shut the door.

When I went down-stairs, Molly Maguire was waiting in the kitchen, and had the audacity to ask me if I thought the coat needed a new lining!

It was on Monday evening that the strangest event in years happened to me. I went to my sister's house! And the fact that I was admitted at a side entrance made it even stranger. It happened in this way:

Supper was over, and I was cleaning up, when an automobile came to the door. It was Alma's car. The chauffeur gave me a note:

> *"DEAR MRS PITMAN—I am not at all well, and very anxious. Will you come to see me at once? My mother is out to dinner, and I am alone. The car will bring you. Cordially,*
> *"LIDA HARVEY."*

I put on my best dress at once and got into the limousine. Half the neighborhood was out watching. I leaned back in the upholstered seat, fairly quivering with excitement. This was Alma's car; that was Alma's card-case; the little clock had her monogram on it. Even the flowers in the flower holder, yellow tulips, reminded me of Alma—a trifle showy, but good to look at! And I was going to her house!

I was not taken to the main entrance, but to a side door. The queer dream-like feeling was still there. In this back hall, relegated from the more conspicuous part of the house, there were even pieces of furniture from the old home, and my father's picture, in an oval gilt frame, hung over my head. I had not seen a picture of him for twenty years. I went over and touched it gently.

"Father, father!" I said.

Under it was the tall hall chair that I had climbed over as a child, and had stood on many times, to see myself in the mirror above. The chair was newly finished and looked the better for its age. I glanced in the old glass. The chair had stood time better than I. I was a middle-aged woman, lined with poverty and care, shabby, prematurely gray, a little hard. I had thought my father an old man when that picture was taken, and now I was even older. "Father!" I whispered again, and fell to crying in the dimly lighted hall.

Lida sent for me at once. I had only time to dry my eyes and straighten my hat. Had I met Alma on the stairs, I would have passed without a word. She wouldn't have known me. But I saw no one.

Lida was in bed. She was lying there with a rose-shaded lamp beside her, and a great bowl of spring flowers on a little stand at her elbow. She sat up when I went in, and had a maid place a chair for me beside the bed. She looked very childish, with her hair in a braid on the pillow, and her slim young arms and throat bare.

"I'm so glad you came!" she said, and would not be satisfied until the light was just right for my eyes, and my coat unfastened and thrown open.

"I'm not really ill," she informed me. "I'm—I'm just tired and nervous, and—and unhappy, Mrs. Pitman."

"I am sorry," I said. I wanted to lean over and pat her hand, to draw the covers around her and mother her a little,—I had had no one to mother for so long,—but I could not. She would have thought it queer and presumptuous—or no, not that. She was too sweet to have thought that.

"Mrs. Pitman," she said suddenly, "*who was* this Jennie Brice?"

"She was an actress. She and her husband lived at my house."

"Was she—was she beautiful?"

"Well," I said slowly, "I never thought of that. She was handsome, in a large way."

"Was she young?"

"Yes. Twenty-eight or so."

"That isn't very young," she said, looking relieved. "But I don't think men like very young women. Do you?"

"I know one who does," I said, smiling. But she sat up in bed suddenly and looked at me with her clear childish eyes.

"I don't want him to like me!" she flashed. "I—I want him to hate me."

"Tut, tut! You want nothing of the sort."

"Mrs. Pitman," she said, "I sent for you because I'm nearly crazy. Mr. Howell was a friend of that woman. He has acted like a maniac since she disappeared. He doesn't come to see me, he has given up his work on the paper, and I saw him to-day on the street—he looks like a ghost."

That put me to thinking.

"He might have been a friend," I admitted. "Although, as far as I know, he was never at the house but once, and then he saw both of them."

"When was that?"

She sat up in bed suddenly.

"Sunday morning, the day before she disappeared. They were arguing something."

She was looking at me attentively. "You know more than you are telling me, Mrs. Pitman," she said. "You—do you think Jennie Brice is dead, and that Mr. Howell knows—who did it?"

"I think she is dead, and I think possibly Mr. Howell suspects who did it. He does not *know*, or he would have told the police."

"You don't think he was—in love with Jennie Brice, do you?"

"I'm certain of that," I said. "He is very much in love with a foolish girl, who ought to have more faith in him than she has."

She colored a little, and smiled at that, but the next moment she was sitting forward, tense and questioning again.

"If that is true, Mrs. Pitman," she said, "who was the veiled woman he met that Monday morning at daylight, and took across the bridge to Pittsburgh? I believe it was Jennie Brice. If it was not, who was it?"

"I don't believe he took any woman across the bridge at that hour. Who says he did?"

"Uncle Jim saw him. He had been playing cards all night at one of the clubs, and was walking home. He says he met Mr. Howell and spoke to him. The woman was tall and veiled. Uncle Jim sent for him, a day or two later, and he refused to explain. Then they forbade him the house. Mama objected to him, anyhow, and he only came on sufferance. He is a college man of good family, but without any money at all save what he earns. And now—"

I had had some young newspaper men with me, and I knew what they got. They were nice boys, but they made fifteen dollars a week. I'm afraid I smiled a little as I looked around the room, with its gray grass-cloth walls, its toilet-table spread with ivory and gold, and the maid in attendance in her black dress and white apron, collar and cuffs. Even the little nightgown Lida was wearing would have taken a week's salary or more. She saw my smile.

"It was to be his chance," she said. "If he made good, he was to have something better. My Uncle Jim owns the paper, and he promised me to help him. But—"

So Jim was running a newspaper! That was a curious career for Jim to choose. Jim, who was twice expelled from school, and who could never write a letter without a dictionary beside him! I had a pang when I heard his name again, after all the years. For I had written to Jim from Oklahoma, after Mr. Pitman died, asking for money to bury him, and had never even had a reply.

"And you haven't seen him since?"

"Once. I—didn't hear from him, and I called him up. We—we met in the park. He said everything was all right, but he couldn't tell me just then. The next day he resigned from the paper and went away. Mrs. Pitman, it's driving me crazy! For they have found a body, and they think it is hers. If it is, and he was with her—"

"Don't be a foolish girl," I protested. "If he was with Jennie Brice, she is still living, and if he was *not* with Jennie Brice—"

"If it was *not* Jennie Brice, then I have a right to know who it was," she declared. "He was not like himself when I met him. He said such queer things: he talked about an onyx clock, and said he had been made a fool of, and that no matter what came out, I was always to remember that he had done what he did for the best, and that—that he cared for me more than for anything in this world or the next."

"That wasn't so foolish!" I couldn't help it; I leaned over and drew her nightgown up over her bare white shoulder. "You won't help anything or anybody by taking cold, my dear," I said. "Call your maid and have her put a dressing-gown around you."

I left soon after. There was little I could do. But I comforted her as best I could, and said good night. My heart was heavy as I went down the stairs. For, twist things as I might, it was clear that in some way the Howell boy was mixed up in the Brice case. Poor little troubled Lida! Poor distracted boy!

I had a curious experience down-stairs. I had reached the foot of the staircase and was turning to go back and along the hall to the side entrance, when I came face to face with Isaac, the old colored man who had driven the family carriage when I was a child, and whom I had seen, at intervals since I came back, pottering around Alma's house. The old man was bent and feeble; he came slowly down the hall, with a bunch of keys in his hand. I had seen him do the same thing many times.

He stopped when he saw me, and I shrank back from the light, but he had seen me. "Miss Bess!" he said. "Foh Gawd's sake, Miss Bess!"

"You are making a mistake, my friend," I said, quivering. "I am not 'Miss Bess'!"

He came close and stared into my face. And from that he looked at my cloth gloves, at my coat, and he shook his white head. "I sure thought you was Miss Bess," he said, and made no further effort to detain me. He led the way back to the door where the machine waited, his head shaking with the palsy of age, muttering as he went. He opened the door with his best manner, and stood aside.

"Good night, ma'am," he quavered.

I had tears in my eyes. I tried to keep them back. "Good night," I said. "Good night, *Ikkie*."

It had slipped out, my baby name for old Isaac!

"Miss Bess!" he cried. "Oh, praise Gawd, it's Miss Bess again!"

He caught my arm and pulled me back into the hall, and there he held me, crying over me, muttering praises for my return, begging me to come back, recalling little tender things out of the past that almost killed me to hear again.

But I had made my bed and must lie in it. I forced him to swear silence about my visit; I made him promise not to reveal my identity to Lida; and I told him—Heaven forgive me!—that I was well and prosperous and happy.

Dear old Isaac! I would not let him come to see me, but the next day there came a basket, with six bottles of wine, and an old daguerreotype of my mother, that had been his treasure. Nor was that basket the last.

CHAPTER NINE
The Curious Scar

The coroner held an inquest over the headless body the next day, Tuesday. Mr. Graves telephoned me in the morning, and I went to the morgue with him.

I do not like the morgue, although some of my neighbors pay it weekly visits. It is by way of excursion, like nickelodeons or watching the circus put up its tents. I have heard them threaten the children that if they misbehaved they would not be taken to the morgue that week!

I failed to identify the body. How could I? It had been a tall woman, probably five feet eight, and I thought the nails looked like those of Jennie Brice. The thumb-nail of one was broken short off. I told Mr. Graves about her speaking of a broken nail, but he shrugged his shoulders and said nothing.

There was a curious scar over the heart, and he was making a sketch of it. It reached from the center of the chest for about six inches across the left breast, a narrow thin line that one could hardly see. It was shaped like this:

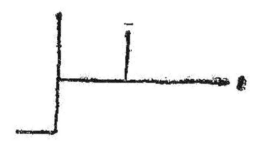

I felt sure that Jennie Brice had had no such scar, and Mr. Graves thought as I did. Temple Hope, called to the inquest, said she had never heard of one, and Mr. Ladley himself, at the inquest, swore that his wife had had nothing of the sort. I was watching him, and I did not think he was lying. And yet—the hand was very like Jennie Brice's. It was all bewildering.

Mr. Ladley's testimoney at the inquest was disappointing. He was cool and collected: said he had no reason to believe that his wife was dead, and less reason to think she had been drowned; she had left him in a rage, and if she found out that by hiding she was putting him in an unpleasant position, she would probably hide indefinitely.

To the disappointment of everybody, the identity of the woman remained a mystery. No one with such a scar was missing. A small woman of my own age, a Mrs. Murray, whose daughter, a stenographer, had disappeared, attended the inquest. But her daughter had had no such scar, and had worn her nails short, because of using the typewriter. Alice Murray was the missing girl's name. Her mother sat beside me, and cried most of the time.

One thing was brought out at the inquest: the body had been thrown into the river *after* death. There was no water in the lungs. The verdict was "death by the hands of some person or persons unknown."

Mr. Holcombe was not satisfied. In some way or other he had got permission to attend the autopsy, and had brought away a tracing of the scar. All the way home in the street-car he stared at the drawing, holding first one eye shut and then the other. But, like the coroner, he got nowhere. He folded the paper and put it in his note-book.

"None the less, Mrs. Pitman," he said, "that is the body of Jennie Brice; her husband killed her, probably by strangling her; he took the body out in the boat and dropped it into the swollen river above the Ninth Street bridge."

"Why do you think he strangled her?"

"There was no mark on the body, and no poison was found."

"Then if he strangled her, where did the blood come from?"

"I didn't limit myself to strangulation," he said irritably. "He may have cut her throat."

"Or brained her with my onyx clock," I added with a sigh. For I missed the clock more and more.

He went down in his pockets and brought up a key. "I'd forgotten this," he said. "It shows you were right—that the clock was there when the Ladleys took the room. I found this in the yard this morning."

It was when I got home from the inquest that I found old Isaac's basket waiting. I am not a crying woman, but I could hardly see my mother's picture for tears.—Well, after all, that is not the Brice story. I am not writing the sordid tragedy of my life.

That was on Tuesday. Jennie Brice had been missing nine days. In all that time, although she was cast for the piece at the theater that week, no one there had heard from her. Her relatives had had no word. She had gone away, if she had gone, on a cold March night, in a striped black and white dress with a red collar, and a red and black hat, without her fur coat, which she had worn all winter. She had gone very early in the morning, or during the night. How had she gone? Mr. Ladley said he had rowed her to Federal Street at half after six and had brought the boat back. After they had quarreled violently all night, and when she was leaving him, wouldn't he have allowed her to take herself away? Besides, the police had found no trace of her on an early train. And then at daylight, between five and six, my own brother had seen a woman with Mr. Howell, a woman who might have been Jennie Brice. But if it was, why did not Mr. Howell say so?

Mr. Ladley claimed she was hiding, in revenge. But Jennie Brice was not that sort of woman; there was something big about her, something that is found often in large women—a lack of spite. She was not petty or malicious. Her faults, like her virtues, were for all to see.

In spite of the failure to identify the body, Mr. Ladley was arrested that night, Tuesday, and this time it was for murder. I know now that the police were taking long chances. They had no strong motive for the crime. As Mr. Holcombe said, they had provocation, but not motive, which is different. They had opportunity, and they had a lot of straggling links of clues, which in the total made a fair chain of circumstantial evidence. But that was all.

That is the way the case stood on Tuesday night, March the thirteenth.

Mr. Ladley was taken away at nine o'clock. He was perfectly cool, asked me to help him pack a suit case, and whistled while it was being done. He requested to be allowed to walk to the jail, and went quietly, with a detective on one side and I think a sheriff's officer on the other.

Just before he left, he asked for a word or two with me, and when he paid his bill up to date, and gave me an extra dollar for taking care of Peter, I was almost overcome. He took the manuscript of his play with him, and I remember his asking if he could have any typing done in the jail. I had never seen a man arrested for murder before, but I think he was probably the coolest suspect the officers had ever seen. They hardly knew what to make of it.

Mr. Reynolds and I had a cup of tea after all the excitement, and were sitting at the dining-room table drinking it, when the bell rang. It was Mr. Howell! He half staggered into the hall when I opened the door, and was for going into the parlor bedroom without a word.

"Mr. Ladley's gone, if you want him," I said. I thought his face cleared.

"Gone!" he said. "Where?"

"To jail."

He did not reply at once. He stood there, tapping the palm of one hand with the forefinger of the other. He was dirty and unshaven. His clothes looked as if he had been sleeping in them.

"So they've got him!" he muttered finally, and turning, was about to go out the front door without another word, but I caught his arm.

"You're sick, Mr. Howell," I said. "You'd better not go out yet."

"Oh, I'm all right." He took his handkerchief out and wiped his face. I saw that his hands were shaking.

"Come back and have a cup of tea, and a slice of home-made bread."

He hesitated and looked at his watch. "I'll do it, Mrs. Pitman," he said. "I suppose I'd better throw a little fuel into this engine of mine. It's been going hard for several days."

He ate like a wolf. I cut half a loaf into slices for him, and he drank the rest of the tea. Mr. Reynolds creaked up to bed and left him still eating, and me still cutting and spreading. Now that I had a chance to see him, I was shocked. The rims of his eyes were red, his collar was black, and his hair hung over his forehead. But when he finally sat back and looked at me, his color was better.

"So they've canned him!" he said.

"Time enough, too," said I.

He leaned forward and put both his elbows on the table. "Mrs. Pitman," he said earnestly, "I don't like him any more than you do. But he never killed that woman."

"Somebody killed her."

"How do you know? How do you know she is dead?"

Well, I didn't, of course—I only felt it.

"The police haven't even proved a crime. They can't hold a man for a supposititious murder."

"Perhaps they can't but they're doing it," I retorted. "If the woman's alive, she won't let him hang."

"I'm not so sure of that," he said heavily, and got up. He looked in the little mirror over the sideboard, and brushed back his hair. "I look bad enough," he said, "but I feel worse. Well, you've saved my life, Mrs. Pitman. Thank you."

"How is my—how is Miss Harvey?" I asked, as we started out. He turned and smiled at me in his boyish way.

"The best ever!" he said. "I haven't seen her for days, and it seems like centuries. She—she is the only girl in the world for me, Mrs. Pitman, although I—" He stopped and drew a long breath. "She is beautiful, isn't she?"

"Very beautiful," I answered "Her mother was always—"

"Her mother!" He looked at me curiously.

"I knew her mother years ago," I said, putting the best face on my mistake that I could.

"Then I'll remember you to her, if she ever allows me to see her again. Just now I'm *persona non grata*."

"If you'll do the kindly thing, Mr. Howell," I said, "you'll *forget* me to her."

He looked into my eyes and then thrust out his hand.

"All right," he said. "I'll not ask any questions. I guess there are some curious stories hidden in these old houses."

Peter hobbled to the front door with him. He had not gone so far as the parlor once while Mr. Ladley was in the house.

They had had a sale of spring flowers at the store that day, and Mr. Reynolds had brought me a pot of white tulips. That night I hung my mother's picture over the mantel in the dining-room, and put the tulips beneath it. It gave me a feeling of comfort; I had never seen my mother's grave, or put flowers on it.

CHAPTER TEN
Eliza Shaeffer Appears

I have said before that I do not know anything about the law. I believe that the Ladley case was unusual, in several ways. Mr. Ladley had once been well known in New York among the people who frequent the theaters, and Jennie Brice was even better known. A good many lawyers, I believe, said that the police had not a leg to stand on, and I know the case was watched with much interest by the legal profession. People wrote letters to the newspapers, protesting against Mr. Ladley being held. And I believe that the district attorney, in taking him before the grand jury, hardly hoped to make a case.

But he did, to his own surprise, I fancy, and the trial was set for May. But in the meantime, many curious things happened.

In the first place, the week following Mr. Ladley's arrest my house was filled up with eight or ten members of a company from the Gaiety Theater, very cheerful and jolly, and well behaved. Three men, I think, and the rest girls. One of the men was named Bellows, John Bellows, and it turned out that he had known Jennie Brice very well.

From the moment he learned that, Mr. Holcombe hardly left him. He walked to the theater with him and waited to walk home again. He took him out to restaurants and for long street car rides in the mornings, and on the last night of their stay, Saturday, they got gloriously drunk together—Mr. Holcombe, no doubt, in his character of Ladley—and came reeling in at three in the morning, singing. Mr. Holcombe was very sick the next day, but by Monday he was all right, and he called me into the room.

"We've got him, Mrs. Pitman," he said, looking mottled but cheerful. "As sure as God made little fishes, we've got him." That was all he would say, however. It seemed he was going to New York, and might be gone for a month. "I've no family," he said, "and enough money to keep me. If I find my relaxation in hunting down criminals, it's a harmless and cheap amusement, and—it's my own business."

He went away that night, and I must admit I missed him. I rented the parlor bedroom the next day to a school-teacher, and I found the periscope affair very handy. I could see just how much gas she used; and although the notice on each door forbids cooking and washing in rooms, I found she was doing both: making coffee and boiling an egg in the morning, and rubbing out stockings and handkerchiefs in her wash-bowl. I'd much rather have men as boarders than women. The women are always lighting alcohol lamps on the bureau, and wanting the bed turned into a cozy corner so they can see their gentlemen friends in their rooms.

Well, with Mr. Holcombe gone, and Mr. Reynolds busy all day and half the night getting out the summer silks and preparing for remnant day, and with Mr. Ladley in jail and Lida out of the city—

for I saw in the papers that she was not well, and her mother had taken her to Bermuda—I had a good bit of time on my hands. And so I got in the habit of thinking things over, and trying to draw conclusions, as I had seen Mr. Holcombe do. I would sit down and write things out as they had happened, and study them over, and especially I worried over how we could have found a slip of paper in Mr. Ladley's room with a list, almost exact, of the things we had discovered there. I used to read it over, "rope, knife, shoe, towel, Horn—" and get more and more bewildered. "Horn"—might have been a town, or it might not have been. There *was* such a town, according to Mr. Graves, but apparently he had made nothing of it. *Was* it a town that was meant?

The dictionary gave only a few words beginning with "horn"—hornet, hornblende, hornpipe, and horny—none of which was of any assistance. And then one morning I happened to see in the personal column of one of the newspapers that a woman named Eliza Shaeffer, of Horner, had day-old Buff Orpington and Plymouth Rock chicks for sale, and it started me to puzzling again. Perhaps it had been Horner, and possibly this very Eliza Shaeffer—

I suppose my lack of experience was in my favor, for, after all, Eliza Shaeffer is a common enough name, and the "Horn" might have stood for "hornswoggle," for all I knew. The story of the man who thought of what he would do if he were a horse, came back to me, and for an hour or so I tried to think I was Jennie Brice, trying to get away and hide from my rascal of a husband. But I made no headway. I would never have gone to Horner, or to any small town, if I had wanted to hide. I think I should have gone around the corner and taken a room in my own neighborhood, or have lost myself in some large city.

It was that same day that, since I did not go to Horner, Horner came to me. The bell rang about three o'clock, and I answered it myself. For, with times hard and only two or three roomers all winter, I had not had a servant, except Terry to do odd jobs, for some months.

There stood a fresh-faced young girl, with a covered basket in her hand.

"Are you Mrs. Pitman?" she asked.

"I don't need anything to-day," I said, trying to shut the door. And at that minute something in the basket cheeped. Young women selling poultry are not common in our neighborhood. "What have you there?" I asked more agreeably.

"Chicks, day-old chicks, but I'm not trying to sell you any. I—may I come in?"

It was dawning on me then that perhaps this was Eliza Shaeffer. I led her back to the dining-room, with Peter sniffing at the basket.

"My name is Shaeffer," she said. "I've seen your name in the papers, and I believe I know something about Jennie Brice."

Eliza Shaeffer's story was curious. She said that she was postmistress at Horner, and lived with her mother on a farm a mile out of the town, driving in and out each day in a buggy.

On Monday afternoon, March the fifth, a woman had alighted at the station from a train, and had taken luncheon at the hotel. She told the clerk she was on the road, selling corsets, and was much disappointed to find no store of any size in the town. The woman, who had registered as Mrs. Jane Bellows, said she was tired and would like to rest for a day or two on a farm. She was told to see Eliza Shaeffer at the post-office, and, as a result, drove out with her to the farm after the last mail came in that evening.

Asked to describe her—she was over medium height, light-haired, quick in her movements, and wore a black and white striped dress with a red collar, and a hat to match. She carried a small brown valise that Miss Shaeffer presumed contained her samples.

Mrs. Shaeffer had made her welcome, although they did not usually take boarders until June. She had not eaten much supper, and that night she had asked for pen and ink, and had written a letter. The letter was not mailed until Wednesday. All of Tuesday Mrs. Bellows had spent in her room, and Mrs. Shaeffer had driven to the village in the afternoon with word that she had been crying all day, and bought some headache medicine for her.

On Wednesday morning, however, she had appeared at breakfast, eaten heartily, and had asked Miss Shaeffer to take her letter to the post-office. It was addressed to Mr. Ellis Howell, in care of a Pittsburgh newspaper!

That night when Miss Eliza went home, about half past eight, the woman was gone. She had paid for her room and had been driven as far as Thornville, where all trace of her had been lost. On account of the disappearance of Jennie Brice being published shortly after that, she and her mother had driven to Thornville, but the station agent there was surly as well as stupid. They had learned nothing about the woman.

Since that time, three men had made inquiries about the woman in question. One had a pointed Vandyke beard; the second, from the description, I fancied must have been Mr. Graves. The third without doubt was Mr. Howell. Eliza Shaeffer said that this last man had seemed half frantic. I brought her a photograph of Jennie Brice as "Topsy" and another one as "Juliet". She said there was a resemblance, but that it ended there. But of course, as Mr. Graves had said, by the time an actress gets her photograph retouched to suit her, it doesn't particularly resemble her. And unless I had known Jennie Brice myself, I should hardly have recognized the pictures.

Well, in spite of all that, there seemed no doubt that Jennie Brice had been living three days after her disappearance, and that would clear Mr. Ladley. But what had Mr. Howell to do with it all? Why had he not told the police of the letter from Horner? Or about the woman on the bridge? Why had Mr. Bronson, who was likely the man with the pointed beard, said nothing about having traced Jennie Brice to Horner?

I did as I thought Mr. Holcombe would have wished me to do. I wrote down on a clean sheet of note-paper all that Eliza Shaeffer said: the description of the black and white dress, the woman's height, and the rest, and then I took her to the court-house, chicks and all, and she told her story there to one of the assistant district attorneys.

The young man was interested, but not convinced. He had her story taken down, and she signed it. He was smiling as he bowed us out. I turned in the doorway.

"This will free Mr. Ladley, I suppose?" I asked.

"Not just yet," he said pleasantly. "This makes just eleven places where Jennie Brice spent the first three days after her death."

"But I can positively identify the dress."

"My good lady, that dress has been described, to the last stilted arch and Colonial volute, in every newspaper in the United States!"

That evening the newspapers announced that during a conference at the jail between Mr. Ladley and James Bronson, business manager at the Liberty Theater, Mr. Ladley had attacked Mr. Bronson with a chair, and almost brained him.

CHAPTER ELEVEN
On Trial

Eliza Shaeffer went back to Horner, after delivering her chicks somewhere in the city. Things went on as before. The trial was set for May. The district attorney's office had all the things we had found in the house that Monday afternoon—the stained towel, the broken knife and its blade, the slipper that had been floating in the parlor, and the rope that had fastened my boat to the staircase. Somewhere—wherever they keep such things—was the headless body of a woman with a hand missing, and with a curious scar across the left breast. The slip of paper, however, which I had found behind the base-board, was still in Mr. Holcombe's possession, nor had he mentioned it to the police.

Mr. Holcombe had not come back. He wrote me twice asking me to hold his room, once from New York and once from Chicago. To the second letter he added a postscript:

"Have not found what I wanted, but am getting warm. If any news, address me at Des Moines, Iowa, General Delivery.   H."

It was nearly the end of April when I saw Lida again. I had seen by the newspapers that she and her mother were coming home. I wondered if she had heard from Mr. Howell, for I had not, and I wondered, too, if she would send for me again.

But she came herself, on foot, late one afternoon, and the school-teacher being out, I took her into the parlor bedroom. She looked thinner than before, and rather white. My heart ached for her.

"I have been away," she explained. "I thought you might wonder why you did not hear from me. But, you see, my mother—" she stopped and flushed. "I would have written you from Bermuda, but—my mother watched my correspondence, so I could not."

No. I knew she could not. Alma had once found a letter of mine to Mr. Pitman. Very little escaped Alma.

"I wondered if you have heard anything?" she asked.

"I have heard nothing. Mr. Howell was here once, just after I saw you. I do not believe he is in the city.

"Perhaps not, although—Mrs. Pitman, I believe he is in the city, hiding!"

"Hiding! Why?"

"I don't know. But last night I thought I saw him below my window. I opened the window, so if it were he, he could make some sign. But he moved on without a word. Later, whoever it was came back. I put out my light and watched. Some one stood there, in the shadow, until after two this morning. Part of the time he was looking up."

"Don't you think, had it been he, he would have spoken when he saw you?"

She shook her head. "He is in trouble," she said. "He has not heard from me, and he—thinks I don't care any more. Just look at me, Mrs. Pitman! Do I look as if I don't care?"

She looked half killed, poor lamb.

"He may be out of town, searching for a better position," I tried to comfort her. "He wants to have something to offer more than himself."

"I only want him," she said, looking at me frankly. "I don't know why I tell you all this, but you are so kind, and I *must* talk to some one."

She sat there, in the cozy corner the school-teacher had made with a portière and some cushions, and I saw she was about ready to break down and cry. I went over to her and took her hand, for she was my own niece, although she didn't suspect it, and I had never had a child of my own.

But after all, I could not help her much. I could only assure her that he would come back and explain everything, and that he was all right, and that the last time I had seen him he had spoken of her, and had said she was "the best ever." My heart fairly yearned over the girl, and I think she felt it. For she kissed me, shyly, when she was leaving.

With the newspaper files before me, it is not hard to give the details of that sensational trial. It commenced on Monday, the seventh of May, but it was late Wednesday when the jury was finally selected. I was at the court-house early on Thursday, and so was Mr. Reynolds.

The district attorney made a short speech. "We propose, gentlemen, to prove that the prisoner, Philip Ladley, murdered his wife," he said in part. "We will show first that a crime was committed; then we will show a motive for this crime, and, finally, we expect to show that the body washed ashore at Sewickley is the body of the murdered woman, and thus establish beyond doubt the prisoner's guilt."

Mr. Ladley listened with attention. He wore the brown suit, and looked well and cheerful. He was much more like a spectator than a prisoner, and he was not so nervous as I was.

Of that first day I do not recall much. I was called early in the day. The district attorney questioned me.

"Your name?"

"Elizabeth Marie Pitman."

"Your occupation?"

"I keep a boarding-house at 42 Union Street."

"You know the prisoner?"

"Yes. He was a boarder in my house."

"For how long?"

"From December first. He and his wife came at that time."

"Was his wife the actress, Jennie Brice?"

"Yes, sir."

"Were they living together at your house the night of March fourth?"

"Yes, sir."

"In what part of the house?"

"They rented the double parlors down-stairs, but on account of the flood I moved them up-stairs to the second floor front."

"That was on Sunday? You moved them on Sunday?"

"Yes, sir."

"At what time did you retire that night?"

"Not at all. The water was very high. I lay down, dressed, at one o'clock, and dropped into a doze."

"How long did you sleep?"

"An hour or so. Mr. Reynolds, a boarder, roused me to say he had heard some one rowing a boat in the lower hall."

"Do you keep a boat around during flood times?"

"Yes, sir."

"What did you do when Mr. Reynolds roused you?"

"I went to the top of the stairs. My boat was gone."

"Was the boat secured?"

"Yes, sir. Anyhow, there was no current in the hall."

"What did you do then?"

"I waited a time and went back to my room."

"What examination of the house did you make—if any?"

"Mr. Reynolds looked around."

"What did he find?"

"He found Peter, the Ladleys' dog, shut in a room on the third floor."

"Was there anything unusual about that?"

"I had never known it to happen before."

"State what happened later."

"I did not go to sleep again. At a quarter after four, I heard the boat come back. I took a candle and went to the stairs. It was Mr. Ladley. He said he had been out getting medicine for his wife."

"Did you see him tie up the boat?"

"Yes."

"Did you observe any stains on the rope?"

"I did not notice any."

"What was the prisoner's manner at that time?"

"I thought he was surly."

"Now, Mrs. Pitman, tell us about the following morning."

"I saw Mr. Ladley at a quarter before seven. He said to bring breakfast for one. His wife had gone away. I asked if she was not ill, and he said no; that she had gone away early; that he had rowed her to Federal Street, and that she would be back Saturday. It was shortly after that that the dog Peter brought in one of Mrs. Ladley's slippers, water-soaked."

"You recognized the slipper?"

"Positively. I had seen it often."

"What did you do with it?"

"I took it to Mr. Ladley."

"What did he say?"

"He said at first that it was not hers. Then he said if it was, she would never wear it again—and then added—because it was ruined."

"Did he offer any statement as to where his wife was?"

"No, sir. Not at that time. Before, he had said she had gone away for a few days."

"Tell the jury about the broken knife."

"The dog found it floating in the parlor, with the blade broken."

"You had not left it down-stairs?"

"No, sir. I had used it up-stairs, the night before, and left it on a mantel of the room I was using as a temporary kitchen."

"Was the door of this room locked?"

"No. It was standing open."

"Were you not asleep in this room?"

"Yes."

"You heard no one come in?"

"No one—until Mr. Reynolds roused me."

"Where did you find the blade?"

"Behind the bed in Mr. Ladley's room."

"What else did you find in the room?"

"A blood-stained towel behind the wash-stand. Also, my onyx clock was missing."

"Where was the clock when the Ladleys were moved up into this room?"

"On the mantel. I wound it just before they came up-stairs."

"When you saw Mrs. Ladley on Sunday, did she say she was going away?"

"No, sir."

"Did you see any preparation for a journey?"

"The black and white dress was laid out on the bed, and a small bag. She said she was taking the dress to the theater to lend to Miss Hope."

"Is that all she said?"

"No. She said she'd been wishing her husband would drown; that he was a fiend."

I could see that my testimony had made an impression.

CHAPTER TWELVE
The Pair of Bellows

The slipper, the rope, the towel, and the knife and blade were produced in court, and I identified them all. They made a noticeable impression on the jury. Then Mr. Llewellyn, the lawyer for the defense, cross-examined me.

"Is it not true, Mrs. Pitman," he said, "that many articles, particularly shoes and slippers, are found floating around during a flood?"

"Yes," I admitted.

"Now, you say the dog found this slipper floating in the hall and brought it to you. Are you sure this slipper belonged to Jennie Brice?"

"She wore it. I presume it belonged to her."

"Ahem. Now, Mrs. Pitman, after the Ladleys had been moved to the upper floor, did you search their bedroom and the connecting room down-stairs?"

"No, sir."

"Ah. Then, how do you know that this slipper was not left on the floor or in a closet?"

"It is possible, but not likely. Anyhow, it was not the slipper alone. It was the other things *and* the slipper. It was—"

"Exactly. Now, Mrs. Pitman, this knife. Can you identify it positively?"

"I can."

"But isn't it true that this is a very common sort of knife? One that nearly every housewife has in her possession?"

"Yes, sir. But that knife handle has three notches in it. I put the notches there myself."

"Before this presumed crime?"

"Yes, sir."

"For what purpose?"

"My neighbors were constantly borrowing things. It was a means of identification."

"Then this knife is yours?"

"Yes."

"Tell again where you left it the night before it was found floating down-stairs."

"On a shelf over the stove."

"Could the dog have reached it there?"

"Not without standing on a hot stove."

"Is it not possible that Mr. Ladley, unable to untie the boat, borrowed your knife to cut the boat's painter?"

"No painter was cut that I heard about The paper-hanger—"

"No, no. The boat's painter—the rope."

"Oh! Well, he might have. He never said."

"Now then, this towel, Mrs. Pitman. Did not the prisoner, on the following day, tell you that he had cut his wrist in freeing the boat, and ask you for some court-plaster?"

"He did not," I said firmly.

"You have not seen a scar on his wrist?"

"No." I glanced at Mr. Ladley: he was smiling, as if amused. It made me angry. "And what's more," I flashed, "if he has a cut on his wrist, he put it there himself, to account for the towel."

I was sorry the next moment that I had said it, but it was too late. The counsel for the defense moved to exclude the answer and I received a caution that I deserved. Then:

"You saw Mr. Ladley when he brought your boat back?"

"Yes."

"What time was that?"

"A quarter after four Monday morning."

"Did he come in quietly, like a man trying to avoid attention?"

"Not particularly. It would have been of no use. The dog was barking."

"What did he say?"

"That he had been out for medicine. That his wife was sick."

"Do you know a pharmacist named Alexander—Jonathan Alexander?"

"There is such a one, but I don't know him."

I was excused, and Mr. Reynolds was called. He had heard no quarreling that Sunday night; had even heard Mrs. Ladley laughing. This was about nine o'clock. Yes, they had fought in the afternoon. He had not overheard any words, but their voices were quarrelsome, and once he heard a chair or some article of furniture overthrown. Was awakened about two by footsteps on the stairs, followed by the sound of oars in the lower hall. He told his story plainly and simply. Under cross-examination admitted that he was fond of detective stories and had tried to write one himself; that he had said at the store that he would like to see that "conceited ass" swing, referring to the prisoner; that he had sent flowers to Jennie Brice at the theater, and had made a few advances to her, without success.

My head was going round. I don't know yet how the police learned it all, but by the time poor Mr. Reynolds left the stand, half the people there believed that he had been in love with Jennie Brice, that she had spurned his advances, and that there was more to the story than any of them had suspected.

Miss Hope's story held without any alteration under the cross-examination. She was perfectly at ease, looked handsome and well dressed, and could not be shaken. She told how Jennie Brice had been in fear of her life, and had asked her, only the week before she disappeared, to allow her to go home with her—Miss Hope. She told of the attack of hysteria in her dressing-room, and that the missing woman had said that her husband would kill her some day. There was much wrangling over her testimony, and I believe at least a part of it was not allowed to go to the jury. But I am not a lawyer, and I repeat what I recall.

"Did she say that he had attacked her?"

"Yes, more than once. She was a large woman, fairly muscular, and had always held her own."

"Did she say that these attacks came when he had been drinking?"

"I believe he was worse then."

"Did she give any reason for her husband's attitude to her?"

"She said he wanted to marry another woman."

There was a small sensation at this. If proved, it established a motive.

"Did she know who the other woman was?"

"I believe not. She was away most of the day, and he put in his time as he liked."

"Did Miss Brice ever mention the nature of the threats he made against her?"

"No, I think not."

"Have you examined the body washed ashore at Sewickley?"

"Yes—" in a low voice.

"Is it the body of Jennie Brice?"

"I can not say."

"Does the remaining hand look like the hand of Jennie Brice?"

"Very much. The nails are filed to points, as she wore hers."

"Did you ever know of Jennie Brice having a scar on her breast?"

"No, but that would be easily concealed."

"Just what do you mean?"

"Many actresses conceal defects. She could have worn flesh-colored plaster and covered it with powder. Also, such a scar would not necessarily be seen."

"Explain that."

"Most of Jennie Brice's décolleté gowns were cut to a point. This would conceal such a scar."

Miss Hope was excused, and Jennie Brice's sister from Olean was called. She was a smaller woman than Jennie Brice had been, very lady-like in her manner. She said she was married and living in Olean; she had not seen her sister for several years, but had heard from her often. The witness had discouraged the marriage to the prisoner.

"Why?"

"She had had bad luck before."

"She had been married before?"

"Yes, to a man named John Bellows. They were in vaudeville together, on the Keith Circuit. They were known as The Pair of Bellows."

I sat up at this for John Bellows had boarded at my house.

"Mr. Bellows is dead?"

"I think not. She divorced him."

"Did you know of any scar on your sister's body?"

"I never heard of one."

"Have you seen the body found at Sewickley?"

"Yes"—faintly.

"Can you identify it?"

"No, sir."

A flurry was caused during the afternoon by Timothy Senft. He testified to what I already knew—that between three and four on Monday morning, during the height of the flood, he had seen from his shanty-boat a small skiff caught in the current near the Ninth Street bridge. He had shouted encouragingly to the man in the boat, running out a way on the ice to make him hear. He had told him to row with the current, and to try to steer in toward shore. He had followed close to the river bank in his own boat. Below Sixth Street the other boat was within rope-throwing distance. He had pulled it in, and had towed it well back out of the current. The man in the boat was the prisoner. Asked if the prisoner gave any explanation—yes, he said he couldn't sleep, and had thought to tire himself rowing. Had been caught in the current before he knew it. Saw nothing suspicious in or about the boat. As they passed the police patrol boat, prisoner had called to ask if there was much distress, and expressed regret when told there was.

Tim was excused. He had made a profound impression. I would not have given a dollar for Mr. Ladley's chance with the jury, at that time.

CHAPTER THIRTEEN
The Motive

The prosecution produced many witnesses during the next two days: Shanty-boat Tim's story withstood the most vigorous cross-examination. After him, Mr. Bronson from the theater corroborated Miss Hope's story of Jennie Brice's attack of hysteria in the dressing-room, and told of taking her home that night.

He was a poor witness, nervous and halting. He weighed each word before he said it, and he made a general unfavorable impression. I thought he was holding something back. In view of what Mr. Pitman would have called the denouement, his attitude is easily explained. But I was puzzled then.

So far, the prosecution had touched but lightly on the possible motive for a crime—the woman. But on the third day, to my surprise, a Mrs. Agnes Murray was called. It was the Mrs. Murray I had seen at the morgue.

I have lost the clipping of that day's trial, but I remember her testimony perfectly.

She was a widow, living above a small millinery shop on Federal Street, Allegheny. She had one daughter, Alice, who did stenography and typing as a means of livelihood. She had no office, and worked at home. Many of the small stores in the neighborhood employed her to send out their bills. There was a card at the street entrance beside the shop, and now and then strangers brought her work.

Early in December the prisoner had brought her the manuscript of a play to type, and from that time on he came frequently, sometimes every day, bringing a few sheets of manuscript at a time. Sometimes he came without any manuscript, and would sit and talk while he smoked a cigarette. They had thought him unmarried.

On Wednesday, February twenty-eighth, Alice Murray had disappeared. She had taken some of her clothing—not all, and had left a note. The witness read the note aloud in a trembling voice:

"*DEAR MOTHER: When you get this I shall be married to Mr. Ladley.*

Don't worry. Will write again from N.Y. Lovingly,

"*ALICE.*"

From that time until a week before, she had not heard from her daughter. Then she had a card, mailed from Madison Square Station, New York City. The card merely said:

"*Am well and working. ALICE.*"

The defense was visibly shaken. They had not expected this, and I thought even Mr. Ladley, whose calm had continued unbroken, paled.

So far, all had gone well for the prosecution. They had proved a crime, as nearly as circumstantial evidence could prove a crime, and they had established a motive. But in the identification of the body, so far they had failed. The prosecution "rested," as they say, although they didn't rest much, on the afternoon of the third day.

The defense called, first of all, Eliza Shaeffer. She told of a woman answering the general description of Jennie Brice having spent two days at the Shaeffer farm at Horner. Being shown photographs of Jennie Brice, she said she thought it was the same woman, but was not certain. She told further of the woman leaving unexpectedly on Wednesday of that week from Thornville. On cross-examination, being shown the small photograph which Mr. Graves had shown me, she identified the woman in the group as being the woman in question. As the face was in shadow, knew it more by the dress and hat· she described the black and white dress and the hat with red trimming.

The defense then called me. I had to admit that the dress and hat as described were almost certainly the ones I had seen on the bed in Jennie Brice's room the day before she disappeared. I could not say definitely whether the woman in the photograph was Jennie Brice or not; under a magnifying-glass thought it might be.

Defense called Jonathan Alexander, a druggist who testified that on the night in question he had been roused at half past three by the prisoner, who had said his wife was ill, and had purchased a bottle of a proprietary remedy from him. His identification was absolute.

The defense called Jennie Brice's sister, and endeavored to prove that Jennie Brice had had no such scar. It was shown that she was on intimate terms with her family and would hardly have concealed an operation of any gravity from them.

The defense scored that day. They had shown that the prisoner had told the truth when he said he had gone to a pharmacy for medicine that night for his wife; and they had shown that a woman, answering the description of Jennie Brice, spent two days in a town called Horner, and had gone from there on Wednesday after the crime. And they had shown that this woman was attired as Jennie Brice had been.

That was the way things stood on the afternoon of the fourth day, when court adjourned.

Mr. Reynolds was at home when I got there. He had been very much subdued since the developments of that first day of the trial, sat mostly in his own room, and had twice brought me a bunch of jonquils as a peace-offering. He had the kettle boiling when I got home.

"You have had a number of visitors," he said. "Our young friend Howell has been here, and Mr. Holcombe has arrived and has a man in his room."

Mr. Holcombe came down a moment after, with his face beaming.

"I think we've got him, Mrs. Pitman," he said. "The jury won't even go out of the box."

But further than that he would not explain. He said he had a witness locked in his room, and he'd be glad of supper for him, as they'd both come a long ways. And he went out and bought some oysters and a bottle or two of beer. But as far as I know, he kept him locked up all that night in the second-story front room. I don't think the man knew he was a prisoner. I went in to turn down the bed, and he was sitting by the window, reading the evening paper's account of the trial—an elderly gentleman, rather professional-looking.

Mr. Holcombe slept on the upper landing of the hall that night, rolled in a blanket—not that I think his witness even thought of escaping, but the little man was taking no chances.

At eight o'clock that night the bell rang. It was Mr. Howell. I admitted him myself, and he followed me back to the dining-room. I had not seen him for several weeks, and the change in him startled me. He was dressed carefully, but his eyes were sunken in his head, and he looked as if he had not slept for days.

Mr. Reynolds had gone up-stairs, not finding me socially inclined.

"You haven't been sick, Mr. Howell, have you?" I asked.

"Oh, no, I'm well enough, I've been traveling about. Those infernal sleeping-cars—"

His voice trailed off, and I saw him looking at my mother's picture, with the jonquils beneath.

"That's curious!" he said, going closer. "It—it looks almost like Lida Harvey."

"My mother," I said simply.

"Have you seen her lately?"

"My mother?" I asked, startled.

"No, Lida."

"I saw her a few days ago."

225

"Here?"

"Yes. She came here, Mr. Howell, two weeks ago. She looks badly—as if she is worrying."

"Not—about me?" he asked eagerly.

"Yes, about you. What possessed you to go away as you did? When my—bro—when her uncle accused you of something, you ran away, instead of facing things like a man."

"I was trying to find the one person who could clear me, Mrs. Pitman." He sat back, with his eyes closed; he looked ill enough to be in bed.

"And you succeeded?"

"No."

I thought perhaps he had not been eating and I offered him food, as I had once before. But he refused it, with the ghost of his boyish smile.

"I'm hungry, but it's not food I want. I want to see *her*," he said.

I sat down across from him and tried to mend a table-cloth, but I could not sew. I kept seeing those two young things, each sick for a sight of the other, and, from wishing they could have a minute together, I got to planning it for them.

"Perhaps," I said finally, "if you want it very much—"

"Very much!"

"And if you will sit quiet, and stop tapping your fingers together until you drive me crazy, I might contrive it for you. For five minutes," I said. "Not a second longer."

He came right over and put his arms around me.

"Who are you, anyhow?" he said. "You who turn to the world the frozen mask of a Union Street boarding-house landlady, who are a gentlewoman by every instinct and training, and a girl at heart? Who are you?"

"I'll tell you what I am," I said. "I'm a romantic old fool, and you'd better let me do this quickly, before I change my mind."

He freed me at that, but he followed to the telephone, and stood by while I got Lida. He was in a perfect frenzy of anxiety, turning red and white by turns, and in the middle of the conversation taking the receiver bodily from me and holding it to his own ear.

She said she thought she could get away; she spoke guardedly, as if Alma were near, but I gathered that she would come as soon as she could, and, from the way her voice broke, I knew she was as excited as the boy beside me.

She came, heavily coated and veiled, at a quarter after ten that night, and I took her back to the dining-room, where he was waiting. He did not make a move toward her, but stood there with his very lips white, looking at her. And, at first, she did not make a move either, but stood and gazed at him, thin and white, a wreck of himself. Then:

"Ell!" she cried, and ran around the table to him, as he held out his arms.

The school-teacher was out. I went into the parlor bedroom and sat in the cozy corner in the dark. I had done a wrong thing, and I was glad of it. sitting there in the darkness, I went over my own life again. After all, it had been my own life; I had lived it; no one else had shaped it for me. And if it was cheerless and colorless now, it had had its big moments. Life is measured by big moments.

If I let the two children in the dining-room have fifteen big moments, instead of five, who can blame me?

CHAPTER FOURTEEN
A Surprise Witness

The next day was the sensational one of the trial. We went through every phase of conviction: Jennie Brice was living. Jennie Brice was dead. The body found at Sewickley could not be Jennie Brice's. The body found at Sewickley *was* Jennie Brice's. And so it went on.

The defense did an unexpected thing in putting Mr. Ladley on the stand. That day, for the first time, he showed the wear and tear of the ordeal. He had no flower in his button-hole, and the rims of his eyes were red. But he was quite cool. His stage training had taught him not only to endure the eyes of the crowd, but to find in its gaze a sort of stimulant. He made a good witness, I must admit.

He replied to the usual questions easily. After five minutes or so Mr. Llewellyn got down to work.

"Mr. Ladley, you have said that your wife was ill the night of March fourth?"

"Yes."

"What was the nature of her illness?"

"She had a functional heart trouble, not serious."

"Will you tell us fully the events of that night?"

"I had been asleep when my wife wakened me. She asked for a medicine she used in these attacks. I got up and found the bottle, but it was empty. As she was nervous and frightened, I agreed to try to get some at a drug store. I went down-stairs, took Mrs. Pitman's boat, and went to several stores before I could awaken a pharmacist."

"You cut the boat loose?"

"Yes. It was tied in a woman's knot, or series of knots. I could not untie it, and I was in a hurry."

"How did you cut it?"

"With my pocket-knife."

"You did not use Mrs. Pitman's bread-knife?"

"I did not."

"And in cutting it, you cut your wrist, did you?"

"Yes. The knife slipped. I have the scar still."

"What did you do then?"

"I went back to the room, and stanched the blood with a towel."

"From whom did you get the medicine?"

"From Alexander's Pharmacy."

"At what time?"

"I am not certain. About three o'clock, probably."

"You went directly back home?"

Mr. Ladley hesitated. "No," he said finally. "My wife had had these attacks, but they were not serious. I was curious to see how the river-front looked and rowed out too far. I was caught in the current and nearly carried away."

"You came home after that?"

"Yes, at once. Mrs. Ladley was better and had dropped asleep. She wakened as I came in. She was disagreeable about the length of time I had been gone, and would not let me explain. We— quarreled, and she said she was going to leave me. I said that as she had threatened this before and had never done it, I would see that she really started. At daylight I rowed her to Federal Street."

"What had she with her?"

"A small brown valise."

"How was she dressed?"

"In a black and white dress and hat, with a long black coat."

"What was the last you saw of her?"

"She was going across the Sixth Street bridge."

"Alone?"

"No. She went with a young man we knew."

There was a stir in the court room at this.

"Who was the young man?"

"A Mr. Howell, a reporter on a newspaper here."

"Have you seen Mr. Howell since your arrest?"

"No, sir. He has been out of the city."

I was so excited by this time that I could hardly hear. I missed some of the cross-examination. The district attorney pulled Mr. Ladley's testimony to pieces.

"You cut the boat's painter with your pocket-knife?"

"I did."

"Then how do you account for Mrs. Pitman's broken knife, with the blade in your room?"

"I have no theory about it. She may have broken it herself. She had used it the day before to lift tacks out of a carpet."

That was true; I had.

"That early Monday morning was cold, was it not?"

"Yes. Very."

"Why did your wife leave without her fur coat?"

"I did not know she had until we had left the house. Then I did not ask her. She would not speak to me."

"I see. But is it not true that, upon a wet fur coat being shown you as your wife's, you said it could not be hers, as she had taken hers with her?"

"I do not recall such a statement."

"You recall a coat being shown you?"

"Yes. Mrs. Pitman brought a coat to my door, but I was working on a play I am writing, and I do not remember what I said.

The coat was ruined. I did not want it. I probably said the first thing I thought of to get rid of the woman."

I got up at that. I'd held my peace about the bread-knife, but this was too much. However, the moment I started to speak, somebody pushed me back into my chair and told me to be quiet.

"Now, you say you were in such a hurry to get this medicine for your wife that you cut the rope, thus cutting your wrist."

"Yes. I have the scar still."

"You could not wait to untie the boat, and yet you went along the river-front to see how high the water was?"

"Her alarm had excited me. But when I got out, and remembered that the doctors had told us she would never die in an attack, I grew more composed."

"You got the medicine first, you say?"

"Yes."

"Mr. Alexander has testified that you got the medicine at three-thirty. It has been shown that you left the house at two, and got back about four. Does not this show that with all your alarm you went to the river-front first?"

"I was gone from two to four," he replied calmly. "Mr. Alexander must be wrong about the time I wakened him. I got the medicine first."

"When your wife left you at the bridge, did she say where she was going?"

"No."

"You claim that this woman at Horner was your wife?"

"I think it likely."

"Was there an onyx clock in the second-story room when you moved into it?"

"I do not recall the clock."

"Your wife did not take an onyx clock away with her?"

Mr. Ladley smiled. "No."

The defense called Mr. Howell next. He looked rested, and the happier for having seen Lida, but he was still pale and showed the strain of some hidden anxiety. What that anxiety was, the next two days were to tell us all.

"Mr. Howell," Mr. Llewellyn asked, "you know the prisoner?"

"Slightly."

"State when you met him."

"On Sunday morning, March the fourth. I went to see him."

"Will you tell us the nature of that visit?"

"My paper had heard he was writing a play for himself. I was to get an interview, with photographs, if possible."

"You saw his wife at that time?"

"Yes."

"When did you see her again?"

"The following morning, at six o'clock, or a little later. I walked across the Sixth Street bridge with her, and put her on a train for Horner, Pennsylvania."

"You are positive it was Jennie Brice?"

"Yes. I watched her get out of the boat, while her husband steadied it."

"If you knew this, why did you not come forward sooner?"

"I have been out of the city."

"But you knew the prisoner had been arrested, and that this testimony of yours would be invaluable to him."

"Yes. But I thought it necessary to produce Jennie Brice herself. My unsupported word—"

"You have been searching for Jennie Brice?"

"Yes. Since March the eighth."

"How was she dressed when you saw her last?"

"She wore a red and black hat and a black coat. She carried a small brown valise."

"Thank you."

The cross-examination did not shake his testimony. But it brought out some curious things. Mr. Howell refused to say how he happened to be at the end of the Sixth Street bridge at that hour, or why he had thought it necessary, on meeting a woman he claimed to have known only twenty-four hours, to go with her to the railway station and put her on a train.

The jury was visibly impressed and much shaken. For Mr. Howell carried conviction in every word he said; he looked the district attorney in the eye, and once when our glances crossed he even smiled at me faintly. But I saw why he had tried to find Jennie Brice, and had dreaded testifying. Not a woman in that court room, and hardly a man, but believed when he left the stand, that he was, or had been, Jennie Brice's lover, and as such was assisting her to leave her husband.

"Then you believe…" The district attorney said at the end, "…you believe, Mr. Howell, that Jennie Brice is living?"

"Jennie Brice was living on Monday morning, March the fifth," he said firmly.

"Miss Shaeffer has testified that on Wednesday this woman, who you claim was Jennie Brice, sent a letter to you from Horner. Is that the case?"

"Yes."

"The letter was signed 'Jennie Brice'?"

"It was signed 'J.B.'"

"Will you show the court that letter?"

"I destroyed it."

"It was a personal letter?"

"It merely said she had arrived safely, and not to let any one know where she was."

"And yet you destroyed it?"

"A postscript said to do so."

"Why?"

"I do not know. An extra precaution probably."

"You were under the impression that she was going to stay there?"

"She was to have remained for a week."

"And you have been searching for this woman for two months?"

He quailed, but his voice was steady. "Yes," he admitted.

He was telling the truth, even if it was not all the truth. I believe, had it gone to the jury then, Mr. Ladley would have been acquitted. But, late that afternoon, things took a new turn. Counsel for the prosecution stated to the court that he had a new and important witness, and got permission to introduce this further evidence. The witness was a Doctor Littlefield, and proved to be my one-night tenant of the second-story front. Holcombe's prisoner of the night before took the stand. The doctor was less impressive in full daylight; he was a trifle shiny, a bit bulbous as to nose and indifferent as to finger-nails. But his testimony was given with due professional weight.

"You are a doctor of medicine, Doctor Littlefield?" asked the district attorney.

"Yes."

"In active practise?"

"I have a Cure for Inebriates in Des Moines, Iowa. I was formerly in general practise in New York City."

"You knew Jennie Ladley?"

"I had seen her at different theaters. And she consulted me professionally at one time in New York."

"You operated on her, I believe?"

"Yes. She came to me to have a name removed. It had been tattooed over her heart."

"You removed it?"

"Not at once. I tried fading the marks with goat's milk, but she was impatient. On the third visit to my office she demanded that the name be cut out."

"You did it?"

"Yes. She refused a general anesthetic and I used cocaine. The name was John—I believe a former husband. She intended to marry again."

A titter ran over the court room. People strained to the utmost are always glad of an excuse to smile. The laughter of a wrought-up crowd always seems to me half hysterical.

"Have you seen photographs of the scar on the body found at Sewickley? Or the body itself?"

"No, I have not."

"Will you describe the operation?"

"I made a transverse incision for the body of the name, and two vertical ones—one longer for the J, the other shorter, for the stem of the h. There was a dot after the name. I made a half-inch incision for it."

"Will you sketch the cicatrix as you recall it?"

The doctor made a careful drawing on a pad that was passed to him. The drawing was much like this.

Line for line, dot for dot, it was the scar on the body found at Sewickley.

"You are sure the woman was Jennie Brice?"

"She sent me tickets for the theater shortly after. And I had an announcement of her marriage to the prisoner, some weeks later."

"Were there any witnesses to the operation?"

"My assistant; I can produce him at any time."

That was not all of the trial, but it was the decisive moment. Shortly after, the jury withdrew, and for twenty-four hours not a word was heard from them.

CHAPTER FIFTEEN
A Fantastic Hoax

After twenty-four hours' deliberation, the jury brought in a verdict of guilty. It was a first-degree verdict. Mr. Howell's unsupported word had lost out against a scar.

Contrary to my expectation, Mr. Holcombe was not jubilant over the verdict. He came into the dining-room that night and stood by the window, looking out into the yard.

"It isn't logical," he said. "In view of Howell's testimony, it's ridiculous! Heaven help us under this jury system, anyhow! Look at the facts! Howell knows the woman: he sees her on Monday morning, and puts her on a train out of town. The boy is telling the truth. He has nothing to gain by coming forward, and everything to lose. Very well: she was alive on Monday. We know where she was on Tuesday and Wednesday. Anyhow, during those days her gem of a husband was in jail. He was freed Thursday night, and from that time until his rearrest on the following Tuesday, I had him under observation every moment. He left the jail Thursday night, and on Saturday the body floated in at Sewickley. If it was done by Ladley, it must have been done on Friday, and on Friday he was in view through the periscope all day!"

Mr. Reynolds came in and joined us. "There's only one way out that I see," he said mildly "Two women have been fool enough to have a name tattooed over their hearts. No woman ever thought enough of me to have *my* name put on her."

"I hope not," I retorted. Mr. Reynold's first name is Zachariah.

But, as Mr. Holcombe said, all that had been proved was that Jennie Brice was dead, probably murdered. He could not understand the defense letting the case go to the jury without their putting more stress on Mr. Howell's story. But we were to understand that soon, and many other things. Mr. Holcombe told me that evening of learning from John Bellows of the tattooed name on Jennie Brice and of how, after an almost endless search, he had found the man who had cut the name away.

At eight o'clock the door-bell rang. Mr. Reynolds had gone to lodge, he being an Elk and several other things, and much given to regalia in boxes, and having his picture in the newspapers in different outlandish costumes. Mr. Pitman used to say that man, being denied his natural love for barbaric adornment in his every-day clothing, took to the different fraternities as an excuse for decking himself out. But this has nothing to do with the door-bell.

It was old Isaac. He had a basket in his hand, and he stepped into the hall and placed it on the floor.

"Evening, Miss Bess," he said. "Can you see a bit of company to-night?"

"I can always see you," I replied. But he had not meant himself. He stepped to the door, and opening it, beckoned to some one across the street. It was Lida!

She came in, her color a little heightened, and old Isaac stood back, beaming at us both; I believe it was one of the crowning moments of the old man's life—thus to see his Miss Bess and Alma's child together.

"Is—is he here yet?" she asked me nervously.

"I did not know he was coming." There was no need to ask which "he." There was only one for Lida.

"He telephoned me, and asked me to come here. Oh, Mrs. Pitman, I'm so afraid for him!" She had quite forgotten Isaac. I turned to the school-teacher's room and opened the door. "The woman who belongs here is out at a lecture," I said. "Come in here, Ikkie, and I'll find the evening paper for you.

"'Ikkie'!" said Lida, staring at me. I think I went white.

"The lady heah and I is old friends," Isaac said, with his splendid manner. "Her mothah, Miss Lida, her mothah—"

But even old Isaac choked up at that. I closed the door on him.

"How queer!" Lida said, looking at me. "So Isaac knew your mother? Have you lived always in Allegheny, Mrs. Pitman?"

"I was born in Pittsburgh," I evaded. "I went away for a long time, but I always longed for the hurry and activity of the old home town. So here I am again."

Fortunately, like all the young, her own affairs engrossed her. She was flushed with the prospect of meeting her lover, tremulous over what the evening might bring. The middle-aged woman who had come back to the hurry of the old town, and who, pushed back into an eddy of the flood district, could only watch the activity and the life from behind a "Rooms to Let" sign, did not concern her much. Nor should she have.

Mr. Howell came soon after. He asked for her, and going back to the dining-room, kissed her quietly. He had an air of resolve, a sort of grim determination, that was a relief from the half-frantic look he had worn before. He asked to have Mr. Holcombe brought down, and so behold us all, four of us, sitting around the table—Mr. Holcombe with his note-book, I with my mending, and the boy with one of Lida's hands frankly under his on the red table-cloth.

"I want to tell all of you the whole story," he began. "To-morrow I shall go to the district attorney and confess, but—I want you all to have it first. I can't sleep again until I get it off my chest. Mrs. Pitman has suffered through me, and Mr. Holcombe here has spent money and time—"

Lida did not speak, but she drew her chair closer, and put her other hand over his.

"I want to get it straight, if I can. Let me see. It was on Sunday, the fourth, that the river came up, wasn't it? Yes. Well, on the Thursday before that I met you, Mr. Holcombe, in a restaurant in Pittsburgh. Do you remember?"

Mr. Holcombe nodded.

"We were talking of crime, and I said no man should be hanged on purely circumstantial evidence. You affirmed that a well-linked chain of circumstantial evidence could properly hang a man. We had a long argument, in which I was worsted. There was a third man at the table—Bronson, the business manager of the Liberty Theater."

"Who sided with you," put in Mr. Holcombe, "and whose views I refused to entertain because, as publicity man for a theater, he dealt in fiction rather than in fact."

"Precisely. You may recall, Mr. Holcombe, that you offered to hang any man we would name, given a proper chain of circumstantial evidence against him?"

"Yes."

"After you left, Bronson spoke to me. He said business at the theater was bad, and complained of the way the papers used, or would not use, his stuff. He said the Liberty Theater had not had a proper deal, and that he was tempted to go over and bang one of the company on the head, and so get a little free advertising.

"I said he ought to be able to fake a good story; but he maintained that a newspaper could smell a faked story a mile away, and that, anyhow, all the good stunts had been pulled off. I agreed with him. I remember saying that nothing but a railroad wreck or a murder hit the public very hard these days, and that I didn't feel like wrecking the Pennsylvania Limited.

"He leaned over the table and looked at me. 'Well, how about a murder, then?' he said. 'You get the story for your paper, and I get some advertising for the theater. We need it, that's sure.'

"I laughed it off, and we separated. But at two o'clock Bronson called me up again. I met him in his office at the theater, and he told me that Jennie Brice, who was out of the cast that week, had asked for a week's vacation. She had heard of a farm at a town called Horner, and she wanted to go there to rest.

"'Now the idea is this,' he said. 'She's living with her husband, and he has threatened her life more than once. It would be easy enough to frame up something to look as if he'd made away with her. We'd get a week of excitement, more advertising than we'd ordinarily get in a year; you get a corking news story, and find Jennie Brice at the end, getting the credit for that. Jennie gets a hundred dollars and a rest, and Ladley, her husband, gets, say, two hundred.'

"Mr. Bronson offered to put up the money, and I agreed. The flood came just then, and was considerable help. It made a good setting. I went to my city editor, and got an assignment to interview Ladley about this play of his. Then Bronson and I went together to see the Ladleys on Sunday morning, and as they needed money, they agreed. But Ladley insisted on fifty dollars a week extra if he had to go to jail. We promised it, but we did not intend to let things go so far as that.

"In the Ladleys' room that Sunday morning, we worked it all out. The hardest thing was to get Jennie Brice's consent; but she agreed, finally. We arranged a list of clues, to be left around, and Ladley was to go out in the night and to be heard coming back. I told him to quarrel with his wife that afternoon,—although I don't believe they needed to be asked to do it,—and I suggested also the shoe or slipper, to be found floating around."

"Just a moment," said Mr. Holcombe, busy with his note-book. "Did you suggest the onyx clock?"

"No. No clock was mentioned. The—clock has puzzled me."

"The towel?"

"Yes. I said no murder was complete without blood, but he kicked on that—said he didn't mind the rest, but he'd be hanged if he was going to slash himself. But, as it happened, he cut his wrist while cutting the boat loose, and so we had the towel."

"Pillow-slip?" asked Mr. Holcombe.

"Well, no. There was nothing said about a pillow-slip. Didn't he say he burned it accidentally?"

"So he claimed." Mr. Holcombe made another entry in his book.

"Then I said every murder had a weapon. He was to have a pistol at first, but none of us owned one. Mrs. Ladley undertook to get a knife from Mrs. Pitman's kitchen, and to leave it around, not in full view, but where it could be found."

"A broken knife?"

"No. Just a knife."

"He was to throw the knife into the water?"

"That was not arranged. I only gave him a general outline. He was to add any interesting details that might occur to him. The idea, of course, was to give the police plenty to work on, and just when they thought they had it all, and when the theater had had a lot of booming, and I had got a good story, to produce Jennie Brice, safe and well. We were not to appear in it at all. It would have worked perfectly, but we forgot to count on one thing—Jennie Brice hated her husband."

"Not really hated him!" cried Lida.

"*Hated* him. She is letting him hang. She could save him by coming forward now, and she won't do it. She is hiding so he will go to the gallows."

There was a pause at that. It seemed too incredible, too inhuman.

"Then, early that Monday morning, you smuggled Jennie Brice out of the city?"

"Yes. That was the only thing we bungled. We fixed the hour a little too late, and I was seen by Miss Harvey's uncle, walking across the bridge with a woman."

"Why did you meet her openly, and take her to the train?"

Mr. Howell bent forward and smiled across at the little man. "One of your own axioms, sir," he said. "Do the natural thing; upset the customary order of events as little as possible. Jennie Brice went to the train, because that was where she wanted to go. But as Ladley was to protest that his wife had left town, and as the police would be searching for a solitary woman, I went with her. We went in a leisurely manner. I bought her a magazine and a morning paper, asked the conductor to fix her window, and, in general, acted the devoted husband seeing his wife off on a trip. I even..." He smiled, "...I even promised to feed the canary."

Lida took her hands away. "Did you kiss her good-by?" she demanded.

"Not even a chaste salute," he said. His spirits were rising. It was, as often happens, as if the mere confession removed the guilt.

I have seen little boys who have broken a window show the same relief after telling about it.

"For a day or two Bronson and I sat back, enjoying the stir-up. Things turned out as we had expected. Business boomed at the theater. I got a good story, and some few kind words from my city editor. Then—the explosion came. I got a letter from Jennie Brice saying she was going away, and that we need not try to find her. I went to Horner, but I had lost track of her completely. Even then, we did not believe things so bad as they turned out to be. We thought she was giving us a bad time, but that she would show up.

"Ladley was in a blue funk for a time. Bronson and I went to him. We told him how the thing had slipped up. We didn't want to go to the police and confess if we could help it. Finally, he agreed to stick it out until she was found, at a hundred dollars a week. It took all we could beg, borrow and steal. But now—we have to come out with the story anyhow."

Mr. Holcombe sat up and closed his note-book with a snap. "I'm not so sure of that," he said impressively. "I wonder if you realize, young man, that, having provided a perfect defense for this man Ladley, you provided him with every possible inducement to make away with his wife? Secure in your coming forward at the last minute and confessing the hoax to save him, was there anything he might not have dared with impunity?"

"But I tell you I took Jennie Brice out of town on Monday morning."

"*Did you?*" asked Mr. Holcombe sternly.

But at that, the school-teacher, having come home and found old Isaac sound asleep in her cozy corner, set up such a screaming for the police that our meeting broke up. Nor would Mr. Holcombe explain any further.

CHAPTER SIXTEEN
A Final Statement

Mr. Holcombe was up very early the next morning. I heard him moving around at five o'clock, and at six he banged at my door and demanded to know at what time the neighborhood rose: he had been up for an hour and there were no signs of life. He was more cheerful after he had had a cup of coffee, commented on Lida's beauty, and said that Howell was a lucky chap.

"That is what worries me, Mr. Holcombe," I said. "I am helping the affair along and—what if it turns out badly?"

He looked at me over his glasses. "It isn't likely to turn out badly," he said. "I have never married, Mrs. Pitman, and I have missed a great deal out of life."

"Perhaps you're better off: if you had married and lost your wife—" I was thinking of Mr. Pitman.

"Not at all," he said with emphasis. "It's better to have married and lost than never to have married at all. Every man needs a good woman, and it doesn't matter how old he is. The older he is, the more he needs her. I am nearly sixty."

I was rather startled, and I almost dropped the fried potatoes. But the next moment he had got out his note-book and was going over the items again. "Pillow-slip," he said, "knife *broken*, onyx clock—wouldn't think so much of the clock if he hadn't been so damnably anxious to hide the key, the discrepancy in time as revealed by the trial—yes, it is as clear as a bell. Mrs. Pitman, does that Maguire woman next door sleep all day?"

"She's up now," I said, looking out the window.

He was in the hall in a moment, only to come to the door later, hat in hand. "Is she the only other woman on the street who keeps boarders?"

"She's the only woman who doesn't," I snapped. "She'll keep anything that doesn't belong to her—except boarders."

"Ah!"

He lighted his corn-cob pipe and stood puffing at it and watching me. He made me uneasy: I thought he was going to continue the subject of every man needing a wife, and I'm afraid I had already decided to take him if he offered, and to put the school-teacher out and have a real parlor again, but to keep Mr. Reynolds, he being tidy and no bother.

But when he spoke, he was back to the crime again: "Did you ever work a typewriter?" he asked.

What with the surprise, I was a little sharp. "I don't play any instrument except an egg-beater," I replied shortly, and went on clearing the table.

"I wonder if you remember the village idiot and the horse? But of course you do, Mrs. Pitman; you are a lady of imagination. Don't you think you could be Alice Murray for a few moments? Now think—you are a stenographer with theatrical ambitions: you meet an actor and you fall in love with him, and he with you."

"That's hard to imagine, that last."

"Not so hard," he said gently. "Now the actor is going to put you on the stage, perhaps in this new play, and some day he is going to marry you."

"Is that what he promised the girl?"

"According to some letters her mother found, yes. The actor is married, but he tells you he will divorce the wife; you are to wait for him, and in the meantime he wants you near him; away from the office, where other men are apt to come in with letters to be typed, and to chaff you. You are a pretty girl."

"It isn't necessary to overwork my imagination," I said, with a little bitterness. I had been a pretty girl, but work and worry—

"Now you are going to New York very soon, and in the meantime you have cut yourself off from all your people. You have no one but this man. What would you do? Where would you go?"

"How old was the girl?"

"Nineteen."

"I think," I said slowly, "that if I were nineteen, and in love with a man, and hiding, I would hide as near him as possible. I'd be likely to get a window that could see his going out and coming in, a place so near that he could come often to see me."

"Bravo!" he exclaimed. "Of course, with your present wisdom and experience, you would do nothing so foolish. But this girl was in her teens; she was not very far away, for he probably saw her that Sunday afternoon, when he was out for two hours. And as the going was slow that day, and he had much to tell and explain, I figure she was not far off. Probably in this very neighborhood."

During the remainder of that morning I saw Mr. Holcombe, at intervals, going from house to house along Union Street, making short excursions into side thoroughfares, coming back again and taking up his door-bell ringing with unflagging energy. I watched him off and on for two hours. At the end of that time he came back flushed and excited.

"I found the house," he said, wiping his glasses. "She was there, all right, not so close as we had thought, but as close as she could get."

"And can you trace her?" I asked.

His face changed and saddened. "Poor child!" he said. "She is dead, Mrs. Pitman!"

"Not she—at Sewickley!"

"No," he said patiently. "That was Jennie Brice."

"But—Mr. Howell—"

"Mr. Howell is a young ass," he said with irritation. "He did not take Jennie Brice out of the city that morning. He took Alice Murray in Jennie Brice's clothing, and veiled."

Well, that is five years ago. Five times since then the Allegheny River, from being a mild and inoffensive stream, carrying a few boats and a great deal of sewage, has become, a raging destroyer, and has filled our hearts with fear and our cellars with mud. Five times since then Molly Maguire has appropriated all that the flood carried from my premises to hers, and five times have I lifted my carpets and moved Mr. Holcombe, who occupies the parlor bedroom, to a second-floor room.

A few days ago, as I said at the beginning, we found Peter's body floating in the cellar, and as soon as the yard was dry, I buried him. He had grown fat and lazy, but I shall miss him.

Yesterday a riverman fell off a barge along the water-front and was drowned. They dragged the river for his body, but they did not find him. But they found something—an onyx clock, with the tattered remnant of a muslin pillow-slip wrapped around it. It only bore out the story, as we had known it for five years.

The Murray girl had lived long enough to make a statement to the police, although Mr. Holcombe only learned this later. On the statement being shown to Ladley in the jail, and his learning of the girl's death, he collapsed. He confessed before he was hanged, and his confession, briefly, was like this:

He had met the Murray girl in connection with the typing of his play, and had fallen in love with her. He had never cared for his wife, and would have been glad to get rid of her in any way possible. He had not intended to kill her, however. He had planned to elope with the Murray girl, and awaiting an opportunity, had persuaded her to leave home and to take a room near my house.

Here he had visited her daily, while his wife was at the theater.

They had planned to go to New York together on Monday, March the fifth. On Sunday, the fourth, however, Mr. Bronson and Mr. Howell had made their curious proposition. When he accepted, Philip Ladley maintained that he meant only to carry out the plan as had been suggested. But the temptation was too strong for him. That night while his wife slept he had strangled her.

I believe he was frantic with fear, after he had done it. Then it occurred to him that if he made the body unrecognizable, he would be safe enough. On that quiet Sunday night, when Mr. Reynolds reported all peaceful in the Ladley room, he had cut off the poor wretch's head and had tied it up in a pillow-slip weighted with my onyx clock!

It is a curious fact about the case that the scar which his wife incurred to enable her to marry him was the means of his undoing. He insisted, and I believe he was telling the truth, that he did not know of the scar: that is, his wife had never told him of it, and had been able to conceal it. He thought she had probably used paraffin in some way.

In his final statement, written with great care and no little literary finish, he told the story in detail: of arranging the clues as Mr. Howell and Mr. Bronson had suggested; of going out in the boat, with the body, covered with a fur coat, in the bottom of the skiff: of throwing it into the current above the Ninth Street bridge, and of seeing the fur coat fall from the boat and carried beyond his reach; of disposing of the head near the Seventh Street bridge: of going to a drug store, as per the Howell instructions, and of coming home at four o'clock, to find me at the head of the stairs.

Several points of confusion remained. One had been caused by Temple Hope's refusal to admit that the dress and hat that figured in the case were to be used by her the next week at the theater. Mr. Ladley insisted that this was the case, and that on that Sunday afternoon his wife had requested him to take them to Miss Hope; that they had quarreled as to whether they should be packed in a box or in the brown valise, and that he had visited Alice Murray

While his wife slept...

instead. It was on the way there that the idea of finally getting rid of Jennie Brice came to him. And a way—using the black and white striped dress of the dispute.

Another point of confusion had been the dismantling of his room that Monday night, some time between the visit of Temple Hope and the return of Mr. Holcombe. This was to obtain the scrap of paper containing the list of clues as suggested by Mr.

Howell, a clue that might have brought about a premature discovery of the so-called hoax.

To the girl he had told nothing of his plan. But he had told her she was to leave town on an early train the next morning, going as his wife; that he wished her to wear the black and white dress and hat, for reasons that he would explain later, and to be veiled heavily, that to the young man who would put her on the train, and who had seen Jennie Brice only once, she was to be Jennie Brice; to say as little as possible and not to raise her veil. Her further instructions were simple: to go to the place at Horner where Jennie Brice had planned to go, but to use the name of "Bellows" there. And after she had been there for a day or two, to go as quietly as possible to New York. He gave her the address of a boarding-house where he could write her, and where he would join her later.

He reasoned in this way: That as Alice Murray was to impersonate Jennie Brice, and Jennie Brice hiding from her husband, she would naturally discard her name. The name "Bellows" had been hers by a previous marriage and she might be able to resume it somewhat easily. Thus, to establish his innocence, he had not only the evidence of Howell and Bronson that the whole thing was a gigantic hoax; he had the evidence of Howell that he had started Jennie Brice to Horner that Monday morning, that she had reached Horner, had there assumed an incognito, as Mr. Pitman would say, and had later disappeared from there, maliciously concealing herself in order to work his undoing.

In all probability he would have gone free, the richer by a hundred dollars for each week of his imprisonment, but for two things: the flood, which had brought opportunity to his door, had brought Mr Holcombe to feed Peter, the dog. And the same flood, which should have carried the headless body as far as Cairo, or even farther on down the Mississippi, had rejected it in an eddy below a clay bluff at Sewickley, with its pitiful covering washed from the scar.

Well, it is all over now. Mr Ladley is dead, and Alice Murray, and even Peter lies in the yard. Mr Reynolds made a small wooden cross over Peter's grave, and carved "Till we meet again" on it. I dare say the next flood will find it in Molly Maguire's kitchen.

Mr Howell and Lida are married. Mr Howell inherited some money, I believe, and what with that and Lida declaring she would either marry him in a church or run off to Steubenville, Ohio, Alma had to consent. I went to the wedding and stood near the door, while Alma swept in, in lavender chiffon and rose point lace. She has not improved with age, has Alma. But Lida? Lida, under my mother's wedding veil, with her eyes like stars, seeing no one in the church in all that throng but the boy who waited at the end of the long church aisle-I wanted to run out and claim her, my own blood, my more than child.

I sat down and covered my face. And from the pew behind me some one leaned over and patted my shoulder.

"Miss Bess!" old Isaac said gently. "Don't take on, Miss Bess!"

He came the next day and brought me some lilies from the bride's bouquet, that she had sent me, and a bottle of champagne from the wedding supper. I had not tasted champagne for twenty years!

That is all of the story. On summer afternoons sometimes, when the house is hot, I go to the park and sit. I used to take Peter, but now he is dead. I like to see Lida's little boy; the nurse knows me by sight, and lets me talk to the child. He can say "Peter" quite plainly. But he does not call Alma "Grandmother." The nurse says she does not like it. He calls her "Nana."

Lida does not forget me. Especially at flood-times, she always comes to see if I am comfortable. The other day she brought me, with apologies, the chiffon gown her mother had worn at her wedding. Alma had never worn it but once, and now she was too stout for it. I took it; I am not proud, and I should like Molly Maguire to see it.

Mr. Holcombe asked me last night to marry him. He says he needs me, and that I need him.

I am a lonely woman, and getting old, and I'm tired of watching the gas meter; and besides, with Peter dead, I need a man in the house all the time. The flood district is none too orderly. Besides, when I have a wedding dress laid away and a bottle of good wine, it seems a pity not to use them.

I think I shall do it.

THE END

.

Made in the USA
Lexington, KY
31 May 2017